CW01653593

Off Limits

By
Sawyer Bennett

Published by Big Dog Books

ISBN: 978-0-9894164-0-5

Find Sawyer on the web!
sawyerbennett.com
www.twitter.com/bennettbooks
www.facebook.com/bennettbooks

Contents

Dedication

This one has to go out to my fans.

I actually have fans!!!

I can't believe how fortunate I am to have people that read Off Sides and demanded, in the nicest way possible, for me to write a follow up novel. You asked, I answered. I hope you love it as much as I enjoyed writing it.

Special thanks for my amazing Beta readers. Your input into this work was invaluable. Hugs to Alyssa, Kris, Shannon, Kizzy, Amy, Shamiran, Sarah and Amber.

Finally, thanks to my dad, retired Marine Jerry Leone for helping me with the Marine Corps and military terminology. I tried to take all of your advice to make my book as accurate as possible but without losing the romance. And thank you for your service to our country!

CHAPTER 1

Emily

"EMILY…HURRY UP, OR we're going to be late."

I groan as I hear my mother call up the stairs to me. I am just putting my jewelry on and glance at my Patek Philippe watch. I still have ten more minutes before we have to leave and I grit my teeth that my mother is so controlling.

Taking a deep breath, I repeat to myself, *Just one more week, and then I'm out of here.*

"I'll be down in just a moment, Mother." I try to keep my voice lilting so she won't sense the frustration I'm feeling toward her.

This summer has been absolutely brutal coming back to Boston. I had wanted to stay in New York after finishing my second year at Columbia but my mother insisted I come home so I could attend an array of political and social functions with them. My father, Congressman Alex Burnham, will hopefully be making a bid for the White House in two years and my life has been overtaken by my mother's need to present the perfect Presidential family to the press.

So, all summer I have been polished, shined and instructed on the best way to behave in front of the camera. I've had my clothes chosen for me and I've been assigned young, affluent bachelors to escort me to parties. My mother will not let me leave the house unless she approves of what I'm wearing and with whom I'm going to be.

And I am suffocating.

Just one more week, and then I'm out of here.

It's a bit surreal to think about how much I've changed in the past few years. I used to adore my life as a socialite with all of the fancy clothes, the snobby friends and the endless stream of parties. Now, I would give anything to just be a normal, college girl who could fade into obscurity anytime I wanted to.

I owe a lot of my change to my older brother, Ryan. Three years ago, he met and fell deeply in love with his one and only, Danny. I admit…I didn't like her at first and I'm equally as embarrassed to say that I decided not to like her without knowing a damn thing about her. My mother told me to hate her and so I did.

And it wasn't hard to follow my mother's orders. I mean, she told me that Danny worked in a diner, had dyed purple hair and piercings in her face. Skank-a-rific! Right?

Wrong!

Oh, how wrong I was.

I had never been that close to Ryan as we grew up. We were almost four years apart in age and he never was one to completely conform to my parents' dictates.

Unlike me. The rat that followed the Pied Piper.

At any rate, Ryan fell utterly and completely in love with Danny and I just didn't understand it. But it intrigued me and I decided I had to find out why.

It took two very important moments in my life to completely re-evaluate the type of person I wanted to be.

First, Ryan had an honest conversation with me explaining all of the reasons why he loved Danny. They were fairytale reasons…reasons I didn't believe were possible. In my world, people married because they were suitably matched on paper and if they were lucky, they grew to love each other. But not Ry…he wanted love first and to hell with everything else.

So Ryan told me that he loved Danny because she was kind, generous, witty and caring. Yeah, yeah. Easy for a guy to say if he's getting some, right?

Wrong, again!

The second thing that happened to change my life was that I decided to check Danny out for myself. My mother had successfully broken Danny and Ryan up, but I guess true love always prevails and that didn't last long. After Danny and Ryan got back together, I called Danny and asked her out to lunch.

Behind my mother's back, of course.

I can still remember that day, sitting across the table from Danny. She was remarkably beautiful, but I knew that. I had seen her once before and I was such a bitch to her then. I didn't apologize to her right away, because I still wanted to know if what Ryan saw in her was legitimate.

So during lunch, while being sidetracked a few times by looking at her nose ring and purple hair, I actually was able to listen to Danny. I mean really listen.

And it became abundantly clear to me why Ryan was in love with her. Hell, by the end of lunch, I was in love with her.

She was everything I was not. The kindest and most non-judgmental soul I had ever met. She had suffered tragedy time and again, yet she still looked at the world as if it was her personal oyster bed. I know a few times during our conversation, I just sat there with my mouth hanging open over some of the things she was telling me about her life. Horrible, horrible things that she had suffered…and yet, she still wore a genuine smile on her face.

By the end of that lunch, two things happened. I apologized profusely to Danny for my behavior and my thoughts. Danny—being Danny—didn't even bother to accept the apology. Instead, she insisted that there was nothing to apologize for. She understood that I had been influenced, and that my loyalties should have been to family. And then she told me that she would very much like to start over with me and become my friend.

See why I fell in love with her?

The other thing that happened after that lunch was an immediate, embarrassing and crushing realization that I was a complete bitch. Danny's open acceptance of all people, most notably myself, made me vow that I needed to change. I needed to knock down those walls of invincibility and entitlement that I had put around myself, and I needed to open up to people. All kinds of people.

And the next two years I was at Columbia were the happiest of my life. I made it my goal to open myself up to experience. I wanted to try everything that I had always been denied.

And the freedom was intoxicating.

I was away from my parents and I had made new and very, very interesting friends that my mother would surely hate if I ever brought them home. That filled me with joy beyond measure for if my mother was sure to disapprove, that meant it was probably perfect for the new Emily.

Best of all, Ryan had signed with the New York Rangers and Danny returned to Julliard so I got to spend a lot of time with them. I had a lot of lost time to make up for with Ryan, and I had a new and blossoming friendship with Danny to build.

The only thing that sucked about my life was having to return home to Boston in the summers.

Don't get me wrong. I love Boston. It's my home. But it also means that I am back under my mother's watch and I now have to put on an act. The Emily that they sent off to Columbia no longer existed and they had no clue of her demise. Perhaps a future in Hollywood was in the cards for me because I had my snotty, debutante act down to an actual science when I was around my mother. I was even able to hang with some of the people in my old crowd and they still thought me to be one of them.

Luckily, I had only one more week of summer break and then I was heading back to Columbia. I missed New York so much. I missed Ryan and Danny, and I missed my crazy roommate, Fil.

Fil was a prime example of my zeal to try all things new and to be accepting of those things with which I had no experience. We were paired together as dorm mates our first year at Columbia and she was my first real test as the new, accepting and non-judgmental Emily. Thinking back at our first meeting, I'm surprised we didn't kill each other.

I had already moved into my dorm. My parents couldn't be bothered to help me so Ryan and Danny came over and got me settled in. Not ten minutes after they had left, my dorm room burst open. I had been busy making my bed and turned to see a tall, lithe woman standing there. She was wearing a pair of ratty, Levi jeans, a plain white t-shirt and dirty sneakers. She was really quite pretty with an olive toned complexion and very short, very black hair that couldn't have been more than an inch in length. She wore no makeup and had beautiful blue eyes.

Once I got past my initial perusal, I noticed that she was sneering at me. I can't say I was overly shocked when she said, "Oh, great. I got stuck with little Miss Debbie Debutante."

I looked down at my clothes wondering how she could guess that. I was wearing jeans, but they were a three hundred dollar pair of True Religion's. I then inwardly groaned when I realized I was also wearing a Chanel blouse, a Hermes scarf, Louis Vuitton shoes and of course, my Patek Philippe watch.

But I couldn't let her intimidate me. So I responded, "Looks like I got stuck with a supercilious bitch."

I tensely waited a few seconds to see if she would punch me, but she did nothing more than grin when she said, "You got balls. I like that."

She then threw her backpack on her bed and walked over to me. Sticking her hand out, she said, "I'm Fil Larson."

I shook her hand, responding, "Emily Burnham."

"Sorry if I came off strong," she said. "It's a bad habit of mine. I'd tell you I'm working to overcome it, but I'm not."

I don't know what possessed me to respond with brutal honesty but I said, "Well, I actually am a snotty, rich brat, but I am seriously working hard to overcome that."

Fil's grin turned evil. "I can definitely help you with that."

I smiled back and returned to making my bed. "So, your name is Phil? Is that short for like Philamena or something?"

"Nope. It's even worse than that. First, it's Fil. F-I-L. It's short for Filet."

My mouth gaped open. "You're parents named you after a steak?"

"Yup. But they didn't name me Filet. They named me Mignon. Which I hate. I abhor. I will do bodily harm to anyone that calls me that. My friends—and I use that term loosely—used to call me Filet Mignon when I was growing up and it eventually shortened to Fil. So that's what I go by now."

"Okay. Fil it is."

Breaking free of my memories of Fil, I give myself one last glance in the mirror and pick up my purse before heading downstairs. I really miss Fil and cannot wait to see her in a few days. We bonded fast and she is my bestie. We moved out of the dorm after our freshman year and got an apartment instead. It made me feel more…grown-up.

I snicker to myself as I walk down the stairs. I can't even imagine bringing Fil home to meet my parents. She is crass and borderline rude. Oh, and she is out of the closet, in your face gay. Celia Burnham, for sure, would have a heart attack.

I reach the bottom of the stairs and my mother is waiting there for me. She is a beautiful woman but her face holds an icy veneer that I've rarely seen crack.

"Honestly, Emily, why do you always have to be late," my mother chastises me.

I sigh. "I'm not late, Mother. I'm here at the exact time you told me to be here."

She picks up her purse and gives herself a quick once over in the foyer mirror. Patting her chignon for non-existent stray hairs, she says, "Well, you know I don't like to be late and what if we hit traffic?"

I sigh again, a little more loudly this time. "Then you should have told me to be ready a bit earlier."

"Don't patronize me," she snaps. "I'm under a lot of stress right now trying to organize the Boston Hospice Charity Gala and I don't need you making it worse."

It would serve me no purpose in arguing, so I merely said, "Yes, Mother. I'm sorry."

But I'm not.

It is so rotten of me but sometimes I like getting under my mother's skin, just so I can see something other than her plastic exterior. If I can get her to show emotion, any emotion, then I can convince myself that she has the capacity to feel things other than disdain, judgment or antipathy.

I follow her out of the house and we get into the waiting limousine. As soon as we are seated, she starts in on me. "It's time for you to declare your major at Columbia. Have you decided yet?"

I know what this means. She's not asking me what my choice is…she wants me to tell her that I will agree to her choice. My mother expects me to go to law school or medical school. Or, she would actually be perfectly happy if I met and married a wealthy bachelor and raised perfect little, wealthy babies.

"I'm still undecided," I say vaguely.

I'm not, actually. My mind has been made up for months that I wanted to pursue a Journalism degree. I want to be a sports writer and that's about akin to me telling my parents I want to be a topless dancer.

"How can you not be decided? We talked about this. You are either pre-med or pre-law."

I really don't want to fight with her about this so I just tell her, "I can't decide between the two. I'm still thinking."

"Well, don't wait too long. I want to release it to the press as soon as you declare. It will be a nice, domestic piece your father can use in the media."

Of course. It's all about what will help my father's political aspirations, not what will make me happy and fulfilled.

Just one more week, and I'm out of here.

My mother changes the subject to one that is equally abhorrent to me. "Remember your father will be home this weekend and we are attending that fundraising dinner at Stan and Margot Craft's house. I've invited Todd to be your date."

I feel my face redden as I sputter, "Todd?"

"Yes, he's such a nice man and if you give him half a chance, he'll prove himself to you."

I am beyond furious. "You cannot set me up with my ex-boyfriend, Mother. I will not go with him."

She doesn't even blink when she responds. "You will go with him because his father is one of your father's biggest contributors."

I take a deep breath and try to calm myself. Todd Fulgram was my boyfriend during my junior and senior years of high school. Although at first, our relationship was nice, we parted on very bad terms the summer before I left for college. He used to be charming—in a rich and cultured way—and he was very cute. He also pressured me for months and months to give my virginity up to him and I did near the end of our senior year.

And it was horrible.

And then he turned horrible.

Todd became mean and verbally abusive. He always seemed to be angry at me, his parents and at the world. I took the brunt of his angst because I was the most accessible and frankly, I was able to ignore his tirades most of the time. I was the perfect outlet for him.

Sex with Todd sucked because it was all about him. I never once had even achieved an orgasm when we were together because the two-minute man couldn't last long enough and he couldn't be bothered to spend any extra time on me. After that first time I gave in to his pressures, I was always the one that had to initiate any sort of intimacy. Sometimes, I felt like it was a chore for him, which didn't do anything for my sexual ego. Luckily, back then, I had enough of an elitist ego that I could let that one roll off my back. This meant we had sex very infrequently, which ultimately became fine with me. I never really felt I was missing anything with him.

The old Emily could easily overlook the lackluster sex. I mean, back in those days, I was only thinking about my wealthy, socialite future and Todd Fulgram was a great catch. But his abuse was something I would not tolerate. It started out as verbal but soon escalated. He never hit me but there was no doubt in my mind that real violence was just over the horizon. He mostly just grabbed me hard or shoved me, particularly when he was drinking. And he drank a lot.

One month before I left for college, we got into a major fight and he went ballistic. He shoved me up against the wall of my bedroom so hard my head bounced off it and it knocked a painting to the floor. I kneed him in the nuts and then ran out of my room. I love to reflect back on that moment as I consider that move to be my official breakup notice.

Since then, I have painstakingly tried to avoid Todd. After that incident, he turned to stalking me. Begging me to take him back, offering the sappiest and most insincere of apologies. And I'm not really sure why. In hindsight, he always seemed to be angry with me and didn't really seem to legitimately care about me as a person. The old Emily was so wrapped up in her own sense of self-importance, that she never noticed her unimportance to Todd. On top of that, I couldn't tell my parents the real reason I broke up with him, so for the past two years, my mother has been pressuring me to give him another chance.

The absolute worst thing of all though, is the fact that Todd goes to Columbia as well. When we were together, we both decided to go to the same university so we could be close to each other.

Unfortunately, Columbia is not a very large school so I tend to run into Todd more times than I would like. I merely walk the other way when I see him. He's tried to corner me a few times but luckily, there has always been someone around. The best is when I'm with Fil. She scares the crap out of Todd, I can tell. If he even starts approaching when she's around, she merely growls at him, "Walk the other way, Shithead, or I'll sneak into your dorm room at night and cut your balls off."

Oh, I love Fil!

Luckily, I haven't seen Todd all summer and he's been noticeably quiet. No creepy texts about how he misses me, or voice mails begging to see me. And now…my mother wants me to go on a date with him? This is just going to get him hopeful again and I can barely stomach the thought of being in the same room with him, much less on an actual date.

I try one more time to appease my mother. "I can't go out with Todd. Things were terrible between us. Frankly, he's a little scary. How about I find someone else instead?"

I know what Ryan means when he constantly complains that our mother never listens to us. She just scoffs and says, "Nonsense. He's a perfectly nice man. Don't disappoint me on this, Emily."

"I'm not going to do it, Mother," I say in a spurt of wild bravery.

Celia Burnham turns her icy blue eyes on me. She's silent for just a minute as she appraises me and a thin sheen of sweat breaks out on my forehead. Then she lowers the bomb. "You will do this, Emily, and you will do it with a smile on your face. If you do not show up Saturday with Todd Fulgram on your arm, the following Monday I will meet with our attorney and have your trust revoked."

I stare at her in stunned silence. I try hard not to be materialistic anymore. I mean, I can't help the tons of designer clothes and expensive jewelry I already have, but that trust fund is my means of independence from my family. I inherit control over it when I turn twenty-one, just a mere ten months away. Once I get my hands on that money, I can be free of my mother's rule and I can go to grad school for Journalism.

Ten more months.

I can do this.

Just one more week and one sickening date with Todd Fulgram, and then I'm out of here.

CHAPTER 2

Nix

I DUMP THE cardboard box out on the floor and start pushing the junk around, searching for my target. My index finger on my right hand is wrapped in a paper towel to staunch the flow of blood while I paw through the stuff looking for Band-Aids.

I know I don't have a chance of finding them. Hell, I can't find anything in my house. It's been a disaster for the past three months due to a major leak in my upstairs plumbing that essentially caved in most of the first-floor ceiling.

Since then, I salvaged what I could, which basically meant throwing all of my shit that wasn't wet into cardboard boxes. I had packed up my clothes and moved into my little brother's condo until I could get the repairs done. He has a sweet place on the Hudson with amazing views of Manhattan. The only thing that sucks is Harley doesn't have room to run as he does here.

Right now, that lazy dog is snoozing underneath an

oak tree in the backyard. I'm glad Linc loves dogs and doesn't mind Harley living in his condo. Otherwise, I'd be living in my soggy house, sleeping on the plywood floors I've just managed to install on the second floor.

It's no use. I'm never going to find a Band-Aid so what's a former Marine to do? I'm going to MacGyver the hell out of it, that's what.

I walk out of my house and go back to my workshop…back to the scene of my injury. I had been hammering a piece of sheet metal that I was forming into a gas tank for a custom motorcycle and carelessly sliced my finger along the edge. It was, oh, only about the millionth time that something like that has happened to me.

Grabbing some duct tape, I walk over to the sink. I throw the bloody paper towel in the garbage can, give a quick rinse of my finger under the tap, then wrap some more paper towels around the cut, pulling tight. I rip off a piece of duct tape with my teeth and wrap it around my finger. I don't have to worry about a tetanus shot. In my line of work, I'm always up to date on that.

There. Good as new.

Turning back to the metal tank, I run my other hand through my hair in frustration. It immediately falls back into my face and I mentally make a note to myself to get a haircut. I had not cut my hair since I got out of the Marines two years ago, so it's probably time for a trim. I scrub my hand over my face and the soft beard reminds me I haven't shaved in about a week. That tends to happen when I work on a new piece. I get so involved that I lose track of time. This means that I don't shave, I hardly sleep and I'm lucky if I remember to eat.

The tank is giving me nothing but fits today and the cut to my finger means I need to take a break. I should probably grab some lunch but I'm too lazy to walk the fifty feet to my house. My kitchen is about the only room that doesn't have any water damage, so I can at least eat while I'm here at my shop working.

Foregoing a trip back to the house for food, I open the small refrigerator I have in my workshop and pull out a Budweiser. It's the King of Beers after all. Popping the top, I take a healthy swallow.

Yup. Way better than a sandwich.

Walking over to my old, tattered recliner, I throw my body in it and stare at the gas tank. This is normally a project I could do with my eyes closed, yet I seem to be fumbling. I take another sip of beer and glance around my work area. This is my haven. It's the place I can come to be alone with my thoughts and where I can work my sheets of metal, forging and hammering them into art.

I bought this property when I left the Marine Corps at the young in body, old in heart age of twenty-four. I had saved up a hell of a lot of money during my two tours in Afghanistan, particularly because of the extra hazard duty pay I was receiving. I was able to get the property dirt-cheap. The house needed a lot of work but I bought it because of the large garage and workshop in the backyard. It was the perfect place for me to set up my custom metal smith business.

When people see what I do for a living, and then they hear I was in the Marine Corps, they automatically assume I must have been a welder during my time in service. They couldn't be farther from the truth but I don't disabuse them of the notion. That would require further conversation about my time with the Corps and that is not something I like to do.

No, when I got out of the Marine Corps, my skills were not transferable. There wasn't much call for someone that could shoot a target from a thousand yards away or make a HALO jump from a plane at thirty thousand feet. My ability to evade capture and withstand torture wouldn't work in the real world. Well, except maybe on Wall Street, but I'm not cut out to wear a suit every day of my life.

Thus, I did the only other thing I knew…metalwork. You see, my old man had been a welder all of his life, so I thought, what the hell. If it was good enough for Pop, it was good enough for me.

Except, I didn't actually follow in his footsteps. My dad still toils after nearly thirty years in a shipyard, welding the hulls of barges and other water vessels. It's backbreaking and brutal work. It's also boring with no outlet for expression, so it's something I have no intention of ever doing.

Nope. I decided to use my welding certificate to make custom pieces of art from metal. That includes anything from custom-built motorcycles to outdoor water fountains to massive pieces of wall art. I had enough money saved up from my time in the Corps that I could afford to take the time to build up this niche business, and I was doing quite well for someone with nothing more than a high school education and years of war under my belt. My bikes sell on the cheap side for $25,000 and go on up from there.

I really am leading a dream life. I'm doing work that I love, making great money, and I answer to no one. What could make my world any more perfect?

I glance over at my desk in the corner of the shop. There is a pile of paperwork at least a foot tall that I need to do. I hate fucking paperwork. Despise it even.

Luckily, all of my bills are on auto-draft so all I have to worry about is depositing my earnings into the bank. But I tend to ignore the little things like balancing my bank accounts, filing sales tax forms, and making the necessary supply orders. I suppose I could do that now since I wouldn't get any more work done on the gas tank today.

That thought lasts only two seconds and then I dismiss it. I'd rather just sit here and stare at the unfinished tank and drink my beer.

Just as I'm finishing the last of my Bud, I hear someone knocking on the back door to my house. I stand up and peek out my shop window.

Oh, shit.

I sit back down and hope like hell she doesn't come out here to where I am now hiding.

A few seconds pass by and then I hear, "Nix…are you back here?"

Shit, shit. No such luck.

I reluctantly stand up and open the shop door.

"What do you need, Lyla?" I say, with as much politeness as is humanly possible for Nix Caldwell to give.

"Is that any way to greet me, sugar?" She runs a fingertip down the middle of my chest and it's not exactly unpleasant but it doesn't have the punch it used to. Lyla is a beautiful girl, with long blond hair and a slammin' body. She and I went to high school together, and we fooled around a lot back then. Just like many of my classmates, she stuck around Hoboken after graduation. I think she cuts hair in a local beauty salon or something. We've hooked up a few times since I've been back, but I've been very clear that it's nothing but sex. No-strings-attached. Each time she says that's all she wants too, but then she keeps coming around wanting to do things together. I expect that is why she is here now and it's baffling to me. Lyla has a few other guys on the side that she has no-strings sex with, too. So why doesn't she go bother one of them?

I'm sure they are a lot nicer than I am.

"I'm working right now," I explain to her.

"Oh, don't be such a drag, Nix. Let's go to the movies and then out for some beers."

"Sorry, Lyla. I've just got too much to do."

She steps in a little closer to me and I can smell her perfume. It's overpowering and burns the inside of my nose. She stands on her tiptoes in an effort to get her lips up near my ear. At six-foot-five, I could bend over and help her out but I don't. She gets close enough though and whispers suggestively, "We could bypass the movies and do something else instead."

There was a time when just those words would have caused my dick to stand at attention and I would have taken her up against the wall but clearly my time with Lyla is about to come to a screeching halt. I didn't have a shred of interest and she's clearly wanting more than no-strings sex.

I step back from her and let her down as gently as Nix Caldwell possibly can.

Which is not very gentle at all.

"Look, Lyla…I'm sorry. I'm just not interested in you, okay?"

Her face falls and the seductive smile she had been

sporting instantly vanishes. "But…I don't understand…"

The biggest lesson that Lyla is about to learn from post-war Nix Caldwell is that he has little patience. And when it's gone, he doesn't hold back. "What's to understand? I have no interest in you. Period. None. Do me a favor and don't come back around."

Lyla's face looks like it's about to crumble, then rage fills her eyes. "You're an asshole, Nixon Caldwell."

I look at her, my eyes probably as dead as I feel on the inside sometimes. "I know. Now, get out of here."

I turn my back on her, assuming she's going to leave. Instead, an empty bucket hits me in the back of my head. It bounces off and lands on the floor with a clatter. I look back at Lyla and she is wearing a very self-satisfied look, with her hands on her hips and her lips pouted out. For a split second, I think about retaliating…not physically…but verbally.

And just as quickly, it's gone. I simply don't care enough to engage and truth be told, I deserved to have her throw the bucket at me. I just stare impassively at her until she turns around in a huff and leaves my shop.

I reach back into the fridge and grab another beer. I'll have to call it quits today. No working with metal tools or fire when I've had something to drink. It's too dangerous.

Even for someone like me, who has been through Hell and back.

CHAPTER 3

Emily

CRAP! I'M LATE.

I hate the drive from Manhattan over to Hoboken and there's construction going on at the Lincoln Tunnel that has traffic backed up.

I shouldn't be nervous. I'm only going to see one of Ryan's best buddies, Lincoln Caldwell. He's the goalie for the New York Rangers and he graciously granted an interview to Ryan's little sister. I have to get it completed for one of my elective classes, The Economics of Sports.

I went ahead and officially declared my major in Journalism with an emphasis on Sports Journalism. Now, when I say I "officially declared", that just means I declared it to the university and to myself. There is no way in hell I'm telling my parents until I absolutely have to.

It really helps having a brother that plays professional sports and it would have been super easy to just interview him. But I don't share with many people that I'm related to Ryan Burnham. I want to keep my relationship with my brother private because I'm really enjoying the bond we've developed. And I don't want people trying to be friends with me just because my brother plays in the NHL.

So Ryan suggested I interview Lincoln. They became fast friends when Ryan signed on with the team and are pretty tight. I've met him a few times at some of the players' parties and he's a nice guy. A little bit of a ladies' man, but nothing I can't handle. Plus, he probably knows Ryan will kick his ass if he ever makes a move on me. I don't think Ryan will ever tolerate one of his teammates dating his baby sister. Which is fine by me. I may love all things related to sports but I have no desire to ever date an athlete. With the exception of my wonderful brother, most of them are just too full of themselves.

I mentally calculate my time frames. I'll need only about half an hour of Lincoln's time and that will get me back over to Manhattan in time for dinner. I'm eating at Ryan and Danny's tonight and I am so excited. This will be the first time we've been able to get together since the Fall semester started for me.

Ryan and Danny got married last December in a beautiful but simple Christmas wedding. The only ones in attendance, other than the happy bride and groom, were me, Ryan's best friend, Mike, and Danny's friends,

Paula and Sarge from Boston. My parents weren't invited because my father was out of the country but I know my mother would not have come. She's still pouting over Ryan's "abandonment of his family" in favor of "that woman with the purple hair". At this point, I think it's safe to say that my mother has completely written Ryan off and that makes my heart hurt for Ryan and Danny. My father, however, has been talking to Ryan so maybe he can talk some sense into my mother. He's the only person with any sway over her and really, it's because my mother adores her husband. Truly.

I find Lincoln's condo easy enough and pull into a parking spot. I pull my visor down and check my face in the mirror. No stray mascara marks and my lip-gloss is still shiny enough.

I pull my phone from my purse and check my texts and emails briefly.

Great! There's another text from Todd.

Em...pls call me. I miss u so much. I luv u. We belong 2gether.

Ever since my mother made me go to that fundraiser with him, he's started his stalker behavior again. He keeps insisting that we belong together. He sounds…frantic. As if his life depends upon hitching me to his hip. Right now, it's just emails and texts, which I have been ignoring. But maybe I need to get tough with him.

I punch out a quick reply.

Stop texting me. We r over.

Short and sweet. Hopefully, he'll get the message. Hopping out of the car, I make my way up to the top floor apartment.

Lincoln, of course, welcomes me in and I'm struck by how beautiful his place is. I expected it to be littered with dirty clothes, beer cans, and posters of naked women. Instead, his walls are painted a warm, taupe color and he has stylish, black leather furniture. Tastefully framed art prints grace the wall, and the only ode I can see to the fact that this is a bachelor pad is that he has an Xbox 360 hooked up to a massive seventy-inch television.

Lincoln Caldwell, goalie for the New York Rangers, is as beautiful as his condo. He's a favorite subject for the newspapers and sports magazines, probably because his face could be considered a work of art in most museums. Hazel eyes, and dark brown sexy hair that's cut into a gazillion layers, perfectly framing his rugged face. He'd be a dream guy to have if it wasn't for the whole "I don't date athletes" thing I have going on.

I'm welcomed in and Linc chooses to have us sit in his living room for the interview. As soon as I take a seat, a huge, furry bundle of what I later learn is a dog comes barreling at me. He…she…it…hops the coffee table and crashes into my chest, sending me backward into the plush, couch cushions.

I'm gasping for air and the dog is licking my face from top to bottom. I hear Lincoln yell, "damn dog" and then he pulls the golden mass of muscle and quivering nerves off of me. I can now see it's a beautiful Golden Retriever…a boy, I believe…and he's staring at me with a big, goofy dog grin on his face.

"It's okay. I love dogs," I assure him.

Lincoln cautiously lets go of the dog's collar and I'm rewarded with the big lug—not Lincoln—coming over to lay his head in my lap.

"Sorry about that. Dog has no manners whatsoever."

I give the furry monster a quick scratch behind the ears and I get a well-behaved canine that promptly lays at my feet and goes to sleep.

The next half hour goes by quickly and Lincoln provides me with an engaging interview. Of course, he can't help by finishing it off with an offer to go out to dinner. I politely decline and he gives me a sad, tortured look. I'm sure that works on a lot of women, but not me. Instead, I give him a professional handshake, thanking him for his time. I do, however, lean over and give the dog a big hug and a goodbye scratch.

Walking back to my car, I glance at my watch. I need to hurry if I want to beat rush hour, although it won't be so bad heading into Manhattan as opposed to coming out.

I get in my little BMW 335i—a high school graduation present from my parents—and put my seatbelt on. I check my phone before heading out. Todd sent me three more texts while I was in Lincoln's condo.

U don't mean that. U still need me.

U need to call me. Now!

Why r u ignoring me?

Reading the last text, I feel an icy shiver go up my spine. Todd is sounding a little unhinged and I'm afraid I might find a dead rabbit in my stew pot when I get home. Gosh, *Fatal Attraction* was an awesomely creepy movie. I hope that it isn't turning into a real-life event for me.

Turning the car on, I look in my rearview and side mirrors. Putting the car in reverse, I start to back out. At the same time, my phone rings and I can see on the screen that it's Danny calling. Keeping one hand on the wheel, I grab the phone and answer it, still backing out of my parking spot.

I barely get the words out, "Hi Danny" when I hear a sickening crunch of metal and my car jolts to a stop.

"Shit!" I yell.

"Are you okay?" Danny asks.

"No," I wail. "I just hit something. I'll call you back."

Looking in my rearview mirror, I can't see anything. I throw my phone down and jump out of my car. Rounding the back corner, I am horrified to see a motorcycle lying on the ground with its driver laying a few feet away. I immediately take in that he appears to be okay as he's getting up from the ground.

My heart is thundering in my chest as the crashing realization that I could have just killed a person sinks into me. My legs start to wobble and my head spins.

"Fuck, lady. Don't you watch where you're going?"

I look at the man who is standing up now and looking down at his bike. He takes his helmet off and throws it to the ground in anger.

I vaguely notice that he glares at me but it's like he's in slow motion. He sounds like he's in a tunnel and his voice is getting fainter when he says, "Hey…are you okay?"

His words say he is concerned but I still have barely enough of my wits to discern his tone of voice says he's still very pissed.

I try to answer him but I can't make my voice work. Then I realize my legs are giving way and I see the ground rushing up to meet me. Before I can hit though, the angry man is there, catching me in his arms. I'm vaguely aware that he picks me up and walks over to a grassy area adjacent to the parking lot where he lays me down very gently.

I can feel him put his palm to my cheek, and he taps it lightly. For some reason, I notice he has what looks like a paper towel duct-taped to his finger.

Weird.

The guy stands up and walks away. I start to sit up and before I know it, he's back squatting down beside me. He hands me a bottle of water. "Here, drink this. I had it in my saddlebag."

I take a few sips, and immediately start feeling better. I look back again at the man, and it's like I'm seeing him for the first time.

My mouth goes dry and my skin prickles with awareness. He is unbelievably gorgeous. Almost super-model perfection, but with a hint of danger and darkness. His hair is long, coming to rest right above his shoulders. It's a dark, brown color with glints of warm, golden highlights running throughout. His eyes are the color of spring ferns and framed by lashes so thick, I'm briefly jealous. His face is perfection. He has perfectly slashed brows, and a perfectly straight nose, and a perfectly square jaw.

He must have been cut from butter is my first thought. Or marble. Or buttery marble.

Best of all, he has at least a week's worth of dark stubble on his face, which makes him look menacing and sexy all at the same time. I take in with appreciation the tight fit of his Harley Davidson t-shirt and dark jeans, showcasing a lean and well-muscled body. He is the exact opposite of any man I have ever thought of dating, and my mother would consider him the Anti-Christ on just his dark looks alone.

I feel dowdy next to him and my hand subconsciously comes up to smooth my hair.

"Are you injured, Lady?"

I'm dumbfounded looking at him. I'm sure he probably thinks I swallowed my tongue in the accident but I have just been blindsided, by what I believe to be, the most physically splendid specimen of a man I have ever seen.

Seriously.

"Maybe I should call an ambulance," he says.

"Emily."

His eyebrows cinch together in confusion. "Excuse me?"

"My name's not Lady…it's Emily."

He gives me an exasperated look and I swear I hear him grumble, "I don't have time for this shit."

I take another sip of water and I'm feeling much, much better now. The fact that I was so petrified I could have killed someone and then almost fainted has completely left my mind. I'm just sitting here enjoying this magically, hot man in front of me.

He stands up and glares down at me. "Do you think you can stand up?"

I nod my head, expecting him to gallantly hold his hand out to me. It doesn't come and after a few seconds, I realize it's never going to come. So I push myself up from the ground, brushing blades of grass from the seat of my jeans.

"I'm assuming you're okay?" he asks.

I nod my head. "Yeah. It just freaked me out when I thought I had killed you. I've never fainted before."

"You didn't faint," he snaps. "You just got a little wobbly."

Okay. What was this asshole's problem?

"You think I'm an asshole? You just ran me and my bike over."

Oh, crap. Did I voice that asshole comment out loud? Apparently, my brain is a little more addled than I thought.

I take a deep breath and then I start rambling…like an idiot. "I'm really sorry. I was distracted. I'm getting these crazy, stalker messages from my ex-boyfriend, and I'm afraid there may be a dead rabbit in a pot when I get back to my apartment. And then I got a call from my sister-in-law, but I know that's no excuse. I thought I had looked. I'll pay for the repairs. Are you injured?"

He's looking at me as if I was an alien. He shakes his head and sighs. "Let's go see what the damage is."

I follow him back over to our vehicles. My back bumper is crumpled in but his bike is a mess. It's dented all over and the front wheel is turned at a weird angle.

I can't think of anything to say, so I offer lamely, "It's a beautiful motorcycle."

He looks at me incredulously. "It was a beautiful

motorcycle, you mean."

"Yes, that's what I mean," I respond politely. I feel like such a tool.

"Look, just give me your insurance information and we won't even bother to call the cops."

What? No! He cannot have my insurance information. You see, I've had a little problem with speeding tickets back in Boston along with two other wrecks, that technically were my fault but I could push some blame too on the other drivers if I was that type of person. Which I'm not…anymore. If I get any more insurance points, I can probably kiss my license goodbye.

"No. We can't put it on the insurance," I say adamantly. "I'll pay you for the damage myself."

He smirks at me and it makes me want to slap his face.

No, kiss his face.

Wait…definitely slap his face.

"Lady, do you know how much that motorcycle costs? There's no way you can afford it out of your pocket, and I don't care how much designer clothing or expensive jewelry you wear."

"For the second time, my name isn't Lady. It's Emily," I grit out. "And for your information, you have no clue what I can and can't afford."

"Do you have about $10,000 you can cough up?" he asks. "Because that's what it's going to cost in materials and labor. The front axle is completely destroyed."

Ten-freakin-thousand-dollars? Oh shit, I was in trouble. There is no way I can come up with that amount at one time. My parents let me draw two thousand dollars a month from my trust fund if I need it but he would have to agree to accept payments.

I put on my most conciliatory face. "Look...I am really, really sorry I did this. But I cannot put this on my insurance. I'll lose my car if I do."

"And this is my problem how?" he taunts.

"It's not. I'm just asking you for a little understanding. I can pay you in installments. Two thousand dollars a month until we are square." I end on a pleading tone but I can't help it. I have no room for pride here.

I watch fascinated as he runs a hand through the hair on top of his head, pulling the long locks back and holding them there. His hair is long enough he could put it in a short ponytail if he wanted. With his hair pulled back, his face is thrown into stark relief, so that his sculpted cheekbones say, "BAM" to me. The angels were definitely singing on the day this guy was created.

I wait with bated breath.

He finally releases the hold on his hair and it gracefully glides back around his face. I wonder if it's as soft as it looks.

"Fine. But I need your information so you can't welsh on me."

As if. "Fine, whatever."

I pull my wallet out and he copies down my license information. I give him my phone number, and he gives me his.

"What's your name?" I ask, so I can program it in my phone.

"Nix."

"Nix what?"

"Just Nix…that's all you need to know."

This man is infuriating. Hot, but infuriating. "Then how can I make a check out to you if I don't know your last name?"

"You don't," he says in a low, husky voice. "Bring me cash. Just call me when you have the first two thousand. I expect it within thirty days or else I'll come looking for you. And trust me…you don't want that to happen."

A shiver involuntarily runs through me and I can't tell if I'm scared or turned on by the danger in his voice.

And even though I'm pissed as hell that I've just blown $10,000 over my own stupidity, I can't help the fact that I'm looking forward to seeing this man again.

CHAPTER 4

Emily

I KNOCK ON Danny and Ryan's door and wait for them to open it. I've finally gotten my heart rate under control after that terrifying but surreal experience with Nix.

And what the hell kind of name is Nix anyway?

The door is thrown open and Ryan is standing there. I throw my arms around his neck and he picks me up, swinging me around.

"There's my baby sister," he says with overt fondness and I love it. I love how much our relationship has changed over the last few years. "How did the interview with Linc go?"

Ryan drops me to the floor and I put my purse and keys on his foyer table. "It was fine. Lincoln's a nice guy. Got exactly what I needed."

"Awesome. Well, come on into the kitchen. Danny is pulling stuff out of the oven right now."

I follow Ryan back into the kitchen. Danny is bent

over the oven, pulling out what looks like an amazing pork tenderloin. Ryan notices her position and immediately goes over to her. "Here, let me get that for you."

Danny swats his hand away. "I can do it. I'm not an invalid you know."

My eyes narrow as I watch Danny pull the pan out, her hands dwarfed by two huge oven mitts. Ryan stands nearby, holding his hands out as if she might fall.

What. The. Hell?

"What's going on with you two?" I demand.

Both of them turn to look at me, guilty expressions on their faces. They look at each other then back at me. Neither of them says a word.

"I repeat…what…is…going…on?" I punctuate every word with enough menace that they know I'm expecting a truthful answer.

Ryan seems to have forgotten that Danny is holding a steaming pan of pork loin in her hand. "Um…well…um…"

I turn to Danny and raise my eyebrows. She'll need to answer because Ryan has apparently been struck stupid.

"That pan looks hot, Danny. Put it down."

Danny turns and sets the roast on the countertop. She turns back to me and she has a little smirk on her face. She's hiding a secret but I can tell she wants to spill.

"Okay, if you two don't tell me what's going on right

this minute…I'm going to…"

What am I going to do? What threat will work?

Oh, I know.

"I'm going to pick up the phone and call Mother. And I'll tell her that Danny cheated on you, Ryan, with a midget from the circus and you are going to have his midget baby. Then you, Ryan, can deal with the fallout."

Danny busts out laughing and Ryan looks horrified. "You wouldn't," he accuses.

"Would."

Danny takes her oven mitts off and slaps them into Ryan's chest. "Get the rest of the vegetables out of the oven."

I start jumping up and down like a kid at Christmas because she's getting ready to spill her guts I can tell. "Tell me, tell me, tell me," I implore. "I can keep a secret."

Ryan pulls the veggies out and shuts the oven with his foot. After setting them down, he takes the mitts off and pulls Danny into his arms. He nestles her backside into him and wraps his arms around her stomach. Placing his lips on her head, they both look at me.

"Think we should tell her?" he asks.

Danny looks at me appraisingly. "I don't know. I'm not sure she could keep the secret."

I pull my iPhone out of my pocket with a flourish. "That's it…I'm calling Mother."

Danny leaps out of Ryan's arms and grabs my phone away. "Fine, you brat. We'll tell you."

Ryan pulls Danny back against his chest and nuzzles her neck. He then looks at me and he has the most joyful smile on his face. Tears are in his eyes. "We're pregnant."

The most delicious, languid and comforting warmth spreads through me. It starts in my chest and seeps outward, touching every nerve in my body with a gentle caress. My breath catches as I watch Danny and Ryan watching me for my reaction.

"HOLY CRAP!" I scream. I dash across the kitchen and throw my arms around both of them, sandwiching Danny in between me and Ryan. "I'm going to be an Aunt!"

All three of us are now crying, and hugging, and laughing. I start hurtling questions, still with my arms wrapped around them.

How? When? Boy? Girl? Names?

Danny finally pushes me back and I release my hold. I stand there—just grinning—and I don't think I've ever felt such happiness in my life. I behold my family…Ryan and Danny…and I hope that one day I can have what they have.

♦

RYAN'S GONE AS he had an evening team meeting. Dinner was fantastic, made better by the wonderful news. I learned more about pregnancy than I ever knew was possible to learn in one sitting.

Danny is only two months along and they are not telling anyone other than me at this point. They want to wait until she gets into her first trimester. I apologize—insincerely, of course—for making them tell me, but Danny admits that they were going to tell me tonight anyway. They felt that I was the one person in the world they wanted to know right now.

That thought alone has me practically melting into a puddle of snotty goo.

We talk about morning sickness, and baby clothes, and whether my niece or nephew will play the violin or hockey. Or both.

We start spouting out names, giggling over the more ridiculous ones like Horowitz and Tangerine.

Danny goes silent for a second and then she looks at me with solemn eyes. "We want you to be the baby's godmother, Emily."

Ohhhh, I think, as I suck in a wisp of air through my teeth.

"I don't know…are you sure…isn't a godmother supposed to be like a good role model or something?"

All of my insecurities come gushing forth. I know I've tried to be a better person…a better woman. But I was rotten for so long. How could they entrust me with something so important?

Danny grabs my hand and holds it to her heart. "Emily…I can't think of a better role model for my baby. You are a spectacularly wonderful person and I hope my child grows up to be just like you."

Okay, here's the waterworks. I smile at her through tear-soaked eyes, and then we are hugging each other. She cradles me to her chest, stroking my hair.

"You are a marvel, Emily Burnham," she says softly.

I pull away from her. "You're my role model, Danny. Always."

The evening ends on a high note. Danny breaks out the wine to celebrate but because she's pregnant, I'm the only one drinking. I get a little bit drunk and Danny insists I stay the night.

We start in on the baby names again, and I throw out, "What do you think about Nix?"

"Nix?" she says, gently letting it roll off her tongue. "For a girl or a boy?"

I shrug my shoulders. "I suppose it could be both, but if your kid is a boy, then Nix will stand for asshole for sure."

"What in the world are you talking about?" she asks.

I shrug my shoulders again and don't answer. I don't want to think about the amazingly perfect looking man I ran over today who turned out to be a world-class jerk. I'd rather keep my fantasies of him on the pleasurable side.

CHAPTER 5

Nix

I POP THE top off my beer and lean up against the wall. I'm watching the party in progress, always comfortable to observe and never to be drawn into conversation. I've always been, by nature, a quiet and introspective person. My time in the Marine Corps, doing deep reconnaissance missions for MARSOC had taught me well the virtues of patience and silence. Some of my time in Afghanistan had been sitting in the frigid mountains, watching the Taliban movement below and reporting it to Command. I could sit for hours at a time and stare at a single spot if I had to. And I had no problems being quiet about it. It was, after all, my nature.

It's not that large, noisy crowds bother me. I like a good party as much as the next guy. As long as I can sit back, drink my beer and observe. And not be bothered. I'm just not overly fond of people in general.

Tonight, my brother Linc has gone all out and thrown a whopper of a party. Almost his entire hockey team is here, along with a slew of beautiful women. Linc never has a hard time coming up with a throng of ladies to ogle. They are basically hockey groupies, accepting the invite with the hope of getting laid and possibly landing themselves a hockey husband. But the ratio of single Rangers to the hungry ladies is vastly disproportionate and I will be able to take one of them to bed if I want.

For now, though, I'm just watching.

Finishing off my beer, I head into the kitchen and throw the empty in the recycle bin. I pull a new beer out of the refrigerator and twist the cap off. I feel like getting shit faced tonight for some reason.

Walking back into the living room, I resume my perch against the wall. Harley is mingling with the crowd. That dog will do anything for a scratch or soft word. And he is so fucking cute, he always gets it. I often wonder if there is something wrong with the fact that I like dogs more than I do people. All I know…Harley has never let me down.

"Having a good time, bro?"

I look over my shoulder and see Linc standing there, holding his typical glass of Scotch. I give him a nod and hold my beer up in acknowledgment.

"Well, it's going to get better tonight. See those two women over there…"

I look to where he's pointing. Sitting on the couch are two ladies that are ferociously gorgeous. They're both wearing tight, short dresses and sky-high heels. I can tell at a glance that both have put copious amounts of money into breast enhancement.

Who says my observational skills in the Corps were wasted?

"Nice," I reply. And I mean it.

"They're for us…tonight …after everyone leaves."

Of course, they are. Linc always looks out for me in that department. He thinks I have no clue how to talk to a woman or get one in bed. He takes my silence and unwillingness to engage people as an inability to get laid. I hate to break it to him, but it's not that hard. There are plenty of women out there who appreciate straight, simple talk without the need to spout poetry at them.

But I don't want to hurt his feelings so I just smile at him and say, "You rock, man."

Linc ambles off and heads straight over to the two women. He plops himself on the couch in between them and I watch as they fawn all over my little brother.

What a player!

I glance around and notice the front door open. More partygoers coming in. I recognize one of Linc's good friends, Ryan Burnham walking in, along with his wife, Danny. Now that is one cool chick. Linc told me she was a graduate of Julliard but she rocks some awesome dyed hair and face metal. So not what I picture a hockey wife and classical musician to look like.

And walking in just behind Danny…

My breath freezes and my bottle of beer stops halfway to my mouth. It's Emily. The girl that ran me over last week.

What the hell is she doing here?

As mad as I was at her last week, I've spent the last several days remembering how beautiful she is. And I see my memory serves me still. Her long hair shimmers like melted dark chocolate and her eyes are the lightest, warmest brown I've ever seen. They look like amber swirled with copper.

The whole incident with Emily was baffling to me. I was fucking pissed that she ran my motorcycle over and part of me wanted to strangle her. And yet, by the end of our meeting, she had convinced me to let her make payments for the damages. I still can't fathom why I agreed to it. Nix Caldwell doesn't cut anyone slack.

I watch in disbelief as Harley barrels through the crowd and jumps up on her. I start to move forward to pull him off but she just grabs him in a big hug and buries her face in his neck.

I'm amazed. Stupefied. Bumfuzzled.

I've never seen a woman react to Harley that way. Usually, his hundred pounds of brute force tends to scare most people.

Emily gently lowers his front paws to the ground and continues to rub his ears as people come up to her to say hello. She clearly knows a lot of the hockey players here and I'm wondering if she's one of those women that are looking to get laid tonight or walk off with a potential husband.

The thought does not set well with me.

And then I see Ryan Burnham turn to her and whisper in her ear. She punches him in the shoulder over whatever he said, and it hits me like a ton of bricks. That's Ryan's sister. Duh…Emily Burnham. Watching them stand next to each other, there is no mistaking the family resemblance.

She must have been here at Linc's place when she hit me that day. He never said a word to me and he usually tells me about all of his sexual exploitations. Maybe Emily is special to him and he's keeping her under wraps.

As I watch her though, she looks over at Linc, who is still wrapped up in the double-trouble beauties. She just shakes her head with a fond smirk. She's clearly not upset that he is with other women. No…she had to have been here for something else that day. Not that I care nor is it any of my business.

So I just sit back…and I watch her.

♦

I NEVER LEAVE my spot, leaning up against the wall. I finish my beer but I don't make a move to get another one. I'm fascinated watching Emily work the crowd.

Ryan brings her a glass of red wine and a bottled water for Danny. Emily then proceeds to mingle around. She clearly knows most of the guys, and even makes small talk with some of the girls. I notice she laughs a lot and it's hard not to notice the way her eyes light up when she finds something amusing.

Probably twenty minutes of her laughing and joking with other people goes by, and then the inevitable happens. She glances my way and locks eyes with me. Instantly, the gregarious smile on her face melts and she actually looks disappointed to see me there.

Can't say as I blame her. I was a real prick to her the last time we met.

Oh, well. It's no skin off my back. That's who I am.

I turn away and walk into the kitchen to get another beer. After opening it up, I take a long swallow and lean back against the countertop. No one is in here and I'm enjoying the blessed quiet. It's my solace. I look down to study the Frye boots I'm wearing. They're getting pretty scuffed, and there's a nice gouge on the heel of the left one, compliments of Miss Emily Burnham running me over.

"Hey, Nix."

My head snaps up and Emily is standing there.

Up close, she's even more beautiful than I remembered. She's wearing a dress but it's not the hooker wear that most of the women in the living room have painted on their bodies. It's butter yellow, fitting nicely across her breasts—which are not surgically enhanced, by the way—and flows softly around her legs. The thin straps showcase creamy, sun-kissed skin. The dress comes demurely to her knees and she has on a pair of gold sandals I notice after dragging my gaze down her shapely calves.

Emily is tall for a girl. She must be close to five-foot-six, as the top of her head comes about to my shoulder. It's the perfect height to pull a woman in close and press up against her body.

I shake my head. What the hell am I thinking?

I fuck women and leave them. I don't take stock of the beauty of their clothing, or how soft their skin looks.

I look her in the eyes and I make myself be me. "Well if it isn't the lady that likes to run people over."

She blushes and averts her eyes from my gaze. I watch as she clasps her hands in front of her then grabs her lower lip between her teeth. The move is innocent and wrings of nervousness, but damn if it doesn't make me want to take her lip in between my own teeth and bite down softly.

I wait for her to say something. Finally, she looks back at me and says, "I have to talk to you about the money I owe you."

I raise my eyebrows at her. "What's to talk about? You owe me the money and you have about three more weeks to make the first payment."

"Yeah, about my ability to get the money…my

source has sort of dried up."

"What do you mean?" I ask. I really shouldn't care about it but I find I want to talk to her more. So this is the perfect excuse.

"I...well...um..." She's stammering with pink cheeks and I find it adorable. Normally, that would be a major turn off for me.

"Spit it out, Emily."

She takes a deep breath and plunges forward. "Okay, here's the deal. I'm a trust fund baby. No surprise there, right? Well, I'm allowed to take out two thousand dollars a month until I turn twenty-one, which is in ten months. When I turn twenty-one, I get full control of the trust. I had planned to just turn over that two thousand every month to you. Unfortunately, I've managed to piss my parents off completely and they cut me off."

Emily blows out a long, slow breath and I see that it is painful for her to admit this to me. But I'm not moved. "You know this isn't my problem. Why don't you just give me your insurance information?"

"No," she exclaims. "I can't."

"Oh, that's right. Mommy and daddy will take away your Beemer, right?" I can't help the sneer in my voice.

She shakes her head. "It's worse than that. If you file an insurance claim, the police will have to do a report. And if I have another accident, I'll lose my license."

I watch her for a minute and she's chewing on that lip again. It makes me want to suck it into my mouth and see how she tastes. I start to feel movement below and holy hell, I'm getting a fucking hard on just by looking at her lower lip. I realize, all of a sudden, that I want this girl.

And I want her bad.

But there is no way. She is clearly not a fuck 'em and leave 'em kind of girl. She's the kind you bring home to meet your parents. And I've never…ever…had a woman I've wanted to do that with. I need to clear my head of Emily Burnham.

She is completely off-limits.

I need to tell her to get the fucking money or else.

Instead, I say, "How would you like to work off the debt?"

I have no clue where that came from but the words are out and I can't take them back. And I'm not sure I want to.

She looks at me, tilting her head to the side in curiosity. "What do you mean?"

"It turns out that I'm a decent welder and metal artist, but I suck at bookkeeping. I have a ton of administrative work that I need help with. How about you give me twenty hours a week and I'll let you work off the amount you owe me."

I watch as she contemplates my offer. I have to clench my fists not to reach out and pull her lower lip out from between her teeth.

Finally, her lip pops free and she says, "That will take

me months to work that kind of debt off."

"A few things you'll learn about me, Emily. I'm not a nice man but I can be a patient one in the right situation."

Her eyebrows close in together as she considers my offer and she licks her lower lip to wet it. I have to bite my own tongue so I don't groan in response.

"Okay," she says. "But it has to work around my class schedule. I can commit Monday, Wednesday and Friday afternoons to you, and Saturdays, too if you want. Oh, and I figured out already that you're not a nice man."

Why those words cut me, I have no idea because they are utterly true. I'm a world-class prick, particularly to the female persuasion. And I've never thought I should be anything different.

"Deal," I say.

I hold my hand out to shake on it and she steps forward to accept. Her hand is warm and delicate but her grip is firm. She's close enough I can smell her and it's a light scent…jasmine, I think. It suits her well.

Releasing her hand, I walk past her. "See you on, Monday."

I reach into the fridge to grab one more beer and I head down the hall to my bedroom. I have no more interest in the party, and I certainly have no interest in hooking up with Linc's women.

The comfort of solitude is what I crave right now.

CHAPTER 6

Emily

I'M DRIVING TO Hoboken for my first day of work for Nix. He texted me his address this morning. That's it…just his address. There was no "Hey. Here's my address. See you later." The man is definitely short on words along with manners and civility.

I'm nervous, no doubt. There is something about Nix that sets me on edge. When I first laid eyes on him at Linc's party this past weekend, I didn't actually connect who he was. I mean, I recognized him as a gorgeous man, and a jolt of pure energy coursed through my body when I made contact with his gaze. I felt instant, sizzling chemistry with this person. And that lasted for two seconds before my brain caught up to my body, and I realized it was Nix.

Our conversation was frustrating. I hated telling him that I couldn't come up with the money. But it was nowhere near as bad as how I lost access to the money.

I shudder even thinking about the conversation I had

with my mother. She called me last Friday, furious. Apparently, Columbia's School of Journalism sent me a letter confirming my major declaration and promptly mailed it to my home address on file. Mother minced no words when I answered the phone.

"Emily…how could you declare journalism as your major? We talked about this and you are supposed to go pre-med or pre-law."

I took a calming breath and counted to five before I answered. "Mother…I don't want to be a lawyer or a doctor. I want to be a sports journalist."

I heard my mother's sharp intake of breath and you would have thought I just told her I murdered someone. She responded to me in the only way that Celia Burnham knows how…with brute force. "That is unacceptable, young lady. You are to go first thing Monday morning and change your major."

There was no amount of oxygen on the planet that would give me a calming breath right then. I gritted my teeth but tried to remain respectful. "I'm sorry, Mother, but I won't do that. I want to pursue a career of my choosing, not yours."

I heard my mother sigh, and I knew she was changing tactics on me. She practically whined to me when she said, "Emily…you know how crucial it is at this time that our family appear as powerful as possible. A daughter in medical school or law school will be a major boost to your father's campaign."

I felt a screeching headache coming on and rubbed gingerly at my temple. "Mother…please don't make me feel guilty about this. There is nothing wrong with a journalism major. It's completely respectable."

And then my mother changed tactics again. This time she got my attention. "I've had enough, Emily. If you do not change your major back, your trust fund is going to be suspended."

I was so tired of her holding that trust fund over me. I wish sometimes it never existed. If she thought that would get me to back down, she had another think coming. In fact, she had made me so mad that I almost told her I was going to drop out of school and become a topless dancer. Instead, I said in a firm voice, "So be it, Mother. Good bye."

I hung up the phone, had a brief moment of glory over standing up to my mother then I had a major panic attack. Two problems came immediately to mind. First, how was I going to pay Nix the money for his motorcycle, and second, how was I going to pay tuition next semester? This semester is no problem. My parents had paid that in full already, along with the lease on my apartment. I can get a part-time job for incidental expenses. I mean, I've never had to work a job in my life, but how hard could it be really? But there was no way I could stay at Columbia next semester without my parents' help and no way to access my trust fund until the following summer.

I hated to do it, but I got in the car and drove over to Ryan's. He wasn't there but Danny sat down and listened to me. After I poured out the story of my mother's phone call, she didn't hesitate. "Emily…you have nothing to worry about. Ryan and I will pay for your tuition next semester if your parents don't come around."

I was so relieved, I jumped up and hugged her hard. She returned it with vigor.

I didn't tell her, though, about owing the money to Nix because she and Ryan didn't need to be burdened with my own stupidity. I was still stewing about that when we went to the party at Linc's condo, and so on top of the shock of seeing him standing there, I now realized I had to confront the dilemma that faced me. And since they say that honesty is the best policy, I figured I should spill my guts to him.

I have to say, based upon my limited experience with him when I flattened his motorcycle, Nix actually took my inability to pay him much better than I thought he would. I could tell he wasn't happy about it but his offer to let me work the debt off was the best I could hope for.

And so, here I am, driving to Nix's house in Hoboken. I've been wondering all weekend why Nix was at that party. I never got a chance to ask him because after we struck our deal, he didn't say another word and just walked away. I didn't see him again for the rest of the night. I would have to remember to ask him why he was there.

I pull into the driveway of the address Nix had sent me. It's a two-story home in a middle class, slightly rundown neighborhood. Large oak trees line the streets and a few kids are riding bicycles on the sidewalk. I pull in behind a dilapidated Ford Bronco that has chunks of the body rusted completely through. Guilt courses through me as I realize this is what Nix is probably driving since I killed his motorcycle.

I knock on the front door but no one answers. I walk around the back and see a large garage and workshop at the rear of the yard. I head that way.

When I get to the workshop, I open the door and walk in. It's spacious and well organized. There's a large worktable with various pieces of equipment all around. I wonder what he does with all this stuff. I notice a desk sits against one wall and it's covered with mounds of paper. My new job, I assume.

Nix isn't in here but there is a door at the back of the shop so I decide to check in there. I open the door and get a brief glimpse of a white, hot light and sparks shooting everywhere.

"Get the fuck out, Emily!"

I jump about a foot in the air when Nix yells at me

and stumble backward through the door. He's stalking through it toward me, even as I'm still stumbling backward. He's furious and I have no clue what I've done.

"Don't ever go in that room when the door is closed. That means I'm welding and you could burn your eyes if you look at that light," he bellows.

My blood is zinging through my body. He scared the crap out of me when he yelled and now he is just pissing me off. "Don't yell at me like that. I had no clue that was dangerous. Maybe if you posted a sign on the door, I wouldn't have gone in there."

He stares at me for several long seconds then seems to deflate. "I'm sorry," he grumbles at me. "I was just worried you'd get hurt."

This appeases me somewhat and I can feel my heart rate slowing. Nix turns his back to me and walks over to a counter mounted on the wall. He removes a pair of gloves and I take the opportunity to check him out. He's wearing a pair of well-faded jeans that look soft as sin. They hang right at his hipbones, held up by a thick, black belt lined with metal studs. He's wearing an olive green t-shirt that is tightly molded to his chest. He reaches up to put his gloves on a shelf and his shirt creeps up just a bit.

Nice!

Black biker boots complete his outfit and while it's

not the attire I normally see on guys I associate with, I have to say it looks damn fine on him. It speaks to who he is…casual and rough. And sexy.

And completely out of my league.

I take in his clothing with just a quick glance but I'm fascinated by the tattoos that are peeking out just under the sleeves of his t-shirt. He has three strands of black barbed wire circling each bicep. Some of the prongs have been inked to look like they are digging into his skin, and there are realistic drops of blood dripping from each wound. It's a terrifying piece of artwork and sinfully erotic just because of its badass look. I've never seen anything like it.

I pull my eyes from his tats and look at him. My face heats up as I realize he's been watching me ogle his arms.

"Like what you see?" The remark should have been a teasing comment but his voice is hard.

I try to play it cool. "Not really. Just fascinated, that's all."

"If you want to see more of my tattoos, you only have to ask. I'll be glad to strip down and show you everything." There…now that was teasing in his voice but his eyes are still hard. It's like he wants to tease me but has no clue how to do it. For some reason, that makes me feel sad for him.

Nix is eyeing me closely for my response. I have to reflexively push my tongue to my lips to keep from swallowing it. The thought of him pulling his t-shirt off so I can see his tattoos causes warmth to rush through my entire body and my gut clenches almost painfully. With every bit of strength that I can muster, I calmly respond, "No, thanks. I'm here to do a job, and that's all."

Nix shrugs his shoulders as if my disinterest doesn't bother him and I suddenly realize his offer to strip was only done to throw me off. He really has no interest in me that way at all.

Which is a relief.

I think.

"So, you won't need the whole tour because you've pretty much seen all there is. Again, don't go in there when the door is closed," he says while pointing at the welding room.

"You clearly made that point already."

He walks over to the desk and waves a hand at it. "This is your job. Organize me."

"That's it? Just organize you? I have no clue what this stuff is."

"Well, that makes two of us. Just go through it and try to make some sense of it. You can obviously throw away junk mail. Once you get it sorted out, I'll give you some more direction. I don't have time to hold your hand on this."

"Okay," I respond, but I'm not okay with this. I'm

going to look like a complete idiot.

Nix turns away and starts back toward the welding room.

"Hey," I call out. "I have a few questions."

He looks irritated when he turns around. "What?"

"What does Nix mean?"

His eyebrows shoot up and it's like no one has ever asked him such a personal question before. "It's short for Nixon."

"Oh. That's cool."

He remains in place, staring at me, and I realize I had said I had questions…as in plural.

"Why were you at Lincoln Caldwell's party last weekend?"

I watch as he smiles at me and it's so surprising I have a momentary feeling of giddiness. I can tell he doesn't do it often…not a true smile anyway. And it is beautiful. "Linc is my younger brother. I'm actually staying with him at his condo until I can make some remodeling repairs on my house."

"Oh," I say. "Okay. Well, I'll get to work."

He gives me a curt nod and closes himself off in his welding room.

Hmmmmm. Nice to meet you, Nixon Caldwell.

♦

AFTER FOUR HOURS of solid work, I've managed to take

the voluminous amount of documents and put them into neat piles. I've thrown away a large amount of junk mail but it really didn't put a dent in my work. So far, I've been able to glean that he has about four months of unpaid bills, about ten months of bank statements that haven't even been opened, and a sales tax booklet where the seal has not even been broken.

I'm sitting at the desk, and I have no clue what to do next. But I hate remaining idle so I start opening all of the bank statements and flattening them out. I'm so engrossed in this menial task that I don't hear the welding door open.

My first awareness that Nix is there is when I feel his breath on the back of my shoulder, which is covered only by the thin strap of my camisole.

I turn my head to the side and I see he is bent down, looking over my shoulder at the paperwork on the desk. I break out in goosebumps from his close proximity. The realization that this man can have an effect on my body just by standing near me is a little intimidating.

"I see you made some progress." The timbre of his voice is rough.

I push forward in my seat to put some distance between us before I answer. "Well, I've got piles. Here are your bills. It doesn't look like they've been paid in months. Frankly, I'm surprised you still have your electricity on."

He surprises me when he laughs. "No worries. I have all of my bills on auto draft. Everything is paid in full. But I will need you to match them up to my bank statements to make sure they match."

I nod. "Which brings me to the next pile. These are your bank statements that date back ten months. You clearly have not reconciled your accounts, so I'm not sure how you know you have enough money in your accounts to pay your bills."

He straightens up and turns, setting one butt cheek on the corner of the desk. He crosses his arms in front of his chest while he looks down at me. I can't help but notice the way the muscles in his arms roll and flex with his movement. Or the way his jeans pull tight against his muscular thighs.

"Again…no worries," he says. "I have plenty of money in my account to cover everything."

"Okay. This," I say, holding up his sales tax book, "is apparently tax forms that you should be filing quarterly. It's dated a year ago and it's clearly never been opened."

Nix scratches his head, ruffling that silky hair. He sighs. "I guess that's probably a good place to start. Call the Department of Revenue and find out what I need to do to get the taxes caught up."

He leans toward me and I start to pull back, but I notice he's only opening the desk drawer. He reaches in and pulls out a checkbook. Throwing it on the desk, he points at it. "Just write a check for whatever the taxes, penalties, and interest are and get it mailed."

My jaw hangs open. I've never met someone that is so cavalier about money. "How do you know you even have enough money in your account to pay the taxes?"

Nix just gives me a patient smile. "You know that motorcycle of mine that you flattened?"

I nod.

"Well, remember me telling you that it would cost $10,000 just to repair it?"

I nod again.

"I build those for a living. I build about five a year, and $25,000 is one of the cheaper bikes. The one you flattened is closer to a $40,000 bike. Do you get what I'm saying?"

I nod and swallow hard. "You make good money."

"Yes. I make good money. Now, all you have to worry your pretty head about is getting me organized and my books in order. The money is there."

Nix stands up from the desk and heads back to the welding room.

I hate that the fact he called me pretty makes me smile inside. He's clearly a man that doesn't hand out compliments very often, which makes them all the sweeter when they come.

CHAPTER 7

Nix

IT'S FRIDAY AND Emily is due to arrive anytime now. I feel jittery and on edge. When I first came up with the hair-brained idea of having her work her debt off to me, I seriously miscalculated my ability to be in her presence.

As someone who constantly avoids interaction and conversation, it was just plain awkward having her in my workspace. Even on Monday, when I spent most of the time welding in a separate room, I could still feel her presence. Just knowing she was sitting out there…in a white "barely there" top and jean shorts so tiny that they should be made illegal. She had her hair up in a ponytail, exposing a delicate neck.

I wanted to bite it. Then lick it to make it better. Then suck on it…hard…just so she'd know how hungry I was.

When she came back on Wednesday, it was no better. I didn't have any welding work to do, so I was in the main shop area while she sat at the desk, doing whatever it was she was doing with my paperwork. After only about thirty minutes, I couldn't stand the tension I was feeling and left. I went ahead and got some work done on my house, expending my frustrated energy by finishing the rest of the plywood base flooring upstairs.

I came back to the shop several hours later and Emily had left, leaving a note on the desk that she was just about finished with everything I had given her so far.

I know what I should do. I should just tell her not to come back and pay me the money when she can. I can wait for her to inherit her trust fund or whatever that pot of money is that she said she would be getting. I'm sure she's good for it and frankly, I don't need the money right now.

And the main reason I should tell her not to come back is because she is making me feel damn uncomfortable in my own space. My haven.

When she's here, I can't help but look at her every minute or so, just to see if the expression on her face has changed, or if her hair has shifted. When her subtle jasmine perfume touches my nose, I think about her lying naked in a bed of flowers. This shit is driving me fucking crazy and it's got no place in my life. It's not who I am.

So the fact that she's almost done with all of the work I had for her and I really don't have anything else, I should be happy our association is almost over.

I hear the tires of Emily's car crunching the gravel in my driveway. My heart rate immediately accelerates and I kick the edge of my workbench in anger. I stand, staring at the door, with my fists clenched.

When she walks in, it's like a punch to my gut. I don't know how it's possible, but she becomes more beautiful…more intriguing…more dangerous, every time I see her. I am out of control and I fucking hate this feeling.

"Why do you look so angry, Nix? I haven't even said anything to you yet."

Angry? No. Frustrated. Yes.

I try to relax my face but I don't think it's working. "I'm not angry. Just got a lot on my mind."

Emily gives me a sage look. "Want to talk about it?"

"No," I answer quickly.

Is it my imagination or does she look disappointed?

Whatever.

I don't talk to people, much less beautiful girls who are way out of my league anyway. She's a trust fund baby. She probably has a trust fund boyfriend all lined up for her.

"So, what do you want me to do today? It only took me two days to organize your desk."

Here's my chance to end it. "Actually, I don't have anything more for you to do."

"There has to be something I can do to work my

debt off. Want me to help work on your house? I'm sure I could learn to swing a hammer."

"Look, Emily. I think it's best we just part ways. I know you're good for the money. You can pay me whenever you can. No rush."

She stares at me and doesn't say anything. My heart rate isn't easing, and I feel like I've made a very bad decision just now. But I have no clue why. I feel completely out of sorts around her and I just want peace in my life.

"So, what's that?" she asks.

Emily is pointing to the new laptop that's sitting on my desk. It's still in the box. I bought it yesterday, when I was having a moment of weakness and trying to come up with more work for Emily to do. So she would have to stick around.

"It's a laptop."

"Yes, I can see that, Sherlock. What do you have it for?"

I shrug my shoulders. I certainly can't say, *"I bought it so I could create work for you, so you would keep coming here and I could be in your amazing presence, and I could figure out what all these weird feelings are"*.

Instead, I opt for ambiguity. "I figured I should put a computer out here to keep all of my bookwork and supply orders organized better that way. My PC is at Linc's condo and I really need something here in the shop."

I don't offer anything more, because at this point I'm torn between making her leave and seeing if she'll stay.

"Well, if you're as good at doing computer work as you were at paperwork…you're going to positively suck, Nix."

I don't say anything. I just watch her, holding my breath to see what she'll do. I've given her the out. *Take it, Emily.*

"So," she drawls. "Why don't you let me set it up and I'll play secretary for you. I'll get all of your stuff organized on the computer."

Play secretary for me?

Holy fuck! Images of her playing secretary for me are completely X-rated at this point and they involve her wearing a short business skirt while she goes down on me behind my desk.

I'm a goner. "Sure. If you want. But I'm completely fine with you just paying me the money later. You don't have to complete this deal we made."

Emily gives me a sweet smile. "No, I'd rather do this. I've always had that trust fund at my disposal. I sort of like the idea of having to work for something."

I groan inside. She couldn't have said anything worse to me. I felt like I would lose interest in her if I kept reminding myself she is a spoiled, rich, brat. Instead, here she is wanting to put a work ethic into play and now I find myself respecting her.

That's just fuckin' great.

"Okay," I say. "I bought some software you can install for the bookkeeping. And I actually need you to inventory my supplies and my stock."

"Sure, no problem. Want to show me where all of that is, then I can get out of your hair?"

I don't think this girl is going to get out of my hair…or my mind. But it's a nice sentiment.

"This way," I say as I head towards the welding room. We walk through it to the door at the back of the workspace. It leads outside and she follows me. Her phone starts ringing and I watch as she pulls it out of her pocket. She looks at the caller and mutters a curse under her breath. Then she pushes a button to disconnect the ring.

I take her to a shed that sits behind the workshop.

"This is where I keep my completed pieces."

"Pieces?" she asks.

I merely open the door, reaching in to flip the light switch and motion her to walk in before me. The room is softly illuminated, showing off all of my metal art.

It's true I build five or so motorcycles a year, but the rest of my time is creating art from metal. Many of my pieces are huge. I've crafted chandeliers, wall fountains, even custom stair railing. Some are small. Wind chimes, garden pieces, small bronze animals and the like. Unless it's a commissioned piece, I create whatever strikes my fancy.

I watch as Emily walks among my stock, running her fingers lightly over a few of them. She stops at one of my favorite sculptures.

It's an outdoor water fountain that stands about six feet tall. It's made of copper and consists of several metal calla lilies, all at varying heights. When it's turned on, water falls from the topmost flower, which is gently arced to the side, streaming into the next awaiting flower. The water goes from flower to flower, until it falls into the copper basin. A stockbroker with a house in the Hamptons commissioned me to make it for him and it would net me several thousand dollars after I deducted the materials. It would be stunning after several months weathering the outdoor elements, when the patina would overtake the copper and color it delicate shades of blue and green.

"Nix," she says softly. "I had no idea you did this."

Her words are reverent, and they make me feel awkward and proud at the same time. She looks at me, and there is something in her eyes that causes my heart to skip a beat.

But then the moment is broken when her phone rings again. She looks at it and anger flashes across her face. She taps the screen and puts the phone to her ear.

"I told you to stop calling me and I mean it," she

snarls. "No more."

Then she hangs up and stuffs her phone into her back pocket.

She looks at me and my eyebrows raise.

"Sorry," she says guiltily.

"Stalker issues?" I ask.

"How did you know?"

"You mentioned something about it the day you hit me."

She looks perplexed. "I did?"

I nod at her, surprised with myself that I even remembered her telling me that. It didn't seem like an important piece of information to me at that time. Most of my interactions with Emily revolve around me wanting more conversation and then less conversation. I'm in the less right now.

"I'm sorry. It's nothing. In fact…" she pulls her phone out of her pocket and shuts it completely off. "…I should have done that before I even came to work. It won't happen again."

She looks tired, angry, and actually a bit scared, all at once, and for the first time I can ever remember in my entire life, I want to take a woman in my arms to just comfort her.

And as I realize that this is something I want to do, I'm immediately doused in frigid mortification as if someone poured a bucket of cold water on me. I do not have time for, nor do I want to have to care for anyone. I care for me and me alone.

I turn my back on her and walk toward the door. "Well, get busy. Inventorying this will take you a few days to get through."

♦

I'M SITTING IN my ratty recliner, enjoying a beer. I deserve it. Not only did I manage to banish Emily from my mind for the last three hours, but I completed a wall sculpture of the Marine Corps Globe & Anchor. Linc asked for it for his condo. He actually tried to commission me to do it but I told him I'd beat his ass if he pushed it. We finally agreed he'd pay for the materials and I would do the piece because, well, he's my brother.

"I'm finished."

I jump at those words, as I had actually forgotten Emily was even here. I like it that way but now she's back in the forefront of my mind. And how can she not be…standing there looking like sex and candy all wrapped into one amazing concoction.

But I'm not in the mood to engage in conversation so I simply say, "Okay. I'll see you on Monday then."

But she's not listening to me. She's walking up to my workbench to look at the Globe & Anchor. She runs her hands lightly across the finish. I've peppered the bronze piece with tiny ball-peen dings that dimple the entire surface. I tried to imagine if someone like Lyla had walked in here and touched my art. I know without a doubt I would have yelled at her to keep her hands off. But the way Emily is stroking the cool metal has me mesmerized.

"This is beautiful. Did you make this for someone who is in the Marine Corps?"

I'm taken aback for a minute. How does little Miss Rich Girl know about the Marine Corps' insignia?

"I made it for my brother."

"Lincoln was in the Marine Corps?" She sounds confused, as she should be.

"No, I was."

She turns quickly and looks at me with awe. "Really? When?"

"I went in when I was eighteen. Got out two years ago at twenty-four."

I watch as she leans back against the workbench and crosses her arms. They lay right below her breasts, which plump up nicely and strain against her blouse. All sorts of lewd thoughts run through my head and I have to keep telling myself to knock it off. Nothing of that nature is going to happen between us.

Besides…Emily is a nice girl and I don't do nice girls.

"Did you serve in Afghanistan?"

"Yes."

She waits for me to say more but she'll wait a long time. I don't talk about my time there…ever. And I can tell by the look on her face she knows not to push it.

"Well, thank you for serving our country. I wish I was brave enough to do something like that."

I'm floored again. She seems to always say something that enthralls me. She always says the opposite of what I think will come out of her completely kissable lips. And she doesn't do it in a calculated way to achieve a certain result. No, it comes out of her perfectly shaped mouth with natural sincerity.

I shrug my shoulders at her but secretly I'm pleased she appreciates the sacrifice it takes to serve. No one's opinion of my service, except for my father and brother, really mattered to me before.

Pointing at the piece I ask, "How did you know that was the Marine Corps Globe & Anchor?"

"Well, you're not the only former Marine I know. It just so happens I know a grumpy Marine veteran who was in the first Gulf War."

She has my interest piqued and for the first time, in a long time, I am actually having a real conversation with someone that interests me. It's a weird feeling but I press on.

"Oh yeah. Who is that?"

"His name is Sarge. He's like Danny's surrogate father. Danny is my sister-in-law. I assume you know my brother, Ryan?"

"Yeah, I know Ryan. I'll have to talk to her about this guy next time I see her."

"Sarge is a hoot. He actually walked Danny down the aisle when they got married. Sometimes Ryan flies him and Danny's friend, Paula down here to visit. You should make an effort to meet him next time he comes."

I smile at her. For fuck's sake. A genuine smile and it feels natural. What the hell is happening to me? "I'll do that. It will be nice to talk to another Marine. It's been a while."

She cocks her head at me. "Don't you keep in touch with the friends who you served with?"

I nod. "Some of them. We're all kind of spread out and moving on with our lives."

"I bet you forged friendships there that will last a lifetime, huh?"

This question makes me stiffen. She is oh, so right about that. When you are in extreme situations, your bonds forge fast and stay strong. But there is a lot of pain and misery that goes along with it. I'm back on guard now and this conversation needs to wind down.

Now.

I stand up from my chair and start walking to the door. "Well, it's late. Go ahead and pack up and I'll see you on Monday."

Emily pushes away from the workbench with an

easygoing smile on her face. "Sure thing, boss."

I watch as she pulls her phone out and turns it on, grabbing her purse while it boots up. She takes a quick glance at the screen and grimaces. I'm assuming there is something stalkerish glaring at her. But I'm not going to ask, even though I sort of want to.

She walks to the door and turns to me. "You got big plans this weekend?"

I needed that question. My priorities come back swiftly in line. My walls go up and slam tight into place. I hope she's not trying to ask me to do something with her. Because that would not be good…in any way.

I answer cautiously. "Not really. I'll probably just hang out at Linc's place."

"That's cool."

Well, damn. I expected her to say something more and that makes me curious now. "What about you?"

Her eyes light up. "Yeah, I'm excited. I'm going with my roommate, Fil, to this new nightclub."

"You live with a guy?" The thought of it raises my hackles a bit but I don't have time to ponder the why of it. It seems all I do lately is analyze every little word that comes out of my mouth around Emily.

She gives a laugh. It sounds like gentle, silver bells, which is a nice change. The laughter of other women always seemed to grate on my nerves.

"No. My roommate is a girl."

"Your roommate is a girl and her parents named her Phil?"

"No. Her parents named her Mignon."

"Wait? They named her after a steak?"

"Yup. Fil is short for Filet. It's this whole nickname thing." She's grinning and I can tell she is enjoying the hell out of this discussion.

I shake my head. This will go down as one of the weirdest conversations I've ever had, and trust me, I've had some weird ones in my head.

"Did she murder her parents for that?"

Emily now lets out a bark of a laugh. It's hoarse and sexy, and I would kill to hear that sound again. "No, although I'm sure she's considered it a time or two."

As her laughter dies down and slides from her eyes, her gaze at me is replaced with something else. Almost as if she's looking at me in awe and delight. It's like she is seeing something inside of me that even I don't understand.

It makes me uncomfortable and pissy.

"What?" I demand.

The joy on her face disappears completely and her eyes go dead.

Yup. I did that. My anger made it go away, just with a singular asshole move on my part. Classic Nix Caldwell and I'm sort of relieved to know he's not completely dead.

"Nothing," she says. "It's just…you have a wonderful smile. Well, you had a wonderful smile just a second ago. Too bad you don't keep it on your face very long."

I was smiling at her? I didn't even realize. Usually, the unnatural feeling of a smile on my face is immediately and completely recognizable to me because it's not something I do often. And then I snapped at her because she dared look at me in a way that was…special. I'm such a shit and I'm sure she thinks I'm nuts. Maybe I am nuts. Maybe she is driving me nuttier.

I can't think of anything to say, so I just head toward the door. "Go ahead and lock up when you leave."

"See you," she says softly.

And damn it if I can't help myself when I say, "Be careful this weekend."

CHAPTER 8

Emily

FIL AND I are headed with a group of our friends to The Blue Room. One of our friends at Columbia knows a friend, who knows a friend whose father owns this nightclub. So we got VIP passes for tonight.

I'm dressed to the hilt for some major dancing and partying. I chose a teal blue dress that comes to mid-thigh. My right arm is covered with a full sleeve while my left arm is bared completely past my shoulder and to my neck. The fabric is ruched across my breasts in crisscross patterns and silver bangle bracelets on my bare arm are the only jewelry I'm wearing. I curled my hair with a large barrel iron so it hangs in soft waves down my back. Three-inch crystal-studded sandals complete my outfit, although, as we walk the four blocks to the club, I'm starting to regret wearing them.

Oh, well. Nothing that a couple of gin and tonics won't cure.

Fil is wearing a borrowed dress of mine and because

she's a bit taller than me, the hem comes up significantly more than mid-thigh. Even though she dresses in shredded jeans and t-shirts most of the time, she does like dressing girly when we go out.

"We're both pretty sizzlin' tonight, aren't we?" I ask as I nudge her in the shoulder.

She smiles at me. "Yup. And the best thing is…we don't have to compete with each other."

"That's right," I exclaim. "Because I likes the guys and you likes the girls."

We both start giggling like two grade-school kids that just uttered our first dirty joke.

I link my arm through hers and she slows her longer legs a bit so I can keep up.

"So, heard anything from Todd today?" she asks.

"No phone calls since yesterday when I told him to cut the crap. But he has sent a few texts apologizing and telling me he just wants to talk."

Fil harrumphs. "That guy is a psycho, I'm telling you. Do not underestimate him. No one spends that much time chasing after a girl that clearly wants nothing to do with him. I hope he doesn't go all John Hinckley on you."

"As long as I have you to protect me, I'm not worried."

"Damned straight," Fil concurs.

We get to The Blue Room around 9:30 p.m. and the

line to get in is wrapped around the building. We walk to the front and hold out our invitations. I feel so sophisticated as the large bouncer unhooks a velvet rope and lets us pass through.

Our group is eclectic, that's for sure. You have me, the rich, snotty girl. Fil the lesbian. Tina and Tonya, twin sisters from Arkansas who were raised on a farm and are still incredibly intimidated by the big city. And finally, my chemistry lab partner, Kevin, who is on Columbia's Lacrosse team, and he brought two of his teammates who I don't know very well, Sam and Breckan.

Our friend who knows a friend whose father owns the place and got us the tickets, reserved two tables for us and we feel like movie stars. We sit on an elevated deck above the dance floor and have our own personal waitress who caters to us all evening. She never asks for our ID's even though we all have our fake ones prepared to deliver at any time.

I don't even finish my first drink when I get pulled out onto the dance floor by Kevin. Before too long, the rest of the gang is there and we are bumpin' and grindin' to Vassy's *We Are Young.* I hold my arms out and twirl in a circle, my face lifted to the flashing electric lights. I feel so alive and thankful to have the freedom to be myself. It wasn't until I came to college that I realized I was a prisoner.

After several dances, I motion to Fil I'm going to take a break and she follows me off the floor. The rest of the group shows no signs of slowing.

We order more drinks and chat while we watch the clubbers.

"So, how did your job go this week?" Fil asks.

She is the only person I told about my accident and my deal to work for Nix. But I haven't told her much about him. With two mixed drinks in my system, I feel like a Chatty Cathy all of a sudden.

"He is about the most gorgeous man I've ever laid eyes on. But he's so distant and he seems on edge all the time. I don't know how to communicate with him."

"Why? What's his childhood trauma?"

I shrug my shoulders. "Hell if I know. I know he served over in Afghanistan and he doesn't want to talk about it. But he's so intriguing that I want to know more."

Fil twirls her fingertip around the edge of her drink glass. I notice she has on black, sparkly nail polish but it's chipping around the edges.

"Well, who says you need to communicate. Just do your job and keep your head down."

I take that in and then say, "I suppose."

"Wait a minute," she exclaims. By the look on her face, I know where she's getting ready to go. "You like him, don't you?"

"What?" I act affronted. "No. No way. He's too…too…he's not someone I'd be interested in."

"Liar!" she yells out, pointing at me. "Liar, liar…pants on fire. I see that look in your eyes. You're smitten." She's laughing because she knows she's busted me.

I smack her arm and she yelps. "No, I'm not. And who uses the word "smitten" these days? I just find him interesting, that's all."

"So do something about it."

I look at her skeptically. "What do you mean?"

"I mean, dummy, make a move on him. If you like him and you're interested, make a move."

I just stare at her. That's preposterous. I couldn't make a move on a guy like that, much less one that radiates an arctic freeze when I'm around him.

"I couldn't…" I say, but I'm pretty sure I want her to push me to do it.

"Em…I love you like you're my own sister. So please believe me it is only with love and affection when I say 'get your head out of your ass'. You're always bitching and moaning that you want to be free. That you want to try new things. That you want to be adventurous. This is your chance, girl."

Her words sort of pump me up. Although it could be the alcohol. "Really? Do you think I should?"

"Absolutely!"

I grin at her. Come Monday afternoon, I think I just might try a little overt flirting with the elusive Mr. Caldwell and see what comes of it.

I slug down the last of my drink and we both hit the dance floor again.

♦

I'M HAVING A blast. Fil ended up getting stinking drunk after slamming several shots and Kevin and his friends left about an hour ago to take her back to our apartment. Poor girl was practically falling out of her chair. I hope there's not going to be a pile of vomit for me to navigate when I get home.

Tina, Tonya and I were burning up the dance floor for quite a while, and then we met some guys. They were a lot of fun and were buying us drinks, so we kept hanging out. We'd all go dance, then come back and do shots, although I stopped drinking over an hour ago so I wouldn't end up sharing the toilet with Fil.

One guy, in particular, James, keeps dancing with me. He's really cute and he's a senior at NYU. His friends have paired off with Tina and Tonya, and they're all getting drunker by the minute. I hope to God that I can get those stumbling fools home. That thought alone makes me break out into a fit of giggles. Which then makes me realize I need to pee. I motion to James and the others that I'll be back, and make my way off the dance floor.

The bathroom line is long and I feel like I stand there forever. I'm so glad I had stopped drinking or else I'd be dying right now. It takes me a good ten minutes to make it to a free toilet, do my business and then freshen up my appearance.

I make my way back out to the dance area and see James sitting at our table. I plop down in the seat next to him. He motions to the waitress to bring another drink but I tell him I'd like a water instead.

Glancing out to the dance floor, I don't see Tina or Tonya anywhere, or the guys they were dancing with.

I lean in toward James so he can hear me over the music. "Where's Tina and Tonya?"

He slides his seat a little closer to mine and puts his arm around my shoulders. "They took off with my buddies. Said they were going to go grab some food."

What? I can't believe Tina and Tonya would leave me here. I dread having to walk home alone this late at night. But I suppose I could just get a cab. Even though my trust was cut off, I still had some cash on me.

"Well, I probably should be heading home." I give James a small smile and reach for my purse.

Before I can grab it, James leans over and places a hand on my knee. He wraps his other arm tighter around my shoulder and draws me close to him. Placing his lips near my ear, he whispers, "Don't go, baby. You and I can still party together."

His hand starts sliding up my leg and when it hits the hem of my dress, I reach down and grab his wrist firmly. "Sorry, James. I'm not into partying like that."

I still have a slight buzz but nothing to the extent that I would miss the flash of anger in his eyes. His hand grips my leg hard for an instant and then he releases me. "It's no problem, baby. How about I walk you home?"

He gazes at me and I note how bleary his eyes look. He has been pounding liquor all night and I hate dealing with drunks and their unpredictability.

He moves his eyes down my body, resting on my breasts while he licks his lips. That's just nasty and I sense danger. I'm not sure why I'm so uncomfortable though. I'm sitting in a packed nightclub. He's released my leg and he's offering to walk me home, but ultimately my instinct tells me to leave this one alone for the night.

"That's alright. I can make my way home," I assure him.

His hand goes back to my leg and he squeezes it again. Not hard, but it's menacing to me. "I insist. It wouldn't be right for me to let you leave out of here all alone." His voice is oily, like a used car salesman.

I sit up straight and try to look as tough as possible. "No, James…I'm going home by myself."

He just grins at me then runs his eyes down to my chest again. His hand squeezes and relaxes, squeezes and relaxes. "Darling…you can walk out of this club, but I'm coming with you. Now, do you want anything before we leave?"

My mind is racing. The intimidation from this guy is causing what little bit of a buzz I had to quickly fade. For all I know, he could just be a weasel that will walk me home and try to cop a feel. Or he could be something far more sinister, hoping to take advantage of me.

I could kill Tina and Tonya for leaving me.

I also know that he's very drunk and I need to deal with him delicately so as not to incite him. I try to put on my most flattering smile. "Okay, have it your way. Let me run to the restroom one more time. All that water just runs right through me."

"Sure thing. I'll settle up our tab. Just meet me back here."

I stand up and I'm dismayed that I'm a little shaky, but it's not from the alcohol. It's from extreme nervousness. I walk toward the bathroom and when I reach the hallway that leads to the facilities, I take a glance back. James is still sitting there, watching me. Leering. I give him a small smile and enter the hallway.

Once I'm in the bathroom, I pull my phone out. I can't call Fil because she's probably passed out. Ryan is at an away game in Philadelphia. There's no way I'm calling Danny since she's pregnant. She's not getting anywhere near this mess.

I call the one person who I shouldn't but more than anything I want here right now to rescue me from this mess.

The phone only rings twice before it's answered.

"Hello," Nix says. I've clearly woken him up.

"Nix. I'm in trouble I think."

"Emily? Where are you?" He sounds worried. Not pissed off, as I'd expected.

I tell him the name of the club and give him the address.

"Do not leave that building. I'll be there soon."

He disconnects without saying anything else. I estimate it will take him a good half hour to make it here and I'm fine hiding in this bathroom until then.

I wait, standing near the sink. I splash cold water on my face and pat my skin dry. I can't believe I just called Nix. He's not even a friend but he seemed like the person I should have called. Part of it was probably that conversation I had earlier tonight with Fil and maybe this was just my first move toward flirting with Nix. Ultimately, James probably would never have done anything to me, but I feel much safer knowing I don't have to even put myself into that position.

The bathroom starts clearing out until I'm the only one left. I am impatiently checking my watch when one of the waitresses comes in and sees me standing there.

"Are you Emily?" she asks.

I nod.

"Your boyfriend is out there waiting for you. And we're closing the club so you two will need to head out."

Oh, crap. I need to stall to give Nix time to get here. There is no way I can walk out of here with James.

"Ummm…I think I might be sick. Can you give me just a few minutes?"

She looks exasperated but says, "Fine. But we're locking up in about fifteen minutes. I'll tell your boyfriend you'll be out soon."

I mutter thanks and walk into one of the stalls, acting as if I'll be sick. As soon as I hear her leave, I open the door and walk back to lean against the sink.

My fifteen minutes goes by too fast and the waitress is back telling me I need to leave. I pick up my purse and catch a glance in the mirror. Wide eyes stare back at me and I realize I'm going to have to handle James on my own. That thought makes my stomach churn.

As soon as I open the door, I see James leaning up against the wall with his arms crossed over his chest. He gives me a devious smile. "Are you okay? The waitress said you were sick."

I nod. "Yeah. I think I drank too much and had to throw up."

Maybe that would gross him out enough to leave me alone. Or maybe it would make him think I was easy prey. His smile turns from devious to practically lecherous. Clearly, he sees me as prey.

"Well, let's get you home and get you to bed. In fact, my apartment is just a few blocks over."

I walk past him and head toward the club's exit.

"No," I reply, trying for nonchalance as if his offer didn't just make my insides squirm with disgust. "I'm going to my apartment."

He appraises me, one eyebrow cocked. "Sure thing, sugar. Let's go."

Unfortunately, the front doors to the club have been locked and we are pointed to an exit that leads out into the side alley. I was hoping there would be a crowd of partygoers loitering around but they've all dispersed and we are alone. At least there is some lighting attached to the top of the building that illuminates the place fairly well.

I turn to head in the direction of the main street but James grabs my arm. I wasn't expecting that and teeter dangerously in my heels. He steps into me, grabbing one shoulder with one hand and one of my breasts with the other. He pushes me back against the wall and doesn't even try any sweet talk before he tries to stick his tongue down my throat.

I start to immediately struggle, fear fueling my strength.

"Get off me you fucking pervert," I yell at him. I manage to push him off of me but he comes back stronger than ever. His hands are squeezing me painfully and he's muttering disgusting words like, "You feel so good" and "Are you gonna make me feel good, baby".

What a slime! Part of me is thinking that he's just a drunk trying to feel me up and another part tells me to take this more seriously than I am. But I just can't believe a guy that I was hanging with peaceably all night would try to assault me in a well-lit alleyway just steps from a main street.

After we engage in a fruitless battle of me trying to push his body away and him trying to feel me up, I finally do what every girl should do in this situation. I try to bring my knee up into his balls. Unfortunately, he's too close and I cannot get enough room to make a solid connection. My knee glances harmlessly off his thigh.

I suppose he gets tired of our banter because he brings his arm up and braces it against my throat, effectively cutting off my supply of oxygen. Now I start to panic as I realize this is so much more than a drunk trying to feel me up. I really start struggling again. This time, when he sticks his tongue into my mouth, I react on pure instinct. I bite down as hard as I can and I taste blood.

CHAPTER 9

Nix

I'M DRIVING THROUGH Manhattan as fast as I can but I don't want to risk getting pulled over by a cop. No telling what type of trouble Emily is in. I didn't bother asking her because I didn't want to waste time. As she was giving me the address of where she was, I was hopping into my jeans and slipping on a pair of flip-flops.

I was out the door and pulling a shirt over my head by the time I disconnected from her.

I make it to The Blue Room in twenty-five minutes and it looks deserted. I pull over to the curb and step out. I walk up to the doors but they are locked.

Figures!

Running my hand through my hair, I look left, then right. There is an alley that runs beside the club and I walk that way. As soon as I turn the corner, I see Emily heading towards me and sigh in relief. She looks fine.

Then I notice a guy behind her and my blood boils

when I see him grab her arm. I take off toward them, murderous rage filling me when I see him mauling her up against the wall. She tries to knee him once but it doesn't hit the mark. He tries to kiss her and before I can reach them, the guy rears back from Emily and screams, "You bitch!"

Emily starts spitting onto the ground. He's holding his hand to his mouth and I can only assume she bit him.

Good girl and that thought alone diminishes a bit of my wrath.

Emily looks scared but she also looks pissed. I'm within just a few feet of them and I see the dude raise his hand like he's going to hit her. She sticks her chin out and stares him down and I am utterly amazed.

He starts to bring his hand down toward her face and that's when I lash out. I catch him by the wrist and shove him backward.

He's surprised and for a split second, I can see he thinks about charging me.

"Man…I wouldn't do it," I warn him. Emily comes to stand behind me and I'm glad I'm between her and this asshole. "You need to turn around and walk the other way."

I'm frighteningly calm despite my anger. There was a time in my life that I would probably have pounded the shit out of him, but I've learned to avoid fights if I can help it. It never seems to solve anything and only creates bruises and cuts.

More shit that needs healing.

The guy sneers at me and then looks at Emily. He thinks he's safe because I've given him a pass to walk away. "That bitch is a fuckin' tease. I was only takin' what she was offering." He punctuates that by wiping the back of his hand across his mouth, blood smearing across his face.

That's it. I'm going to kill the bastard.

I start toward him but Emily takes a hold of my wrist, lightly. It stops me in my tracks and I look over my shoulder at her.

"Please don't", she says softly. "Can you just take me home?"

Even though my blood feels like lava in my veins and I want to pound some respect into this douche bag, I immediately take in that Emily now looks completely overwhelmed by this situation. Her adrenaline is clearly waning and an urgency rises in me to make this all better for her. For once, I don't stop to analyze it.

I don't even glance back at the dude. Taking Emily's hand, I turn around and walk us out of the alley. She's wobbly on her feet and I don't know if it's because she's drunk or because she's teetering around in impossibly high heels. Which make her legs look freakin' amazing, by the way. I slow my pace so she doesn't end up breaking her ankle.

When we get to my Bronco, I unlock the passenger door. I reach in and grab a bottle of water I had sitting in there. I hand it to her and she doesn't hesitate when she takes a huge swig, swishes it around her mouth, and spits it out on the ground.

"Thanks," she says quietly.

It's quite a leg up into my Bronco so I hold onto her hand as she steps a crystal-studded foot up onto the running board then slings herself across the seat. I try not to notice her dress riding up and exposing her leg. I grit my teeth and close the door.

Once I pull myself up into the driver's seat, I look over at her. She's sitting with her hands clasped in her lap and her gaze looks a bit vacant as she stares out the side window.

"Are you okay?" I ask her.

She just nods her head but I see her bottom lip start to quiver a bit. My stomach clenches. Normally, a girl crying will freak me out and I'll do anything to get away. But now, I kind of want to take her in my arms and hold her…to reassure her that everything is okay now. My arm rises up on its own accord and as I reach out to her, I suddenly feel awkward. I'm not built for this. I don't do chivalrous and I don't do reassuring.

I do hard and tough.

My arm drops in my lap and I start the truck. Then I decide to be an asshole to prove I'm still me. "What the hell were you doing out there by yourself? How could you let yourself get in that situation?"

Emily's head snaps around so fast to glare at me, her hair flies in a fluid arc and comes to rest over her bare shoulder. I notice the bottom lip is no longer quivering and if looks could kill, I'd be oh, so dead. But I give myself some praise for my tough methods. She's angry now and doesn't look on the verge of collapse. At least I won't have to deal with tears.

"I didn't choose for this to happen, Nix." Her words are bitter and angry. "My friends ditched me and left me to fend octopus man on my own. I'm really sorry to inconvenience you tonight."

She spits those last words out and then turns her head back to stare out the window. Her shoulders are now stiff and not pitifully sagging the way they were just a few seconds ago. That should make me happy, but it doesn't.

I sigh. "Look, you're not inconveniencing me…I just—"

She cuts me off with another look, but this one is pleading. "Please don't. I've had a really bad night. I just got attacked and I don't need you to lecture me. Can you just take me to my apartment?"

"Is Fil there?"

"Yes. Passed out, I'm sure, but she'll be there."

Her voice…so soft and quiet…it slices straight through me. I usually don't have care or understanding in me, but tonight Emily needs it. She called on me and

I answered. I need to see it through, no matter how hard it cuts against the grain.

"No. I'm not taking you to your apartment. You'll come back home with me. Let's get some food in you and let you get a good night's rest."

I don't even bother to wait for a response. I put the truck in drive and pull away from the curb. After a few blocks, I risk a glance at her. She's still staring out the passenger window and her eerie silence is beginning to spook me.

Mustering every shred of gentleness I may have buried deep somewhere—which is really scraping the bottom of the barrel—I say, "This wasn't your fault, Em."

Em? When did she become Em to me?

"I'm not so sure," she whispers. "Maybe I could have handled it better."

"You handled it just fine. You called someone to help you."

She reaches over and touches my shoulder lightly but I still feel the warmth of her skin coming off in waves. "Thank you for coming."

I look at her, glance back at the road then look at her again. "Sure. Not a problem."

Her hand falls away from me and I feel noticeably chilled with it gone.

♦

WE GET TO Linc's place and I help her out of the truck. Once she steps onto the pavement, I release her and we head inside. As soon as the door opens, Harley comes barreling out of the back bedroom. Rather than jump on me like he usually does, he heads straight to Emily but I'm able to grab his collar before he can leap up on her.

"Easy, Harley. Sit."

He immediately sits down and gives a whine toward Emily. She kneels to the carpeted floor and puts her arms around him. She clearly needs some type of comfort right now and I'm glad Harley can give it to her. Although I do wonder what it would feel like to have her arms wrapped around me like that.

I throw my car keys on the coffee table and head into the kitchen.

"When's the last time you ate?" I call out to her.

Her voice surprises me when it answers not but a few feet away. "I ate dinner around six. I'm not that hungry."

I look at her as I open the refrigerator door. She is so unbelievably gorgeous in that blue dress that fits her body like a second skin, I space out for a second and just stare at her. She returns my look unblinkingly.

Quickly putting my head into the fridge, I pull out some eggs, cheese, onions and peppers. "Well, I'm hungry and you might as well eat something too. It will help absorb some of the alcohol in your stomach."

She shrugs and takes a seat on a kitchen stool. "I

didn't really drink that much tonight but I'll eat something if you are."

That damned dress rides up again, stealing my gaze and scattering my thoughts. I don't get it. It's not like I haven't seen plenty of hot women dressed in even more revealing clothes than what Emily is wearing right now so my reaction to her is bordering on the ludicrous side.

I get out a skillet and set it on the stove, turning the gas on. I throw a couple pats of butter in for good measure. Breaking open the eggs, I begin whisking them together but I keep my back turned to her when I casually ask, "So what happened tonight?"

Emily sighs and I hear her get off the stool. She steps up beside me and my whole body tenses although she does nothing more than takes the onion and starts to chop it. "I don't know. Nothing like this has ever happened to me before. He seemed like a nice enough guy. There was a group of us hanging out and dancing all night. And then all of a sudden, my friends were gone and his were gone, and we were left alone."

She pushes the pile of chopped onions aside and starts on the pepper.

"He just got really weird all of a sudden."

"How?" I ask, although I'm sure the answer is going to piss me off.

I can sense her shudder beside me. "He got grabby and demanding. He was insisting he walk me home…and then he wanted me to go to his apartment. He was pretty drunk so I couldn't talk him down…"

She trails off, sounding bewildered that someone would do that to her. I break the tension by scooping up the onions and peppers and throwing them in the skillet.

"You did the right thing in calling me," I tell her as I push the vegetables around in the pan "You trusted your instinct and it was right."

"I guess."

She doesn't say anything while I continue to cook. After I throw the eggs and some cheese on top of the veggies, I ask, "Why do you sound so unsure?"

Emily walks back and sits on the stool. I'm proud I maintain direct eye contact with her, hitched up skirt be damned. She leans forward onto the counter and rests her chin on her hand. "He just seemed so nice and normal the whole night. How could I have missed it?"

It's a good question and I didn't have the answer. I've learned over the years, and particularly while in Afghanistan, that people can be very good at hiding their true nature. It makes it difficult to ever give anyone the benefit of the doubt.

I flip the mess of cheesy eggs onto a plate and bring it over to where Emily is sitting. I take two forks out of the drawer and hand her one.

"Eat up," I tell her.

She just looks at the huge pile of eggs on a single

plate, and each of us holding a fork. She arches an eyebrow at me in amusement.

"What? No sense in dirtying two plates when we can both eat off the same one."

"Agreed," she responds and digs in.

After we finish, I rinse the plate off and put it in the dishwasher.

"Come on. You can sleep in my room and I'll take the couch."

"I can't let you do that. I'll take the couch."

"I may be an asshole most of the time, but I do know proper manners. You take my bed and I'll sleep on the couch. And that's final."

"Careful, Nix," she teases. "You may lose your asshole status."

I snort. No way was I losing that. I lead her back to my bedroom and reach into one of my drawers, pulling out a large t-shirt.

I throw it at her. "Here. You can wear this tonight. You know where the bathroom is. I'll see you in the morning."

Heading toward the door, she calls after me. "Thank you, Nix. For everything."

I throw my hand over my head in a wave of acknowledgment. Normally, praise or thanks makes me feel awkward, and it's no different here. But I also have a well-satisfied feeling as I walk back into the living room.

CHAPTER 10

Nix

I WAKE UP early, even though I've only been back to sleep for a few hours. The couch is fairly comfortable but it's been hard for me to sleep with Emily in the next room. Harley had started up on the couch with me but that didn't last long. He ended up hopping off and padding back to my room to jump in bed with Emily.

And now I'm slightly envious of the dog. Which is weird, since I don't like sharing my bed with anyone but Harley.

It's perplexing to me why this woman is plaguing my thoughts. Sure, she's beautiful, but that's clearly not it. I've seen and been with my own share before. I wish I could put my finger on it because then I'd be able to fix it.

Rolling off the couch, I stand and stretch. I kept my jeans on to sleep just in case Emily came out of my room. Modesty is normally not one of my virtues but I doubt Emily would appreciate stumbling upon a naked, sleeping man.

Sadly.

I head down the hallway to the bathroom and as I pass my bedroom, I peek in. The door has been left open just a bit, probably when Harley pushed his way in last night. The coming dawn is letting in just enough light that I can see Emily on her back, one arm lying across her stomach and the other on the pillow above her head. Harley is in bed beside her. His head is down at her feet and he has his bottom legs lying across her chest. One foot sits about two inches from her nose. I can't help but grin at the picture before me.

In fact, I have to turn away before I start laughing and wake them up. I'm finding this new emotion called amusement tastes like Sweet Tarts in my mouth.

After I take a quick shower and brush my teeth, I head into the kitchen. A quick peek back in my room shows me that Emily hasn't moved in the past few minutes. Not surprising though. The sun has barely started to rise and I figure Emily has to be exhausted. Harley, however, is wide awake and he trots out of the room to greet me.

"Come on, little man," I whisper. "Let's go for a walk."

I clip on Harley's lead and we head out into the cool morning air. The more I think about what that jackass did to Emily last night—what more he could have done to her had I not shown up—makes my stomach burn. She seemed so lost last night, not willing to believe that monsters can exist in her world. I have a feeling she's been sheltered most of her life and last night may have been a bit of a rude awakening for her.

When we get back to the apartment, it's quiet so I assume Emily must still be sleeping. I brew a pot of coffee and take a cup to the outdoor balcony. I sip at the brew and watch the sky turn from gray, to pink, to light blue by the time I finish. Walking back inside for a refill, I come to a dead stop as I enter the kitchen.

Emily is standing at the coffee pot, pouring herself a cup. She's standing on one leg while resting one foot on top of the other. Her hip is cocked out in a completely "I don't know I'm sexy" way. She's in nothing but the t-shirt I gave her and while it provides her the same coverage, if not more, than the dress she had on last night, she looks fucking sexy as hell wearing it.

Her hair is a mess, and the t-shirt is wrinkled but I'd rather see her like this than that knockout number she had on last night. I wonder how much of that feeling has to do with the fact that it's my clothing she's wearing.

Emily senses me standing there and whips around. She doesn't seem embarrassed to be standing there in only my t-shirt and gives me a sleepy, quiet smile. "Good morning."

"Hey," I say lamely. I walk to the coffee pot and she

picks up her cup, stepping aside. "How'd you sleep last night?"

"Great actually. Thanks again for giving me your bed."

After I pour my cup, I turn around and lean back against the counter. Taking a sip, I watch her over the rim. "After you finish your coffee, I'll take you home."

"It's a plan." She blows lightly on her coffee then takes a sip. "So when do you think you'll have your house ready to move back into?"

"I'm not sure. I'm not on any deadline and just working on it in my free time."

"I bet you're ready to get back though, huh?"

I shrug indifferently. "Sure. I mean, it's closer to my work…just a short walk from the back door to my shop."

She looks strangely at me. "But it's your home. I thought you'd be more comfortable there."

"Why's that?" I ask. I have no clue where she's going with this.

"It's just…you seem like a man that likes his personal space."

Aaahhh. Now I see where she's going. "You'd be right about that. I do like my personal space. But honestly, one bed is just as good as another. I don't have any personal connection to that house."

"It's hard for you to make personal connections, isn't

it?"

Now there's a stark question, brutally honest and cutting to the bone. I almost tell her to mind her own fucking business, because that's what I would normally say to anyone that tries to psychoanalyze me.

Instead, and without a trace of bitterness or scorn in my voice, I say, "Yes."

It's a stupid response on my part because it only invites the inevitable follow up question I know is coming.

"Why is that?" Her question is soft…hesitant…nervous. It makes my skin crawl and leap in turns.

"Making personal connections is easy. Losing them is what's hard. It's easier to avoid."

She's staring at me, her eyes are wide and sympathetic. "I imagine you've lost a lot. I'm sorry."

That's all she says and I don't feel like she needs a response from me. I was expecting her to push, prod, and attempt to pull information from me but she doesn't. And she doesn't because I know she can sense that I won't go any further with my sharing.

And this is what's strange about that. Normally, I cut people off with a glare, or glacial frost in my words. It's the standard cue I give when someone needs to back off. Sort of like hackles rising on a dog.

Here I didn't do that. I apparently didn't need to do that. I answered her questions honestly and she knew, on her own, that I'd had enough. She backed off without me needing to become Nix Caldwell, the prick extraordinaire. Emily has a part of me figured out that most don't.

At that intrigues the hell out of me.

♦

I'M DRIVING EMILY to her apartment. She's changed back into her sexy dress and my mind is having a hard time not considering the miles of leg she is blatantly inviting me to stare at. You would think the harsh light of day would cause some of the sex appeal to diminish but she had scrubbed her face last night before going to bed, so she looks fresh and young. Her hair is pulled up into some kind of messy concoction on top of her head that makes me want to pull it back down again. She looks supremely beautiful and I'm betting Emily Burnham doesn't know how to look bad.

Her beauty, though, is not what makes her interesting. I hate to admit it but she's managed to pound a chink in my armor, which has, in turn, made me curious about her. I'm finding I want to know things about her. Things that I wouldn't normally give a rat's ass about.

"So, what did you do to piss your parents off that got you cut off from your money?" I broach a subject that will result in, what I hope to be fruitful conversation. The type of conversation that will provide some lucidity as to why I find this woman so intriguing.

She snorts. "I tried to have a life."

I glance over at her and there is bitterness and hurt in her voice. I don't know the story but it makes me want to ring her parents' necks.

"Want to expound?"

She turns in the seat and looks at me. I glance once at her, taking in her bourbon colored eyes that are now filled with acerbic memories. I hesitate a little longer than I should, swimming in her eyes when I should be looking at the road. Her next question jolts me back to reality.

"Have you ever been under someone's complete control?"

"Sure," I answer easily enough. "The Marine Corps. I did what they told me to do, no questions asked."

She's silent because I know I make it sound so effortless and I don't want her to think that is the way of all things. So I clarify my statement. "But, I knew that going in and I accepted it."

"Well, I don't accept it and that's what pisses my mother off."

"So, the little girl is rebelling? Nice!" I'm trying to tease her and it goes over like a ton of bricks.

"I'm not rebelling," she snaps. "I'm trying to live my life with freedom. I'm an adult."

The air is heavy with tension and I feel bad that I

made light of what is apparently a very touchy subject for Emily. I didn't mean to hurt her feelings, and the fact I feel badly about it is a new emotion for me. Most of the time, I do mean to hurt people's feelings, so they'll back off and leave me alone. That I want the opposite here has me searching for a way to make this right.

"I'm sorry. I was trying to tease you and apparently, I suck at it. So tell me what you want that is so different than your parents' aspirations."

She takes a deep breath. "My father is Alex Burnham...do you know him?"

I whistle through my teeth. "Uh...yeah...who doesn't know him? He's the ranking member of the House Armed Services Committee. And he's eying the White House."

"Well, when you come from an affluent and political family like mine, you tend to have all of your choices taken away."

I glance over at her skeptically. Surely, she's exaggerating just a bit. "All of your choices?"

"Most of them. I mean, I do get to choose when I can go to the bathroom." Her tone is snide and she's shutting down on me.

"Give me examples," I prompt her. "So I can understand."

I want to see just how bad she really has it. Because it must be so terrible to come from all that money and political standing. And yes, that's the sarcastic Nix Caldwell surfacing for an appearance.

Emily takes a deep breath before making her pitch to me. "Okay. Let's see…well, I am told what to wear, who to socialize with, how to talk, how to act, what friends to have, what degree I can get, and how much food to eat because God forbid I'd get fat and look terrible on camera."

"Is that it?" Which, okay, that's really pretty bad now that I think about it.

"No. One of the worst things is my mother trying to push an ex-boyfriend at me only because his father is one of my father's biggest campaign contributors."

"The stalker?"

"The one and only. And they could care less that he is violent. As long as I don't rock the money boat."

"What the fuck?" I exclaim loudly. "He was violent with you?"

She nods. "Just once, but I broke it off with him immediately."

I'm blown away. "And you're parents still want you to see him?"

"Well," she hedges. "They don't exactly know what he did to me. I just told them that it ended badly. I don't exactly have the type of relationship with my parents where I can confide in them."

Something about her tone of voice makes my heart

hurt a little for her. She is clearly lacking something in her relationship with her parents and I wonder if it's something as simple as love. I throw out just to see what she'll say, "Maybe they would understand if you told them."

"Maybe."

She slouches down in the seat and crosses her arms over her stomach. The move causes her dress to ride up another glorious inch. My mind is still very much involved in this conversation but I can still appreciate the breathtaking view to which I'm being treated.

I decide to change the subject a bit. "So which one of those edicts did you break that caused you to lose your money?"

She actually snickers. "I declared journalism as my major and my mother stroked out. She wanted me to go to law school or medical school."

"What's wrong with journalism? It's not like you're going to stripper school or anything."

She sits up in the seat tall and turns to me with excitement. "Exactly! That's the same thing I've been thinking to myself. You get me, Nix."

I give a short laugh. Maybe I am starting to get her.

"So, have you always been this rebel of a daughter?"

I can see from the corner of my eye that her shoulders slump again and she hangs her head just a bit. I've hit on something that appears to be very demoralizing.

Her body language reads loud and clear.

"No. I never rebelled," she says quietly. "You wouldn't have liked me very much just a few years ago."

I try to lighten the mood a little because her voice sounds so embarrassed. "Who says I like you now?"

I'm rewarded with a solid punch to my arm.

And then she twists my guts. "You like me."

It twists my guts because I'm afraid she may be right. Her voice is soft and sexy. And she's not meaning for it to come across that way, but that's the way I'm choosing to take it.

Time to lighten the mood again. "You're okay, Burnham. For a girl."

She laughs and it's that husky laugh that tightens my stomach even further. My dick starts to twitch and I have to talk him down.

Must think of something else.

"So why wouldn't I have liked you a few years ago?" If she's that bad, it will forestall a hard-on, I'm sure.

"Oh, let's see. I was spoiled, vain, narcissistic, capricious, entitled, bitchy, bratty and snide. And that's just for starters."

Her voice is light but I can tell she really believes she was all of those things.

Surely not? Not the Emily I've seen and come to…admire?

"You're not those things now," I state it emphatically. She may come from money and affluence but she's never once come across as anything but a down to earth kind of woman to me.

"Thanks, Nix. That's the nicest thing you've said to me. I bet that's about the nicest thing you've ever said to anyone."

I glance over and give her a short smile. It's true. That is probably the nicest thing I've said to anyone…at least for a very long time.

CHAPTER 11

Emily

I CAN'T BELIEVE the conversation I've been having with Nix. He's normally so standoffish and reserved. I'm not sure what changed, but he's actually engaging me.

And I like it. This conversational Nix, along with the Nix that saved me last night, has me appreciating him on a whole new level.

I about swallowed my tongue this morning when he walked into the kitchen. He was wearing the same jeans he had on the previous night, except the top two buttons were undone and they were hanging very low on his hips. He wasn't wearing a shirt and I almost got dizzy letting my eyes roll over the peaks and valleys of his abs. His muscles were cut sharp at his hips and angled to a "V", and while his chest was smooth, he had that dark trail of hair that disappeared into Happytown below his fly.

I knew I was staring as I also took in his tattoos. I glanced briefly at the barbed wire on his biceps, but I didn't stay there long as I had already had a peek at them. My gaze was stuck on his chest and ribs.

Starting just below his right shoulder and covering his right, pectoral muscle was a huge skull. It had a banner scroll covering its eyes and the words “See No Evil” were written in heavy, Gothic lettering. The scrollwork curled and wove its way off of the skull and across his ribs, disappearing around his back. I couldn’t see what was written on the scroll but it was small lines of lettering. Maybe a song? A poem?

I was dying to ask what was written there but I was also put off by the warning across the skull. See No Evil. I probably didn’t want to know the rest of the words.

We pull in front of my apartment building and I gather my purse. “Thanks again for saving me last night.”

He snorts. “You pretty much saved yourself. I just gave you a ride.”

I reach my hand out and lay it on his arm. I’m dismayed when I feel him flinch but I don’t move my hand. His muscles are hard and corded under my fingertips and I have the sudden urge to stroke his skin.

But I refrain.

“It was more than just a ride and you know it.”

I watch as he swallows hard and mutters, “It was no biggie.”

I remove my hand and turn to grab the door handle. I look to the door leading into my building and fury seeps into my bones. "Shit!"

"What?" Nix asks with alarm.

"Stalker alert," I respond dryly and open the door to step out of the Bronco, intent on giving Todd a piece of my mind.

By the time my feet hit the sidewalk, Nix is already out of the vehicle and standing beside me. I look to Todd and I notice his hands are clenched as he's watching us. He's seriously pissed and I know it's because I just got out of a man's truck while wearing last night's party dress.

I take a step toward Todd but Nix restrains me by taking hold of my wrist. "Get back in the truck, Emily."

"No," I say firmly. "I can handle him."

"Get back in the fucking truck, Emily." His words are harsh and frankly, they scare the crap out of me. I look at him uneasily but he's not even looking at me. He's staring at Todd as if he's relishing the thought of tearing him apart.

I pull my wrist out of his grip and he finally looks down at me. "This is not your fight, Nix." I keep my words fluid and cajoling.

He glances back at Todd for a second and then turns back to me. "Fine. But I'm staying right here until you get into your building. You've got two minutes to send him on his way or I'm going to do it for you. And I really hope you go over the time limit, Emily."

I don't know why, but his words are a turn on. He sounds dangerous, protective and animalistic. I have this sudden wave of desire come over me and I can't fathom why. A searing image blankets across my brain…of barbed wired biceps wrapped around my naked ribs, holding me tight while he pounds into me.

I shake my head and take a stuttering breath. What the hell was that?

I give Nix one last look—hoping it didn't look as lustful as it felt—and turn to walk toward Todd.

As I approach, his face is livid. I stop just a few feet short of him and hope he doesn't make a threatening move. I know if he does, Nix will be there in a flash and beat the shit out of him. My heart rate is spiking hard and I needed to put a quick end to this unexpected meeting.

"What are you doing here, Todd?"

He doesn't pull any punches. "Are you whoring yourself out for some street thug?"

I know I should be offended. Hell, maybe I should even be scared by the vehemence in his voice. But the fact he called Nix a street thug actually makes me laugh out loud.

My laugh dies suddenly as the look of fury on Todd's face intensifies. I need to nip this now. "You have no say in anything I do, Todd. I need you to get that through your head and just leave me alone."

I watch as the fury slides from his face and his eyes soften. I'm creeped out when his voice turns whiny and pathetic. "But baby…you know we're good together. You need to give us another shot."

I glance quickly at Nix and he's leaning back against his Bronco. He taps his index finger against his watch a few times, indicating that time's ticking.

I decide to go out on a limb and lie my ass off.

"Fine. I didn't want to have to break it to you this way, but I'm seeing someone new." I point back at Nix. "My boyfriend is not happy to have you waiting outside my apartment. And here's the thing…he told me that he is only giving me two minutes to get rid of you, then he is going to come over and stomp the shit out of you. Do us all a favor, Todd…save your own skin and please just leave."

I hope my words are convincing enough. Nix is in no way my boyfriend. Heck, I'm not even sure he's a friend. But there is no doubt he will pound Todd's ass into the concrete if he doesn't leave.

Todd's eyes lose the soft begging and instantly harden once again. He's shown me a variety of emotions in the last minute and I wonder which is the true one that is fueling his actions. He glances at Nix and I can see the muscles in his throat jumping. He looks back at me and then grins, in a coldly malevolent way. I actually cringe inward.

"You just fucked up, Emily." He starts walking backward away from me, holding my eyes. He raises a hand and points his index finger at me. "You fucked up big time, Em."

Then he turns and casually walks away, hands in his pocket.

My heart is pounding. Todd's stalking had always seemed to be childish and spoiled. But there's been a shift. I can feel it and there's a darkness to it that I had not noticed before. It settles over me like a heavy blanket and I shudder, feeling slightly suffocated. I think I'm actually afraid of him.

I look over my shoulder at Nix. Whatever is on my face worries him and he pushes away from his truck to walk toward me. I give him a fast shake of my head and hold my hand up for him to stay. I try to give a reassuring smile and he stops in his tracks. He looks undecided but I turn away and walk into my building.

I don't look back.

When I get into my apartment, I double-lock the door and slide the security chain. I engage the security alarm, something I never do while I'm inside. Throwing my purse down, I kick my heels off and walk to the window that faces the street. I can't see Todd but Nix is still there, just sitting in his Bronco. He's clearly waiting to make sure Todd doesn't come back and it provides me with amazing comfort.

♦

I FINISH WITH a shower and put on a pair of old sweats and a t-shirt. After brushing my hair out, I head into the kitchen to get something to eat. As I'm toasting a bagel, Fil walks into the kitchen. She looks rough.

"How do you feel, Steak-Um?"

She glares at me because she hates that nickname but also because she's quite hungover.

"I feel like crap. How was your night?"

"You wouldn't believe me if I told you." I hold up the toasted bagel and she nods, grabbing it out of my hand. "Do you want some cream cheese too?"

She groans. Dried bread product is all her stomach can apparently handle. Taking a seat at our little kitchen table she repeats, "So, how was your night?"

I bring my bagel to the table and sit across from her. "Well, let's see…after you left, Tina and Tonya ditched me and left me with a guy that wouldn't take no for an answer. So I called Nix to come get me. It took Nix awhile to get there but luckily I was able to avert rape before he showed up by biting a hole in the guy's tongue. I still had to stop Nix from beating the shit out of the guy though. Then he took me home with him. That's about it in a nutshell. The end."

Her eyebrows shoot straight up, a piece of bagel halfway to her mouth. "You're shittin' me, right?"

"Nope."

"Okay, okay…start over. Full story, top to bottom. And I want details. Technicolor details."

I fill her in on everything that happened last night and this morning. She wants to immediately rush out of the apartment and kick Tina and Tonya's asses for ditching me, but I convince her it wasn't their fault. I mean, up until then, James had seemed perfectly nice. Fil then wants to go hunt Todd down and kick his ass. I tell her it's just not worth it.

"So why did you go home with Nix? Why didn't he just drop you here? It's close to the club," she asks.

I shrug. I have no clue why he wanted to take me to his place but I also know that it never even crossed my mind to decline. I knew I was safe with him, and it just seemed like the right thing to do. The man was fascinating times ten and I suppose I wanted an opportunity to learn more about him.

"Oh, my God. You like him, don't you?"

"Of course I like him. He's a nice guy. He saved me last night."

"Don't be a dumbass. You know what I mean. You like him, like him. I mean, last night, I was really just teasing you about liking him, but now I mean it. You really like him! You feel something for him."

"I do not. I'm just…weirdly attracted to him, that's all. He's like the forbidden fruit."

"And you want to pluck his tree." Fil bursts out

laughing over her own double entendre then clutches her temple because that apparently aggravated her hangover headache.

I snicker then I start laughing. When I finally quiet down, I look at her soberly. "Fil…there is something about him…"

She cocks her head at me. "What do you mean?"

"I don't know. He has this really hard exterior, and he's hard to get close to. There's definitely something that keeps him from forging relationships. It makes me want to…I don't know…hug him?"

I ask it as a question, because I'm not really sure that is what I mean. For all of Nix's tough act, there is a vulnerability there hovering just below the surface. And I want to pick at it until I expose it. Then I want to kiss it.

And other things.

Fil and I head into the living room and we spend the rest of the day watching movies on TMC. I check my phone occasionally expecting a text or call from Todd. He's surprisingly quiet and that doesn't make me feel better. It makes me think he's up to something…like planning.

CHAPTER 12

Nix

I SIT OUTSIDE of Emily's apartment for a good twenty minutes to make sure her ex-douche doesn't come back. It occurs to me I don't even know his name, and I obviously don't give a shit. Ex-douche is good enough for me. Once I'm satisfied he won't return, I head back to Linc's place to take a shower and do some laundry. Then I load Harley up in the truck and we head out to my dad's place.

I usually try to spend most Sundays with him. My pop is the only one, other than Linc, who knows the real me.

Hank Caldwell is a great father. At sixty-two, he's a little bit older than my other friends' parents. Well, when I say other friends, I mean those I had in high school. I really don't have any friends now, other than a few Marine buddies that I keep in touch with via text and email.

My father had a previous marriage that had faltered

then disintegrated before he married my mother. That marriage had lasted for eight years before it ended in a bitter divorce. I don't know all the details but mom told me once, before she died, that dad had wanted lots of kids and his first wife didn't want any. That was apparently a recipe for disaster in a marriage.

Dad met and married my mom, Carolyn, just a few years after his divorce and I came along a scant nine months later. My dad apparently didn't want to waste any time in the baby-making department. Linc came along two years later.

My mom died of ovarian cancer when I was just ten. My memories of her are fuzzy but they are warm. Dad raised us on his own after that, never falling in love again. He said he'd never find another woman like his Caro.

My dad provided a solid home for me and Linc. There may not have been a lot of money, but there was a lot of love and a lot of happiness. Dad worked his ass off to support us, putting in sixty-plus hours a week at the shipyard. The crazy coot still works there. Linc and I have been on him trying to get him to retire but he won't listen to us. I think he's afraid that if he stops working, he'll die or something.

I pull into dad's driveway…my childhood home. It hasn't changed much over the years. Dad keeps it spruced up with help from me and Linc. It's a small, two-bedroom bungalow that sits on about a quarter-acre of land. The paint on the eaves and shutters is fresh, thanks to a working party we had last summer. The siding is clean and free from mold thanks to my dad's favorite tool…a portable pressure washer.

Harley runs to the front door before I can even get the door to the truck closed and barks. My dad opens it up, giving Harley an affectionate squeeze. He holds the screen door open for me and we give each other a half hug with lots of back pounding as I walk in.

I follow dad back to the living room and he already has two boxes of Giovanni's pizza on the coffee table and a cooler of beer sitting beside it. I reach in and pull out a bottle, grab a slice of pizza and sit on the couch. Dad is in his recliner that looks like it's about a hundred and fifty years old. Linc was going to buy him a new one a few years ago and he chewed Linc out for even thinking about it. He loves that old beast of a chair like it's one of his own kids.

We spend the next few hours watching the Jets get pounded by the Patriots so we are both left in a semi-bad mood. Dad doesn't help things when he asks, "Are you going to go back to see Dr. Antoniak?"

I try not to stiffen up because I know my dad is only asking because he cares. But he and Linc both know this is a touchy subject with me.

"I don't think so."

Dad stays silent and I can tell he's debating whether to push the subject. He decides to leave it alone but comes circularly at me.

"How about Paul? Have you talked to him lately?"

Fuck! Why can't he leave this shit alone? But I take in a deep breath and exhale it slowly through my nose. My fingers absently rub Harley's head as he sits beside me on the couch. I respect my dad too much to let loose on him. It's not a privilege I give anyone else, including Linc.

"No, Pop. He's called a few times but I've been busy."

My dad doesn't hold back. "You need to call him back. Better yet, get off your ass and go see him."

I sigh. "I know. I'll call him, okay?"

Sitting up in his recliner, my dad leans forward. He has that serious look on his face and he's staring me dead in the eyes. I want to turn my head, to avoid what he's going to say, but I won't puss out.

"Son…you need to do something about this. I'm worried about you. You know I only push at you because I love you, right?"

I smile at my dad. It's ghost thin, but it's still a smile. "I know, Dad, and I love you too. I'll get up with him. Don't worry."

"That's my boy. I'm proud of you, Nix. So damned proud."

A pit forms in my stomach at those words. Why does he have to say things like that? There's nothing to be proud of here. The fact that he tells me he's proud only makes me more shameful. Acid churns and I can feel the beer and pizza wanting to make a re-appearance but I push it back down. Luckily, dad doesn't say anything else and the subject is dropped.

I stick around and watch half of the Pittsburgh/ Baltimore game before heading out. Dad gives me a hard hug again, holding on a little longer this time. I take in a deep breath and smile inside at the hint of Old Spice aftershave. It's one of the smells I remember from my childhood. Back when things were simpler.

Harley jumps in the truck and we head back to Linc's place. He's still out of town and won't be back until tomorrow. Which I'm glad. I think he and dad are in a conspiracy to get me to talk about old wounds. He always grills me after I come back from dad's, wanting to know what we talked about.

I take Harley for a walk around the block and let him do his business before we head in. I'm dreading what I need to do and I decide a little fortification is necessary. I only had two beers at dad's so I need something a little stronger. I pick up a bottle of Jack Daniels from Linc's bar and pour a shot. I toss it back swiftly, enjoying the burn as it goes down. I stare out the window as the night sky darkens, mesmerized by the twinkling lights of

Manhattan across the river. I wonder what Emily is doing right now.

Shaking my head from thoughts of the dark-haired beauty, I pour one more shot and slam it back. The burn is equally as pleasant.

Walking into the living room, I bring the bottle and shot glass with me. I sit down on the couch, drink one more shot, and then put my implements on the coffee table. I pull out my cell phone and dial Paul's number.

It rings four times and I consider hanging up but then he answers. "It's about fucking time you called me back, you prick."

I smile. Only Paul.

"I've been busy, man."

"So damned busy you can't call your best buddy back? Oh, and did I tell you, you are a prick?"

I laugh. "I get told that every day by someone. I don't need you to confirm it."

There's silence there for a minute. Both of us waiting for the other to say something.

I go first. "So, how are you doing?"

"Freakin' peachy keen, jelly bean. Got my new walkin' legs last month. Of course, you'd know that if you ever called me back."

I grimace and my stomach churns. I'm in danger of losing the Jack all over Linc's living room carpet. "That's great. Do they put Lieutenant Dan's to shame?"

He busts a gut laughing at me. "They sure do, Forrest. Titanium steel. Actually, they have these new spring mechanisms in the knee joints that really take a lot of pressure off my hips and lower back. It's like walking on a cloud of air."

I lean back into the couch cushions, close my eyes and listen to Paul talk. He tells me all about his new prosthetics, he tells me about starting college, and he tells me he's going to ask Marie to marry him. He's happy, and well adjusted, and I want to vomit listening to it. Because I'm afraid he's putting on an act just to make me feel better.

And because it's my fault he lost his legs.

We talk for about an hour, and I doubt I hear ninety percent of what he says to me. I promise I'll come visit him soon, but we both know it's probably a lie.

After I hang up, I pour another shot of Jack and drink it down. I stare at the empty glass. It's how I feel. My instinct is to hurl it across the room as hard as I can and watch it shatter into a million pieces. But just as quickly that thought is gone because it just seems like too much work. Instead, I set the glass gently on the coffee table and stand up. I take the bottle of liquor back with me to the bedroom.

I'm not done with it yet. And it doesn't escape my notice the next time I tip the bourbon up to my lips that it's the same color as Emily's eyes.

CHAPTER 13

Emily

IT'S FRIDAY AND I can't believe I'm actually going to be painting Nix's house today. It's not that I mind. Heck, I owe him money so I'll work it off however I can. And part of me is sort of excited to try this. I've never painted anything before. I imagine what my mother would say and I practically cackle with unfettered glee.

I hope I don't screw his walls up too bad, but if I do, that's his problem. I'm just doing what he tells me and if he wants to hire an amateur, so be it.

And while I don't mind doing any type of manual labor at the behest of my employer, what I do mind is the fact that Nix has been a grumpy bastard all week to me. I think he's having me paint inside his house to keep me out of his workshop. And that sort of hurts my feelings.

I thought we were opening up some doors of friendship this past weekend, particularly after he sort of...maybe a little...well not really, opened up to me.

But he had engaged in honest conversation and I was wise enough to know when to back off. And he had genuinely been interested in me, too. All of those things had helped to ratchet up my attraction to him.

Now, I didn't feel so shallow. I was attracted to more than just his body. The thought amused me greatly.

When I had come in to work on Monday, it was with utter disappointment that I found the original, brooding and somewhat offensive Nix Caldwell. I can only assume that something happened to put him in a really bad mood on Sunday. He didn't even bother to try to be polite. He just barked orders at me and then shut himself off in his welding room. He never came back out, even though I loitered around a good fifteen minutes after I had finished my tasks for the day. I thought maybe he was just busy.

But when I returned on Wednesday, I was met with the same thing. He apparently didn't have any welding to do but he practically told me to keep my mouth shut and not bother him while he was working. So I watched him a lot while I worked on setting up vendor accounts in his new Quick Books program on the laptop.

He was meticulous in his work and utterly focused. That I could understand and respect. It was even sort of cute when he was really concentrating hard on something, sometimes the tip of his tongue would stick out from between those generous lips of his. His eyebrows would scrunch together. And when he completed the delicate work he was doing, it was a joy to watch his face smooth out and a small smile curve his lips.

It was practically hypnotizing and difficult to tear my eyes away from him. He actually caught me staring at him once and glared at me with venom. I immediately dropped my head back over the laptop, and typed furiously on the keyboard.

The second time he caught me looking at him, he snapped at me, "What the hell are you looking at, Burnham?"

He didn't even have the grace to call me Emily. He freakin' called me Burnham.

Asshat.

Just before I was preparing to leave that day, he told me to wear old clothes on Friday. When I asked him why, his smile was almost evil when he told me I'd be painting inside his house.

I wasn't about to let him see that I was bothered by this news. First, the only thing that bothered me was that he clearly didn't want me in the same room with him. But if I showed him that I was bothered, he would think I was nothing but a spoiled brat, and I had worked hard the last few years to shed that image.

Hell, I even volunteered with Danny two weekends a month at a homeless shelter. The old Emily Burnham was hopefully nothing more than a faded, somewhat embarrassing, memory.

So here I am. Standing in Nix's living room, watching him lay out all of the painting supplies. And, of course, I'm admiring the way the muscles in his back bunch and ripple underneath his t-shirt as he lifts a bucket of paint up. Or the way his jeans mold to his ass when he bends over to lay the drop cloth on the floor. I shamelessly ogle and I don't have an ounce of guilt. Especially since he's been a jerk all week, it appears the only thing that is appealing about him right now is his body.

I will never admit this in a hundred years, but when Nix told me he wanted me to paint his living room, I did have a moment of panic. I may not have ever done this type of manual labor before, but that fact alone would not fully ease my conscience if I really screwed his walls up. The fact of the matter was, I hated failing at anything. So, I actually diligently studied up on the subject. I read a few articles online and then I went to the god of all internet teachings…YouTube. You'd be amazed at how many videos there are on how to paint walls and trim.

So while it's true I've never done this before, I now actually feel a little confident that I will at least not look like a complete buffoon.

Nix has everything laid out and he stands up straight to look at me. He tersely points out all of the materials and tells me that the walls have already been primed. I can tell that because the faint odor lingers in the air.

He shows me how to use a screwdriver to pop the lid off the paint can, and stirs it up with a wooden stick. Wiping the excess off, he lays it on a corner of the drop cloth. And while I don't need the instruction—again, thank you YouTube—I very much enjoy watching him bending, stooping and straightening back up as he demonstrates to me the finer points of how to use a paint roller versus a paintbrush.

When he's finished, he asks if I have any questions.

"Nope."

His gaze rakes over my body, and he sort of sneers at me, "I told you to wear old clothes because you will get paint on yourself. And that's the best you could do?"

I look down at myself and I can see a little of what he is saying. It's not like I had a pair of paint coveralls in my closet so I'd worn my oldest and most casual clothing. A pair of old khaki cargo pants, a white tank top, and flip-flops. I tell him this, although I leave out the part that I painted my toenails the night before a lovely shade of pink, because it goes well with khaki.

"I don't mind getting these clothes messed up." I try to sound jovial but I sort of want to slap him upside the head for being such an idiot the last few days.

"Whatever. I'll be in my shop working if you need anything. But please…try not to need anything."

"Fine." I snap at him and I do see a little flash of guilt in his eyes but it only makes a brief cameo appearance before it exits stage left. He doesn't respond and walks out the door.

I huff a little to myself over the entire conundrum that is Nix Caldwell as I step up to the task. I don't recall whether YouTube said to do the main wall with a roller or do the trim with a brush first, so I go ahead and opt to start with the roller.

I recall with vivid memory dipping the roller into the pan, pulling it back and rolling it on the slope back and forth to get it evenly covered. I make my first strokes, rolling in diagonal crisscrossing patterns, enjoying the work.

I let my mind drift. It would be nice right now to just reflect over the hotness of Nix, but I'm actually a bit more occupied with the fact that my parents are coming to dinner tomorrow night. This lovely news was just sprung on me this morning when my mother called me.

I was running late for class, something that did not happen often, when my phone started ringing. I wasn't thinking and I pulled the phone out to answer before even looking at the Caller ID.

"Hello, Emily."

I felt guilty that my stomach dropped upon hearing my mother's voice. Plus I was still smarting over the fact she kyboshed my trust just because I dared to declare

Journalism as my major. So, it was no surprise I went in for an early kill.

"Hi, Mom. What's up?"

I could hear my mother suck in her breath just a bit. She hated the title "Mom". I had grown up always calling her "Mother", clearly educated to do so from an age so early I don't remember receiving the edict. But I made the mistake of calling her "Mom" one day several years ago and I got a fifteen-minute lecture on the proper title of a parent.

My mother, Celia Thorne Burnham, is where the old money comes from in our family. Oh, my father made great money as a trial lawyer before he went into politics, but our insane coffers come from my mother's family and goes back generations of Thornes. Thorne Enterprises, run by my Uncle Jim, is a conglomerate of corporations that dabble in everything from shipping to manufacturing to research and development.

In fact, my Uncle Jim is the one that years ago talked my parents into amending the trusts for me and Ryan so we could have full access to them when we turned twenty-one. Until that time, they were controlled by my mother, which is why she had cut off my monthly allowance.

And the funny thing is, outside of not being able to pay Nix the money I owe him, I don't miss the damn thing at all. I didn't use it for anything but buying clothes and trinkets.

Heck, I was kind of enjoying being one of the frugal, working masses now. I had even told Uncle Jim that earlier this week when he called to check in on me. He laughed so hard when I said that, he started choking and coughing. The memory of his amusement makes me smile.

Finally, my mother found her voice. "You know I don't like that, Emily. Please call me Mother."

"Yes, Mother," I dutifully said but I know I didn't sound repentant at all.

"I wanted to let you know that your father and I will be in New York tomorrow and we've made reservations at Le Bernardin for dinner. You need to be there at 7:30pm."

I gritted my teeth that she assumed that I would be available on such short notice. Even though I was. "Okay, Mother. That will be fine."

"I'll see you then."

I hung up and ruminated about the conversation the whole way to class. This conversation would have not bothered me a few years ago. It would have been…normal. But I won't lie…it hurts my feelings that the conversation failed to include her asking how I was, or how school was, or even that she missed me. Living in the real world and out of my sheltered environment, I have come to learn how cold and sterile my family could be. If it wasn't for Uncle Jim, who called me every week just to check in and see how I was doing, I would probably lose my faith in parenthood altogether.

My heart actually clenches up a little thinking about this. It's not like I ever had this type of relationship with my parents. My mother was always there, but emotionally distant. My father was emotionally closer, but never physically there. I wish they could be more normal.

And I wish it didn't hurt so much that they weren't.

Enough of this subject!

I'm getting depressed. I decide to put those thoughts aside for I am now in a mood to turn my attention to the hotness of Nix Caldwell. I am finding the movements of painting to be relaxing and the perfect environment to slip into a sexy daydream about him.

CHAPTER 14

Nix

I CAN'T STAND it anymore. I'm going to go check on Emily.

This week I've tried my damnedest to distance myself from her and I've done a good job of it. But I'm not liking it. And just like everything else in this world, that pisses me off.

I don't like having this unnatural attraction to her. And trust me, it's unnatural for Nix Caldwell to have any sort of passing interest in a female other than trying to get in her pants.

But I'm going to say it, and I'm going to kick myself for saying it. Emily is different.

She is.

I find her utterly fascinating and for a variety of reasons. First, she's apparently done a complete overhaul of her persona and character, because she deemed herself to not be a very nice person not all that long ago. I don't think many people ever go through life having that sort of epiphany and I'm strangely attracted to that.

Second, she is fierce. She's stood up to me, she's stood up to her parents, she's stood up to a guy that was probably intent on raping her, and she stood up to her psycho, stalker ex-boyfriend. She's tough as nails and I like that a lot.

Third, and most importantly, she seems to get me. I don't know the how's or the why's, but I have watched her handle me like a pro. She has found some secret to unlocking my defenses, yet she knows exactly when I've had enough. That, in and of itself, makes me start to trust her just a tiny, tiny bit. I feel like I could open up to her, but when I've had enough, she will back off. My dad is really good at that, too. Linc, not so much, but he's just being a pestering younger brother half the time, so I'll cut him some slack.

I wash my hands in the shop sink and dry them off. I have a ton of other stuff to do, but like I said...I can't stand it anymore and so I'm lifting my self-imposed Emily Exile.

As soon as I enter the house, I hear her singing. And while I've recently come to admire many of Emily's qualities...let's just say singing will never be one of them. I smile to myself as I picture her with earbuds in her ears, bopping to some tune that only she can hear.

As I walk into the living room, I'm momentarily stunned to find she's not singing to any music.

Nope. No earbuds in her ears.

She's just belting out a song on her own. No wonder why she's not in tune.

I have to almost bite into my tongue not to laugh out loud at her. She's singing the theme song from True Blood, and trying to replicate the low, low, baritone of Jace Everett. She's perched on the top rung of the ladder I left out for her. She's got a paintbrush in her right hand and she's balancing herself with her left hand on the ceiling. She's shaking her ass to the song she's singing…badly…

When you came in the air went out.

And every shadow filled up with doubt.

I don't know who you think you are,

But before the night is through,

I wanna do bad things with you.

I watch mesmerized as she belts at the top of her lungs, her gorgeous hips gyrating back and forth. Surprisingly, her paint line is super straight. She's clearly a multi-tasker.

And while her tune is off and she doesn't carry Louisiana hillbilly off very well, the words to the song and just imagining she is singing those words to me sends a wave of hot longing straight below my belt. I walk quietly up behind her and stand at the base of the ladder, looking up.

I don't know what you've done to me,
But I know this much is true.
I wanna do bad things with you.
I wanna do real bad things with you.

I clear my throat. "Who do you want to do bad things with?"

Emily shrieks and turns around so fast, her flip flop gets stuck in the ladder rung and she pitches sideways. The brush flips out of her hand and hits me on the side of my face with a wet slap, before grazing down my neck and bouncing off my shoulder. I reach out instinctively as she falls and she slams into my chest.

I had a brief moment of panic—just a mere second—when she started to fall. Then when I caught her in my arms, panic turned into something hot and carnal.

She comes to rest perfectly with her chest mashed to mine, her arms draped over my shoulders. We came perilously close to banging heads, but I don't even consider that. Instead, I consider the fact that I can feel her heartbeat slamming from her chest into mine…and the fact that her lips are mere inches away.

My arms wrap tight around her waist and although propriety would dictate I should lower her immediately to the floor, I say to myself, *Fuck Propriety!*

I'm staring straight into her eyes and they are warm and languid. I lower my gaze and her lips are slightly parted, and one soft pant comes out. Her legs are hanging down against my crotch and I know she can feel the erection I started sporting the minute I really paid attention to her lyrics.

Neither one of us moves, and I am just considering if I should kiss her or let her slide down, when she does the unbelievable and lowers her mouth to mine.

I didn't expect it. I had no clue Emily even felt the slightest attraction to me. But the minute her lips feather over mine, I know without a doubt she was singing those lyrics with me in mind.

I want to see how far she takes this, because this is new territory for me. If a woman laid her mouth against mine, with the same look that Emily is giving me right now, she'd be in my bed for the rest of the night. But I don't want to make that assumption about her.

I want it to be true, but I don't want to assume.

Emily pushes a little harder against my mouth and I let my lips part. I have blood rushing to my head, and more blood rushing to my other head.

When she slips her tongue into my mouth, it's all over for me. With one hand firmly around her waist to hold her body against mine, I bring the other one up to grab her hair. I fist a good chunk of it right near the nape of her neck and tilt her head to the side with a slight tug. It opens her mouth further and I plunge back.

The contact is explosive. I groan at the same time she

lets out a feminine whimper. Her arms curve all the way around the back of my head and she grips my hair.

Really hard.

Then she uses her arms for leverage to pull her body up, wrapping her legs around my waist, crossing her feet behind my back. She slides down a little and it puts her softness in direct, molten contact with my hardness. I flip our bodies around and push her up against the freshly painted wall. I can feel the wetness against my arms that are probably crushing her right now.

The kiss becomes deeper, hotter, wetter. It goes on for an eternity, yet not long enough. I flex my hips against her, pushing her back into the wall. She rubs herself against me and although she doesn't break the kiss, she somehow manages to push the words, "Oh God" into my mouth.

When I woke up this morning, I never thought in a million years that I would be on the verge of pulling Emily's pants down in the middle of my newly painted living room with the idea in mind of plunging mindlessly into her.

Over and over again.

And now that I'm on the verge of doing that, a small kernel of doubt starts to take hold.

I'm holding Emily Burnham in my arms. Congressman Alex Burnham's daughter is molded to my erection. Insanely wealthy and formerly bratty Emily is rubbing herself all over me.

And while it feels so right…so very, very right, I'm aware that too much of this could be wrong. I'm sure Emily has some wealthy, educated stud in her future that she will marry and with which she will have two point three little, rich babies. I don't have anything in my future except offering her an orgasm…or two…or three.

For tonight.

Because let's face it…I don't do relationships and Emily is built for them. She's too sweet not to be.

I'm too rotten.

My thoughts sound rational but do absolutely nothing to cool the raging lust I'm feeling, so it is with great difficulty I make myself tear my lips from hers and I drop her like a sack of hot potatoes. Luckily, the wall is there to support her because I immediately take one step backward to get some distance. Emily puts her arms back against the wall for support, before sagging completely against it. She's going to be covered in paint when she walks out of here.

Both of us are standing there, our chests heaving with desire and need. We are staring wide-eyed at one another…disbelief on her face…resolve on mine.

"This can't happen, Emily."

The disbelief on her face pours through into her voice. "Why?"

Why indeed?

All of those reasons that were sparking through my brain are lost. I know I had sound logic not just ten seconds ago, but I can't grasp it right now.

"Because…we're not…compatible."

She stuns me when she laughs, genuine delight showing in her eyes. "Oh, we're compatible. Your working parts and mine were in perfect alignment just a few seconds ago."

Damn, that is hot!

She's clearly saying that wasn't just a kiss. She's saying she was imagining those multiple orgasms just the way I was. I almost lunge at her to pull her back in my arms, but I have a shocking moment of clarity.

I shake my head at her. "Our parts are definitely compatible, Em. But that's all it would be. It would never be anything but a fuck."

I expect those words to hurt her…to enrage her…to make her realize that Nix Caldwell is the world's biggest asshole. I hope those words cause her to go running from my house in tears.

Instead, she says, "So?"

Well, shit. I'm kind of incensed—on her behalf—since she's clearly not smart enough to be. "So? Do you understand what I'm saying?"

She looks at me like I'm a dumbass. "Yes," she drawls. "You're saying this would just be casual. No-strings sex."

Yes, that's exactly what I'm saying. Why does she sound so damned okay with that concept? This is sweet, Emily Burnham here. The one that wears buttercup, yellow dresses and sleeps with my dog's foot pressed against her nose.

I don't buy it for a second. "Come on, Emily. You're not a casual sex type of person."

Her eyes flare at me hotly. "What makes you think I'm not? I can do casual sex. If I want, I can do lots of casual sex. And it doesn't even have to be with you."

Shit. I've offended her big time and her comment about implying she can do casual sex with other men pisses me off. But I don't backpedal. I'm determined to talk her out of her foolishness. "Get real. You are flowers and romance. I'm down and dirty."

The hot look in her eyes goes nuclear, and my heart skips a beat with wariness. She bends down and picks up the wet, paintbrush off the floor and takes a step toward me. She slaps it against my chest and I feel little paint splatters against my neck. My hands reach up automatically to grab the brush as she releases it. "You don't know shit about me, Caldwell. I'm done for the day. Clean up your own crap and I'll see you on Monday."

She stomps around me and leaves the living room. Just before she walks out of sight, she turns around and looks at me. Her voice isn't quite as frosty when she says, "You know, Nix. I've made it my mission the last few years to experience as many new things as I can. I bet I can get just as down and dirty as you can. Maybe even more so."

With that, she practically flounces into my kitchen and out of my sight. I hear the back door slam and seconds later, her car pulling out of my driveway.

Fuck. That went well.

I know her last words are going to haunt me for days. And there's not a doubt in my mind her words were calculated on her part to do just that. I've just added deviousness to Emily's list of attributes I'm beginning to admire. Just imagining Emily getting down and dirty with me is going to ensure I stay immersed in a cold shower for the foreseeable future.

CHAPTER 15

Emily

MY CAB PULLS into the front of Le Bernardin about ten minutes early but I know my parents will already be here. They habitually arrive early to everything, just as I do. I pay the cabbie and step out of the car. It's been a while since I've dressed up, as there's not much of a need living the life of a college student.

I smooth down the front of my cream-colored, Valentino dress. It's one of my favorites. It's perfectly tailored to fit my curves and stops just above my knee. It's sleeveless and has a mandarin collar. A lightweight black jacket and black peep-toe pumps complete the look. It's nice to play dress up every now and then, but these clothes represent such a small part of my life now.

I'm finding myself more partial to paint-covered cargo pants than anything.

But just that thought makes me fume over Nix's misplaced sense of decorum. How dare he even place a label on me? I had just spent two years digging myself out of a category, and he was pushing me right back into one.

Bastard.

Maybe I should just show up Monday to work and drop my clothing on the floor and see what he does. I'll show him down and dirty.

I walk into Le Bernardin and scan the bar. My parents are sharing a table and have drinks in front of them. I approach them with nothing less than dread in my stomach. The main topic of our conversation I'm sure will center on my degree and how wrong it is for the family.

My heart hurts a bit that I can't have the type of parents that would be ecstatic just to come and have some quality time with their daughter. As I approach their table, they both look up at me. My father's smile is warm but he stays seated. My mother rakes her scrutiny down my body, taking in my appearance. Approval of my dress is the only thing reflected on her face. What I wouldn't give for both of them to jump up, yell out to everyone in the restaurant, "Emily, we've missed you."

But to be fair, it's not like I'm running to them either. In fact, I feel like my pace is slowing, such is my aversion to this meeting.

When I reach the table, my father stands and gives me a hug. He pulls a chair out for me and I lean over and kiss my mother's cheek before I sit down.

"You look very nice, Emily," my mother comments.

It's a compliment and I greedily soak it in. "Thank you. You both look wonderful as well. What are you doing in New York?"

"Just a few fundraisers. We're staying with Reynolds and Libby Fischer," my father supplies.

My father is a very handsome man. His dark hair has gray at the temples and his brown eyes are welcoming to me. It's a stark contrast to my mother's lovely, Nordic features.

A waiter approaches and asks what I'd like to drink. I ask for some iced water, as my mouth has been dry as hell since I left my apartment. I'm sure it has nothing to do with nerves.

"So, how is school going?" my dad inquires.

My eyebrows rise slightly. I'm not sure if he's baiting me or not, but I cautiously answer.

"It's going great. I really love all of my classes." And then I decide I better break the ice. "I really love Economics of Sports. It's so fascinating and I was lucky to be able to get into it this semester."

I hear my mother make a weird sound in her throat and I see her hands are clenched on the table. My father surprises me when he says, "That's wonderful, Em. I'm glad to see you enjoying your studies."

I suppose my mother couldn't stand this farce any longer. She reaches over and lays her hand over my father's. "Now Alex, don't encourage her."

"Well, why not," my father booms. "That class sounds really interesting."

I'm sort of enjoying this. I can tell my father has no clue that he's talking about a class that directly supports my forbidden major of Journalism. For even if he truly doesn't care what I major in, he would never intentionally say something to upset my mother. One of the reasons he's an awesome politician is because of his ability to keep the peace.

"Alex," my mother warns, in temperatures that range from frigid to downright arctic. "We discussed this."

And then my father shocks the hell out of me. "No, Celia. I believe you discussed this. I didn't seem to have much of a say-so." He then turns to me. "I'm proud of you kiddo. You pursue your dreams as best you see fit."

I stare at my father dumbfounded. He has never, ever, gone against my mother. In fairness, he's usually gone most of the time so governance of their children usually fell to her. My mother gasps over his comment and stares at him as if she's planning which form of murder will be less likely to be traced to her.

"Alex," she says and I didn't think her words could get any colder. "A journalism degree is not the absolute best choice for your campaign."

My father takes a sip of his drink and says, "Screw the campaign, Celia. Stop trying to control everything.

It's not like she's learning how to be a stripper."

I can't help myself but I actually snort out loud. My mother glares at me, and then glares again at my father. My father shoots a wink over at me and I give him a toothy grin.

"Well fine," my mother huffs. "I'm just trying to do the best possible job that I can to help you achieve your goals."

Leaning over to kiss my mother on her temple, my dad smoothes her ruffled feathers. "And you do a marvelous job, darling. I wouldn't be what I am today without you."

Awww. That's so sweet. I'm delighted to see the tension leave my mother's shoulders and she gives him a fond smile. Maybe this dinner won't be so bad after all.

"Hello, Congressman Burnham…Mrs. Burnham…"

I turn in my chair at the voice that just spoke out from behind me and realize that this dinner was about to get very bad.

"Todd!" my father says in surprise. "What are you doing here?"

Indeed! What the hell is he doing here?

My mother stands up and gives Todd a warm hug. It pisses me off because clearly, I didn't rate one. "I invited Todd to join us tonight. Isn't that nice?"

Todd looks down at me with a sly smile on his face. I can see he's happy to have trapped me here in his presence. I can see him mentally patting himself on the back.

"Emily. You look beautiful," Todd says as he leans down to give me a kiss on my cheek. I'm beyond furious that he thinks he can get away with this. I push my chair back abruptly to avoid his kiss and stand up. Todd actually has to jump back a foot so the chair doesn't ram into him.

I look at my mother. "I told you, Mother, that Todd and I are not dating, nor will we be in the future. I will not be having dinner tonight if he's here."

"Emily," my mother hisses at me. "That is completely rude. Todd is our guest and you will not embarrass our family further."

I close my eyes and try to garner as much strength as I can. Opening them back up, I look to my father first. He's looking at me with worry. Glancing at my mother, she's completely affronted. Todd is merely smirking, convinced that I'm going to bow to my mother's declaration.

I muster as much calm and gentility as I can. "Mother…I told you this summer that things ended badly between me and Todd. I don't understand why you can't accept that and stop pushing us together."

"Don't be silly, Emily. Everyone has problems with their relationships. You just need to sit down and talk things through."

God help me, but I've never wanted to throttle my mother before but I was on the verge now. "No, Mother.

Some problems can't be talked through."

My mother completely ignores me. She leans toward my father and says, "Honestly, Alex. Emily can be so dramatic sometimes." She slaps his arm playfully. "I think she gets that from you."

Then my mother actually giggles over that remark.

I, on the other hand, feel like the top of my head is going to blow off. I have no control over my next words. "Mother, would it make you feel any different if I told you that Todd was physically violent toward me? He slammed me into the wall in my bedroom so hard that a painting fell off. How's that for dramatic?"

The patronizing smile slides off her face and my mother's lips press severely together. "That's a very serious accusation."

Deep down, I knew my mother wouldn't believe me. Not necessarily because she thinks I'm dishonest, but because it would ruin all of her plans of matching me with Todd Fulgram and his father's huge war chest. She wants it to be false, therefore, she will do anything in her power to make it false. It still hurts like hell that she doesn't immediately jump up and shove Todd out of the restaurant.

"It's not an accusation, Mother," I say on a heavy sigh, and the full truth of how I feel comes pouring out. "It's a fact. And honestly…I'm a bit heartbroken that my own mother cannot even take my side. You've managed to alienate your son, now you're doing it with your daughter. You need to wake up, Mother, and get your priorities in line. Now, if you will excuse me, I'm going to leave."

I turn around and walk out the door. Tears start pooling and I wipe the back of my hand across my eyes to dash them away. They immediately fill back up again.

Just as I step out onto the sidewalk, I feel someone grab my arm. I wheel around, thinking it's Todd, but it's my father. His eyes are filled with heartache and I know immediately that he believes me.

He holds his arms open and I walk into them, tears now pouring down my face. "I'm sorry, honey. I wish you would have told us."

"Why?" I mumble into his chest. "Mother doesn't believe me."

He kisses me on top of my head and pushes me back just a little so I can look at him. "Your mom tends to get too deeply involved in appearances. It's something she has to work on and it's something I will talk to her about. But don't ever forget, she's your mother first. She'll always be that for you in the end."

His words sound nice but I'm having a hard time accepting them. Just the mere fact she couldn't even hug me but had a warm embrace waiting for Todd told me all I needed to know. That made the tears continue to fall.

My father frames my face with his hands and wipes away the wetness with his thumbs. "We both love you very much, and are proud of you. No matter what we say to you, or anyone else says to you, you go after *your* dreams. You don't let anyone stand in your way of what you want. Not even your parents. Okay?"

I nod my head and give him a shaky smile.

"How about we go get some dinner somewhere else…just the two of us?" my dad offers.

"That's okay, Dad. I think I'm just going to head home."

He's worried…I can tell by the look on his face. "Are you sure?"

I stand on my tiptoes and kiss him on the cheek. "I'm sure. We'll get together next time."

Then he wraps me in a big, bear hug and whispers in my ear. "I love you, Emily."

"I love you too, Dad."

Stepping back from me, my father rakes his hand through his hair. "I guess I need to go back in and threaten Todd if he ever looks at you again I'm going to kick his ass."

I start giggling. "That's awesome."

But then the repercussions of this whole Todd fiasco come crashing down on me. "But what about his father?"

"To hell with him. I don't need him to get elected. Not at the expense of my little girl." He reaches out and strokes my cheek.

"Thanks, Daddy," I whisper and then turn abruptly away to hail a cab before my tears start again.

CHAPTER 16

Emily

THE ENTIRE CAB ride home, I ruminate over what had just transpired. My father has always been loving and supportive of me. It's just he's never around much to give it to me. His words of reassurance were exactly what I needed though, and I'm hoping he can talk my mother into backing off of me a bit.

Best of all, my father has basically sanctioned me to move forward with my Journalism degree. My mother's only argument against it was because it wasn't the "best" degree for his campaign. But that didn't seem to matter to him, so I'm not going to worry about it any further.

As I get out of the cab at my apartment, I reflect on my father's advice. To go after my dreams and the things I want, and to not let anyone stand in my way.

That is damned good advice.

Rather than going up to my apartment, I get in my car and decide to head across the river.

♦

I KNOCK ON the door to Linc's apartment. I have no idea if Nix is even here, and if he is, I have no idea what I'm going to say to him. But I do think we need to talk about what's going on between us. Clearly, there is an insane mutual attraction and frankly, I need him to give me a better reason why we shouldn't act on it.

My father said to go get what I wanted and I want Nix Caldwell. And I don't feel the slightest bit trashy for it. This is all part of my collective plan to experience life and there is something that I believe I can learn from Nix.

And I'm not just talking about sex, although, if I can get him to capitulate, I'm sure it will be amazing. No, there is something about Nix that is captivating me. He's got more facets than the Hope Diamond and he intrigues the hell out of me. I know he says he's not relationship material, and I'm not even sure I'm looking for a relationship, but Nix has experiences and wisdom that go beyond anyone I've ever met. I want to figure him out. I want to learn from him.

And if we have sex along the way…that would be great too.

The door swings open and Nix is standing there. He's clearly surprised to see me and an array of emotions play across his beautiful face. First, something hot flares in his eyes, then it switches to wariness, then—if I'm not mistaken—there's anger.

Just great. He's pissed off that I showed up.

Instead of telling me to leave, however, he grabs my hand and pulls me into the apartment.

"What's wrong?" he asks. His voice is laced with worry, which catches me off guard.

Can't he just think I might want to come over to seduce him?

"What makes you think something is wrong?" I grumble.

"Because you've clearly been crying," he says gently.

Oh!

Now I'm off my game. I was completely empowered driving over here. I was going to go after what I wanted, just like my father told me to do. Although I'm sure he was not specifically thinking for me to go after a man when he told me that. Still, the principle of his advice is solid.

And now I don't know what to say. So I just stand there like an idiot.

"Emily, why were you crying?"

"Um…it's nothing. Just a little run in with my mother."

Still holding my hand, Nix leads me into the kitchen. He releases it and opens the fridge, pulling out a bottle of white wine. He pulls down a glass from the cabinet and fills it. Handing it to me, he says, "What happened?"

I didn't come over here to spill my family dirt to

Nix. I don't want to get sidetracked from my mission. After a small sip of the wine—which is delicious by the way—I look Nix in the eye. "I want to resume discussions with you about us having sex."

"What the fuck, Emily?" Nix literally steps away from me as if I'm diseased. "And that's why you were crying?"

"What? No, that's not why I was crying. I was crying for something else that I don't want to talk about. I want to talk about sex."

Nix is staring at me as if my head is on fire. A combination of horror and odd curiosity. "You want to talk about sex?"

"Yes."

"I don't understand."

I blow out a pent up breath of frustration. "Are you purposely being obtuse?"

Nix doesn't answer but reaches in the fridge and pulls out a beer. He twists the cap off and throws it in the sink. He takes a long swallow and just stares at me. The muscle that sits just along his jawbone is popping.

Finally, he says, "There's nothing to talk about. We are not having sex."

"Now you're just being stubborn," I mutter. "All guys want to have sex."

The corners of his mouth twitch and it's nice to know he finds me so amusing. I clearly need to change tactics because I was hoping he would find me alluring and sexy.

What to do?

I know. I'll try some logic first, and if that doesn't work, maybe I'll just strip naked and see what happens.

"Let me ask you something, Nix."

"What's that?" I can tell he finds this line of questioning from me to be quite entertaining.

"Do you find me attractive?" I don't intend for it to happen necessarily but my voice is throaty…full of promise.

He stares at me hard, the jaw muscle popping faster. "Yes."

I'm thrilled just by that simple admission and it fuels me on.

"Have you thought about us having sex? You know…down and dirty style?" I throw that last bit in there to amp up the heat factor on my logical argument.

He swallows hard and his eyes turn a darker shade of moss. His voice is harsh when he says, "Yes."

"And do you imagine me…doing things to you?"

I'm not sure where that question came from. My plan to lay out a logical path of reasoning seems to have evaporated as I realize my questions are nothing more than an intense seduction so I can get what I want.

Sometimes I don't even realize the depths of depravity I will sink to.

I notice that Nix is gripping his beer bottle so hard that his knuckles are white.

"I imagine you doing a lot of things to me, Emily." Nix's voice is low and guttural and it causes me to shiver. "What's your point in all of this?"

Hmmm…so he wants me to bring this to a logical conclusion after all? Well, you asked for it, Nix Caldwell.

I set my wineglass down on the counter and walk to him. I reach out and take his beer bottle from his hand. It slides easily from his fingers and I set it down next to my wine.

Stepping in close to him, he's looking down at me with such carnality, my knees almost buckle. We aren't touching anywhere but the physical heat swirling between our bodies is palpable, like the waves of hot air that roll off a blazing fire.

"My point is that I want the same things you do. We're not as different as you think we are."

Nix moves suddenly, bringing his hand up to the back of my head and grabs a fistful of hair. I gasp in shock and a thrill of hope runs through me. He slowly pulls my head back so my neck is exposed fully and I can't help but wonder if he's looking for my submission.

"What do you want from me?" His voice is hesitant, maybe a bit distrustful.

"Whatever you're willing to share with me, I'll take it. And I won't ever push you for anything more."

He studies me. His gaze flicks choppily between my eyes, trying to see if there is a lie somewhere. He looks briefly toward my lips, as if considering whether it's safe to kiss me, then he comes back to my eyes again.

Finally, he says, "I don't want to hurt you."

"You won't," I hastily assure him. "You can't. Not if I don't expect anything from you. I'm clear on that Nix, I promise."

He's on the edge, teetering. He needs just a tiny push. I step in closer to him, and press my body into his. His breath comes out in a mass exodus as he closes his eyes and grits his teeth. The man's self-control is amazing and I'm starting to feel like this may be an insurmountable mission on my part.

But before I can consider it any longer, Nix opens his eyes and pins me with a look that is resolute.

"Fuck it," he says, right before he slams his mouth down on mine.

I'm caught off guard. I was trying to gear myself up to either back away gracefully or amp up my seduction, so I am not ready for this onslaught. Regardless, my heart leaps in response to the knowledge he's made a decision and he's acting on it.

Nix loosens the grip on my hair, but it's only to spread his hand wide so he can hold my head in place. He takes his other arm and wraps it around my waist, pulling me tight into his body. I gasp when I feel his thickness press into my belly.

His kiss is brutal and I don't know if he's trying to scare me off or if he's just unleashing a firestorm of passion, but a small sound of pleasure bubbles low in my throat over his possession of me. And it is a possession in every sense of the word.

I notice that my hands are pinned between us and I work them out of the tight space so that I can wrap them around his neck. I scrape my nails along his scalp, feeling the slippery coolness of his hair in between my fingers.

Just as I'm getting accommodated to his body pressed to mine and to the way his tongue is sliding along my own, he drops both hands from me. I have no time to bemoan a protest because they immediately drop to my hips and grab fistfuls of my dress.

In one swift move, he pulls my dress up over my head and cool air blankets my exposed skin. Nix stares at me for a moment, running his eyes down my body. His tongue peeks out as he runs it over his bottom lip and I know he's considering devouring me on the spot.

Nix raises his hands to my shoulders and strokes them feather-light down my arms. My body practically convulses in response. His hands move around to my lower back, moving softly downward until they come to rest over both of my ass cheeks. They are still for just a moment, and then they dig in, almost painfully through my panties. The sensation is not unpleasant and I answer him with a hard yank to his hair. I'm rewarded with a lustful curse that falls from his mouth before he kisses me again.

See…I can do down and dirty.

"Christ, Emily. You're driving me crazy," he groans into my mouth as he grinds his pelvis against mine.

Keeping one hand on my ass, Nix moves the other to my stomach, his knuckles deftly grazing the top band of my underwear. I know the path he intends to take and my hips instinctively move in acknowledgment.

Moving his mouth from mine, he blazes soft kisses across the corner of my mouth, to my jaw, and then down the side of my neck. They are warm and promising kisses, and I start to melt against him. He licks and lightly sucks at my neck, all the while his fingers are flirting with the edge of my underwear. I'm tense, waiting for him to make a further move. I want to scream at him to move his hand but I have a feeling that Nix will always be in control and will only move at his own pace.

He slowly nibbles his way down to the muscle that lies between my neck and shoulder, feathering it lightly with his lips. His hand finally dips down into the front of my underwear and he brushes his fingers lightly over me, back and forth.

I'm about ready to scream from the tension and my muscles seem to be clamping and clenching on their own accord.

And then, without any warning, Nix bites down at that tender muscle on the side of my neck, just as a finger drives into me. The competing sensations have me screaming out and my hips slam hard against his hand, driving him deeper into me. He adds another finger while gently licking at the place where he bit.

I feel liberated as my almost naked body starts riding his fingers. I can feel my climax starting to build fast, centered right where the tips of his fingers are deep inside of me.

Nix lifts his head from my neck and looks at me. His eyes are molten and expectant as they forge a bond with mine. He dips back down, placing his lips against my own and murmurs, "Emily?"

I answer with a half grunt-half moan.

"Remember when you asked me if I thought about us getting down and dirty?"

"Y-e-e-s-s-s," I stammer, finding it difficult to talk while his fingers are pushing against something delicious inside of me.

"Want to know what I think about the most?"

Oh, God did I ever, but I can't even get the words out. I offer up a feline purr in response.

Before answering me, Nix moves his thumb over my center, lightly caressing me. He moves his mouth to my ear and whispers, "I think most about what you will look like when you come. I wonder if your eyes will flutter closed? Will you scream? And if you do scream…will it be my name that falls out of those beautiful lips?"

His thumb pushes against me hard, and the tense buildup inside of me implodes first and then bursts outward as I fragment into oblivion.

I'm pretty sure I call out Nix's name as I throw my head back, numbly taking in the kitchen ceiling lights before closing my eyes. My hips continue to shallowly thrust against his hand while every last spark of my orgasm fires through me.

When I finally open my eyes, Nix's face is hovering over mine. He's wearing a triumphant look and his fingers are still deep inside of me.

"That was beautiful," he says reverently. "I want to see that again."

Those words…they are the most erotic thing I've ever heard and even though I'm deliciously spent, I want more. I jerk my hips against his hand so he knows without a doubt I want more and his eyes widen in surprise.

"Nix…let's move this into your bedroom, okay?"

He gives me the most breathtakingly stunning smile I've ever seen, and leans down to kiss me gently. He removes his hand from my underwear and I give a sad moan over the loss of contact.

"You are so fucking sexy, Emily. There are a million

different ways I want to make you come for me."

He's calling me sexy? Oh, my God…I think I could have an orgasm just from his words. Nix grabs my dress from the floor and takes my hand. Before we even make it out of the kitchen, we hear a key working in the front door and I look to Nix in panic.

The door opens and we hear, "Hey, Nix, you asshole…I'm finally home."

No! No! No! No!

Linc is here…in the living room…with just a tiny wall between him and my near nakedness.

"Son of a bitch," Nix mutters.

My eyes are questioning when I look to him. He simply puts my dress over my head and pulls it down as I thread my arms through. He takes a moment to smooth his hands over it, pushing any wrinkles out of the way. He then looks at me and smoothes his hands over my hair, which must be a mess from the way he was fisting it.

Framing my face with his hands, he leans into me and places his forehead against mine. "I'm sorry," is all he says before walking into the living room to greet Linc.

And I'm left wondering what he is sorry for. For crossing a line with me or for Linc's untimely appearance?

CHAPTER 17

Nix

UN-FUCKING-BELIEVABLE!

Linc would have to come home right now. It kills me to walk away from Emily in the kitchen, with her face all flushed from that climax she just had. I'm sure it's evil of me, but I'm prideful that I put that look on her face. And I will put it there again but apparently not tonight.

I head into the living room, assuming Emily is right behind me. Linc is setting his equipment bag on the floor and he looks up at me.

"Hey, man," I say.

"Wazzup?" He gives me a warm smile and then his eyes widen in surprise. He's looking right over my shoulder and I'm aware that Emily has walked into the room.

"Emily?" Linc asks in surprise, as if he can't believe she's standing here. Hell, I can barely believe it.

I turn to look at her and she appears cool and composed. She's even holding the glass of wine in her hand. "Hey, Linc. How are you?"

Linc is looking back and forth between me and Emily, like he can't put his finger on our connection. And there's no reason why he should. I've never told him that Emily hit me, or that she is working for me.

"I'm good," he says slowly. "What are you doing here?"

He asks the question of Emily but looks at me for the answer, like I must have her here against her will or something. Thankfully, my hard-on has almost completely diminished so he shouldn't be making that connection.

"Emily's working for me part-time," I supply. No sense in hiding the truth. It's not like it's a secret. I've just never told Linc because I never thought to. It wasn't that big of a deal to me.

"She's working for you? Why?" He's now asking me the question, but looking at Emily for the answer. That tells me he's skeptical.

Emily leans up casually against the wall and takes a sip of her wine. She is visually stunning and I'm amazed at how composed she is right now. Just two minutes ago she was riding my hand and screaming out my name. I do get a small sense of satisfaction over the fact that her cheeks are still a little flushed.

"Well…it's kind of a funny story," Emily answers

him. "Would you like to tell him, Nix or should I?"

I turn the palm of one hand face-up and sweep it in a grand gesture toward her, giving her the all-clear to tell him the details.

Emily's gorgeous mouth turns up into a smirk when she says, "I accidentally ran over your brother with my car that day I interviewed you. I happened to mangle his motorcycle pretty badly, and now I'm an indentured servant to him until I work the debt off."

Linc's eyebrows shoot for the stars. "You're kidding?"

"Nope. I almost killed your brother." She's grinning as she takes another sip of wine.

"Why in the hell are you working for him? Aren't the Burnhams richer than God?"

Emily snorts—quite unladylike—but she doesn't even look embarrassed. I like that.

"Let's just say that I've been cut off from my family's riches for a while. Besides, I'm actually enjoying it. I even had a lot of fun painting Nix's living room yesterday."

I almost choke when she says that. She's clearly referencing the scorching kiss we shared, but Linc doesn't know that. It doesn't stop his jaw from dropping just over the thought of wealthy, socialite Emily Burnham painting my living room.

Linc nods his head up and down as if he understands, but his vacant expression says he doesn't. It's actually amusing me to see his consternation.

"Well," Emily says as she hands me her wine glass. "I really need to get going. Thanks for the glass of wine and the talk, Nix. Linc…I'll see you around."

I walk Emily to the door and Linc says goodbye before heading back to his bedroom. As she steps out into the hallway, I walk out with her.

"I'll walk you down to your car," I offer.

"No need. I'm good. I'll see you after school on Monday."

She starts to walk away and I don't like this cool, nonchalant, "I can easily walk away from you after a mind-blowing orgasm", Emily. I reach out and grab her wrist. She stops and looks at me, her head slightly tilted at an inquiring angle.

"Are you okay?" I don't know what makes me ask this, or why I'm even worried about it.

She gives me a soft smile. "I'm good. And…we're cool, Nix. No worries."

Now, what the fuck does that mean?

I release her wrist and watch her walk to the elevator. She stands there staring at the doors, tapping her toe. The smile is still on her face and I wonder if she's thinking about what just happened when we were in the kitchen.

That memory is certainly going to stick with me.

The elevator opens and she steps in. I start to turn away, but she calls my name. I look back, and her head is peeking out the doors at me. She looks like a cat ready to pounce when she says, "Next time…I get to reciprocate." She gives me a little wave then disappears behind the doors.

I walk back into Linc's apartment, shaking my head. The thoughts of her reciprocating are almost too much for me to bear knowing that she's not within arm's length of me.

Heading into the kitchen, I can't help but wonder what would have happened tonight if Linc had not shown up. At the moment he walked in the door, I was dead set on losing myself inside of Emily. But I also wonder if I would have talked myself out of it. I mean, it's one thing to pleasure the hell out of her which was oddly and incredibly gratifying to me as well. But if we had sex, the ballgame would change completely. Would it be worth potential complications that would arise down the road? I'm betting it would be.

I grab the beer I had been drinking and take a long swallow. When I raise the bottle to my mouth, I can smell Emily's sweet scent on my hand and my dick starts twitching again. It doesn't need much encouragement after Emily's last words.

"What the fuck are you doing with Ryan Burnham's baby sister?"

I spin around and see Linc walk into the kitchen. He grabs a beer out of the fridge and pops it open. His words aren't menacing...more disbelieving if anything.

"I'm not doing anything with her. She came by to talk and she had a glass of wine."

"Talk my ass," Linc says. "You were sporting a major woody when you came into the living room and there's no way you got that just by 'talking'. So fess up."

Shit! He saw that, huh?

Well, I'm not going to lie about it further. "Mind your own business. We're two consenting adults."

I haven't admitted details but by telling him to keep his nose out of my affairs pretty much admits that something is going on.

"So, that whole story about her hitting you and working the debt off is fake?"

I smile at him. "Nope. That's true. She almost killed me and now she paints my house as well as a variety of other menial tasks."

"Menial tasks? Please don't tell me she's working it off in the bedroom, Nix! Please, please tell me I'm wrong to be thinking that."

"You're a damned pervert, Linc. Of course, she's not paying her debt off that way. She's doing secretarial stuff for my business...and...well, yeah, one day I had her paint my living room but that was just to keep her out of my hair for the day."

Linc doesn't say anything and takes another sip of his beer. His voice is serious when he says, "Don't hurt her,

Nix."

My blood immediately flares then boils over. "Why? Do you have a thing for her?" There is no way Linc is having Emily!

"No, I don't have a thing for her. I mean, I would have a thing for her if she gave me the time of day but she never has." He pauses, trying to find the right words. "It's just…if you hurt her, it's probably going to ruin my relationship with Ryan. Which, I hate to say, could jeopardize our playing together. Just be considerate of others is all I'm saying."

Wow. I didn't consider that there could be further reaching implications than what I had originally imagined. But I shake it off. "We're good, Linc."

He looks at me with continued worry.

I try to reassure him, and myself. "Emily and I have an understanding. No worries."

♦

EMILY HAS BEEN gone a few hours and I'm lying in my bed, trying to go to sleep. Fat chance of that, seeing as how I can't stop replaying those few minutes we had together in the kitchen. She was so free, so accepting of everything I gave her. I half expected her to be strung a little tight. Like when I pulled her dress off of her…I expected her to be shy, or nervous, or even slightly distressed we were in the middle of the kitchen. But

Emily…she was the opposite. She reveled in her sexual nature.

I have no clue what her level of experience is, and frankly, I don't give a shit. I've already breached that wall of worry and there's no going back now. I tried—very hard—to keep my distance from her. Every logical argument as to why I should stay away from Emily Burnham has played through my head and I've decided to reject them all.

It's like I told Linc. We're both consenting adults. There is nothing standing in our way from exploring our sexual attraction to each other. Hell, those were Emily's very arguments she made to me.

Still…there is that small part of me that wonders if Emily can truly handle a no-strings relationship. I know I won't be able to handle it if she wants to pin me down in any way. Just the thought has me feeling boxed in and anger surges through my veins. My heart rate picks up.

I take a few deep, calming breaths. Just the way Dr. Antoniak taught me. I really need to pay her a visit, and probably soon. My talk with Paul the other day has me spiraling a bit. I'll make sure to call her tomorrow morning and make an appointment.

As if sensing my need for him, Harley gets up from the bottom of my bed and moves his body next to mine. He places his warm head on my chest and just stares at me with those chocolate eyes. I reach up and lazily scratch his head, running my fingertips behind his ears. I concentrate on the softness of his fur.

As I continue to rub Harley's head, my heart rate starts decreasing and after a few minutes, I'm not only calm but feeling drowsy. My thoughts drift back to Emily and the image of her breaking apart under my hand is the last thing I remember thinking about before I fall asleep.

CHAPTER 18

Nix

I CALL FIRST thing Monday morning and luckily, I am able to get an appointment with Dr. Antoniak for the following day due to a cancellation she had. I fire off a text to Emily that I will be gone out of state for a few days and just to come in to work on Wednesday.

My text doesn't say anything else and I actually struggled for a few minutes over whether I should say more. Part of me wanted to ask how the rest of her weekend went, and how she was doing, and was she thinking of me the same way I was thinking of her. Then I scoffed at myself and put my phone back in my pocket.

Any such actions on my part will give Emily the wrong idea. It will push whatever this is between us into a different realm. I decide I'm going to treat Emily the way I would have treated someone like Lyla, for example.

I ask myself, *Would I have asked Lyla how her weekend went?*

The answer is easy. No, I would not.

Therefore, I will not ask Emily.

And it doesn't matter at all that I actually want to know what she did all day Sunday. I never gave a rat's ass what Lyla did once she left my bedroom, but I do think a lot about what Emily is doing.

It's just another source of tension I'll need to deal with, thus making the trip to see Dr. Antoniak even more relevant.

The better part of Monday is spent working on some sketches of a custom metal arbor I've been commissioned to make. Then I pack an overnight bag and Harley and I hit the open road around mid-afternoon.

It takes us about three and a half hours to make the drive from Hoboken to Bethesda and my timing is nothing short of impeccable. I arrive right in the middle of rush hour traffic.

Finally, I pull into a hotel that is conveniently located near Walter Reed National Military Medical Center. Harley and I settle in for the night and I think about all of the things I need to talk about in the precious hour that I have with the good doctor.

♦

THE NEXT MORNING, Harley and I head over to Walter Reed. I graciously pull through McDonald's first to get us each a sausage biscuit. We contentedly eat our breakfast in the parking lot, and when we are finished, I walk to the passenger door.

Harley always sits in the front seat when he rides with me. I clip his leash on and he hops out. I put him in a "sit" and then reach into my pack. I pull out his Service Dog vest and fasten it on him. The damn dog's chest actually puffs with pride when his uniform is on, I swear it.

Harley and I navigate the hallways until we make it to the Neuroscience Department. There was a day when I hated coming here…despised it beyond all measure. Now, it sort of feels like an old glove.

I haven't been to see Dr. Antoniak in a few months. I was officially released from her care over a year ago, but I've made trips back every so often.

It's not long before we are called in and we step into her office. She steps from behind her industrial, military issue desk and comes around to shake my hand.

"It's good to see you, Nix." She bends over and gives Harley a rub on his head. "And you too, Harley."

I take a seat opposite her desk. Her office is small and sterile which makes me feel oddly comforted. She takes her seat behind her desk, appraising me with interest and a slight fondness that has developed over our months of therapy. There was a time she would do that and I wanted to throttle her, so great was my anger in those days.

Dr. Antoniak is an interesting doctor. She's a diminutive woman with steel gray hair cut close to her scalp. She has piercing blue eyes and when I say piercing, I mean they could cut through some of the thickest metal I work with. Her intelligence is a weapon and she will not let me get away with any misstep in what I say. The woman probably has reams of paper dedicated to our meetings and yet she never has to look back to reference our discussions. She can remember something I told her two years ago as it if happened only yesterday. She's been my neuropsychiatrist from the moment I returned from Afghanistan on a military medical flight.

"You look well, Nix. Hair's a little long."

I smirk at her. "That's what my dad says every time he sees me."

"So, what brings you in today?" Her voice is warm, completely at odds with her iron looks.

I shrug my shoulders. "Just like my dad has an opinion about my hair, he suggested it might be time for a tune-up with you."

Dr. Antoniak gives a bark of laughter. "A tune-up? I love it."

"Yeah, well, I wouldn't have come but he's been riding me about it."

"And you don't think you need any follow up treatment or counseling?"

I shrug my shoulders again. "Not really. I think I'm coping well."

"No headaches?"

"Nope."

"Rages?"

"Nope."

"Nightmares?"

I almost say "nope" but she'll know I'm lying. "A few times a month."

She jots that down on a notepad then pins me with her blue lasers. "Have you talked to Paul lately?"

Shit. I knew she'd go there but it still threw me. Thank God I just talked to him. I smile confidently when I reply, "Sure. Just last week."

She returns the smile. "That's wonderful. And you initiated the communication?"

Fuck.

She's too damned insightful and it pisses me off. But truth be told, this is the main reason I made the appointment with her.

"No. I returned his call."

"And how many times had he attempted to call you before you returned his call?"

"Several," I grit out.

"Why are you avoiding him, Nix?"

My anger flares white-hot. I reach for Harley's head and start rubbing it.

"Why are you so nosy?" I ask her.

"Come on, Nix. Quit fucking around. You know we don't have long."

Dr. Antoniak's bluntness is one of the things I appreciate about her. She never would let me escape from the difficult conversations, and she's not about to let me do so now. It's part of the Exposure Therapy she had been torturing me with over the two years I've known her.

Might as well get this over with. She'll never let me leave here without answering the question so I take a deep breath. "He makes me feel uncomfortable."

"Why?" she asks simply and without judgment.

How do I say these words without sounding like the biggest asshole, prick on the planet? "He acts too happy…too well-adjusted. It just makes me feel…bad."

"Do you doubt he's happy and well-adjusted?"

"Yes." The answer pops out before I can analyze it.

"Why?"

"Why? Well, because his legs were fucking blown off. How's that for starters?"

"And why can't someone who lost their legs be happy and well-adjusted?"

Why indeed? Why, why, why?

But I know the answer to that too, and I don't need Dr. Antoniak to shrink me to know it either.

I sigh. "Because…what happened to me wasn't even a tenth of what he's gone through and I'm pretty fucked up."

"Maybe the problem is you're diminishing what you've been through."

I kick my legs out in front of me so she sees them.

"Nope. My legs are working just fine."

"But your legs weren't hurt, Nix," she says softly, bringing me back around to the real issue. "Your brain was hurt. Your chest was hurt. Your mental health was hurt."

I want to scream at her, *So fucking-what?* But I don't. Because, if it's one thing she has taught me over the past two years, it was how to control my rage. Instead, I say, "And here we are back to the beginning. I'm pissed he's doing so well."

"Be honest, Nix. You're not just feeling anger…"

She trails off, waiting for me to finish her thought. I pick it up. "I'm feeling guilt. I know." My voice is heavy and resigned.

She picks up my file and flips through it, taking a few minutes to read something. I don't know who she thinks she's kidding, but she doesn't need to review anything in there. She knows me well.

"The last time we met…four months ago…you had agreed to go visit Paul. I'm assuming you haven't done that?"

"I've been busy."

It's a pathetic excuse. She knows it and I know it.

"We talked about this before, Nix, but let's go over it again. Your guilt is impeding your full recovery. You've made remarkable improvements since your injury. Your brain is fully functioning now and your cognitive therapy has worked wonders to help you deal with your rage issues. But you need to work on this guilt issue over Paul and his injuries. It's holding you back."

I just stare at the floor. I've heard this all before. Many times. I know she's right. Hell, I'll even walk out of here charged up and ready to go see Paul. But then time and doubt will get in the way, and I'll head back to a life of isolation to ease my burden.

"Nix," she says softly and I raise my eyes up to hers. "Guilt is a poison. It will slowly choke out everything you have worked so hard to overcome. And when it's destroyed all of that…it will keep on killing everything that's good in your life."

♦

HARLEY AND I are heading back to Hoboken. I'm lost in my thoughts and Harley is snoozing, curled up into a tight golden ball on the front seat next to me. I reach over and absently rub his hipbone.

Just three months from my enlistment with the Marine Corps ending, my squad and I had been injured in a blitz by the Taliban, normally called a "green on blue" attack. Paul lost his legs.

In some ways, his injuries were easy to treat in that they were palpable…physical…you could see them. The doctors could see the damaged blood vessels and nerves, and knew exactly what they had to do to heal him.

It wasn't as easy for me. In addition to getting shot in

the upper part of my chest, which was the least of my worries, I'd suffered a Traumatic Brain Injury. You couldn't see my injury on films. There was no gaping wound or missing body parts. Just millions of tiny pieces of tissue that were shredded and torn, causing me to turn into a monster.

My injury was complicated by an additional diagnosis of Post-Traumatic Stress Disorder. That's what Harley was for. The Veteran's Administration doesn't pay for psychiatric service dogs, but they are still a legitimate and necessary form of treatment under the American's with Disabilities Act. So after shelling out thousands of my own dollars to get Harley, he's allowed to go everywhere I go by virtue of his status as a service dog. I certainly don't take him everywhere with me, because I have made massive improvements, but I love being able to all the same.

Between the brain injury and the PTSD, the Nix Caldwell that returned to Hoboken, New Jersey was unrecognizable from the fresh-faced kid that left when he was eighteen. I was angry, filled with wrath. The smallest thing would set me off and I'd want to smash something. Nightmares plagued my sleep every night. And if I wasn't raging, I was just plain mean, moody and irritable. Loud sounds would cause me to jump. People walking up behind me would cause me to panic.

After recovering from my chest wound, I started

intensive cognitive and exposure therapy and I'll grudgingly admit, I've made major progress.

And while I'm able to control my temper in almost every situation, I'm still a moody jackass most of the time. My nightmares have diminished a lot and I no longer feel the compulsion to kill someone for looking at me wrong.

Lots of progress.

But not enough apparently.

I ease back into remembering the last fifteen minutes of our session. I told Dr. Antoniak about Emily. It felt silly at first for me to bring her up, considering she seemed to be the one good thing I had going for me right now. But I'd be lying if I didn't say I wasn't very concerned over how she would play in my recovery.

Part of my therapy is confronting my trauma. Confronting trauma means talking about it. Emily is the only person I know of that has come even close to getting me to open up about anything. Frankly, I'm scared shitless that she'll continue to expose my demons.

I have to reiterate to myself that what Emily and I have is nothing more than a sexual relationship. However, I'm not stupid enough to ignore the fact that sex is an emotional activity…particularly for women.

When I see her again, I really, really need to set some boundaries with her and make sure she understands there are certain lines that cannot be crossed.

CHAPTER 19

Emily

DANNY EXITS HER apartment building and sees me. She heads my way with a smile on her face and I stare in marvel at this woman…my sister-in-law. She's always so happy and self-assured. And I'm sure that extra soft look on her face now has something to do with the fact that she's knocked up with my little niece or nephew.

Reaching me, she pulls me into a surprisingly strong hug and says, "I'm so glad you could come tonight. It's going to be so much fun."

"Me, too."

Ryan got us invitations to the owner's box tonight. Usually, they gave out several each game to player's family members but I have yet to sit in such luxury during a hockey game. I'm looking forward to not having to stand in a long line to pee or get a pretzel.

Oh, the little luxuries in life now are surprisingly simple for me.

Danny loops her arm in mine and we take off down W. 33rd. We're both wearing matching Burnham jerseys and the people walking in our direction are all decked out in their Rangers gear. I love looking for my brother's jersey on other people. It makes me so proud.

"So how are you feeling?" I ask her as we walk with the flow of the crowd.

"Surprisingly good. I've had a little nausea but nothing that a few crackers doesn't settle right down. Oh, and my boobs hurt like hell already. I had to tell Ryan to go easy on them last night."

"Whoa, whoa, whoa. T-M-I. Now that image is burned into my brain."

Danny giggles at me and I grin back at her. I love her.

"Heard any more from your mom or dad?"

"A few emails from Dad to check in," I comment.

I'm really liking his shortened title. Dad. It sounds much better than Father.

I had told both Danny and Ryan about the botched dinner a few nights ago. Ryan wasn't surprised by our father's reaction as they've been communicating more and more. It started out with emails and now they've progressed to a few phone calls. Ryan hopes that he can get Dad to come for a visit soon. Maybe our mother will thaw out a bit too. They shouldn't miss the birth of their first grandchild.

We make it into the arena and find the owner's box.

The large wood-paneled room has artfully framed photographs of various players and Rangers executives. There is a full-service bar with bartender and a buffet layout of the most delicious looking foods. I'm starved, I realize.

After Danny makes some small talk with a few of the top dogs, we make up some plates and choose two plush leather chairs in the front row. We got here early so we are enjoying watching the players warm-up. I smile to myself the way Danny's eyes never leave Ryan while he's out on the ice.

I want to pee before the game starts so I make a dash to the uber-luxurious bathroom. They even have sumptuous hand towels and expensive soaps lying out. Nice touch!

When I finish, I head back to the bar to get me and Danny some bottled waters. As I'm standing there, I feel a sudden prickling on the back of my neck and I turn around. My heart comes to a standstill for a painful second then starts beating rapidly.

Nix is standing there, five feet away. He gives me a devilish grin and I smile back. He's standing with an older man, who I'll go out on a limb and guess is his father. Grabbing my waters, I walk over to him and he introduces me.

"Emily…this is my dad, Hank Caldwell. Dad…this is Emily Burnham. She's Ryan Burnham's sister."

Nix's dad pumps my hand in an exuberant shake and

says, "It's a pleasure, Emily. Your brother is a fine man and a damned good hockey player."

"It's good to meet you too, Mr. Caldwell."

"None of that. You call me Hank. All my friends do."

I'm amazed at how outgoing Nix's dad is. But I guess I shouldn't be surprised. Linc is, after all, a people person. Just because Nix is a snarly son-of-a-bitch half the time doesn't mean his family is that way.

I turn to look at Nix. "What are you doing here? I thought you were out of town."

Hank looks at Nix questioningly and all Nix says is, "I went to Bethesda, Dad."

His dad just nods in understanding and makes no comment.

"I had to go to Maryland for a few days for a business trip."

"Oh...well, welcome back."

He smiles at me and it's so nice. He actually looks happy to see me, which is something to say for Nix Caldwell. I know I'm certainly glad to see him. He has practically dominated my thoughts since Saturday night.

The game is getting ready to start so we take our seats. Nix and Hank sit next to me and I make introductions with Danny. Then we settle in to watch the game.

♦

THE FIRST TWO periods are not going well for the

Rangers and they are down by two goals at the end of the second period. We all get up to stretch and get more drinks. I'm waiting for Danny to come out of the bathroom, when I can feel Nix step up behind me. He's standing close and my body tingles just from the prospect that he may brush up against me. He leans down and whispers near my ear, "Have you missed me?"

I turn slowly to look at him and our faces are inches apart. I glance around to make sure his dad isn't standing nearby but we are thankfully alone.

"Maybe," I reply.

"Miss me bad enough you'll let me come home with you tonight?"

I suck in my breath and a rush of warmth courses through me. I don't need to think about this. Here I've been worrying the last few days that Nix was backing off. Here I've been fantasizing the last few days about having sex with Nix. There's no way I'm going to pass this up.

"Okay," I whisper.

The blinding smile that Nix gives me is like nothing I've seen before. I've seen him smile, of course, and it's been beautiful. But the smile he is giving me right now is full of light and joy. It's amazing and I'm momentarily struck stupid.

Did my agreement to take him home tonight do that?

♦

THE GAME IS over and it was a stunner. The Rangers came back with only four minutes left and tied the game up. After a futile overtime period, we ultimately won in a shootout thanks to Linc's overly impressive goalie skills. We were all so crazed with excitement that when Linc stopped the last shot, I threw my arms around Danny and squeezed the daylights out of her. Then I spun the other way, seeing Nix there with his hand raised in the air for a high-five. I ignored it, choosing instead to throw my arms around his neck in a fierce hug. He was momentarily stunned, then his arms wrapped around me tightly, his nose burying briefly in my hair. When he released me, I gave his father a hug as well, although I certainly didn't plaster my body to his the way I had with Nix.

Danny merely raised her eyebrows at me when I told her that Nix was going to give us a ride but she didn't question me. She and Nix talked about the Marine Corps and Sarge on the way to Danny's while I sat in the back seat and listened to them. After we arrived, Danny gave me one fleeting look in her eyes that said "be careful" then she hopped out of Nix's truck.

Now, as Nix and I are walking up to my apartment, I have a sudden case of nervousness. I know we are getting ready to cross a bridge that will not be open to further traffic once we make it over. It feels so weird…walking side by side, not talking, not holding hands. We are both entering this building with the sole purpose of screwing each other's brains out.

I don't know whether to be mortified or titillated.

As I pull my key out, Nix brushes the hair from the back of my neck and leans down to place a warm kiss there. I shiver, almost uncontrollably and can't get the damn key in the door. He covers my hands with his own and deftly helps me insert it into the lock. He pushes the door open and waits for me to go in.

When I walk inside, I'm grateful that the living room is dark. Fil is most likely in her room studying, for when I look down the hall, I see the soft glow of light coming out from underneath her door.

I drop my purse and keys on the kitchen counter and turn to Nix, suddenly nervous and at a loss as to what to do.

"Would you like something to drink?"

He walks toward me, shaking his head. "No."

"Do you want anything?"

My question was said innocently enough but his eyes darken with meaning.

"I want you," he replies as he comes to stand directly in front of me.

And oh, hell…my knees practically give out over the sexy rumble in his voice. I just stare up at him, not sure what to do. He moves even closer, so our bodies are just barely touching—nothing more than a whisper between us—and I can feel my skin tightening all over.

"Take me to your bedroom now, Emily, or we'll have to put on a show for your roommate."

I swallow hard. Taking a step to the side, I walk by him and head down the hall to my room. I can feel him right on my heels…stalking me. I can feel the pulse at the base of my throat starting to thump with anticipation, giving credence to the rush of blood flowing through my veins.

As soon as I step into my bedroom, Nix has his arms banding around me from behind. I can hear him kick the door shut but I can't turn to see it. The front of his body is pressed tightly against my back, his arms circled around me…one forearm tightened across my chest, the other around my waist.

He brings his mouth down, nips at my earlobe and says in a voice so low, I can barely hear it, "You don't know how bad I want inside you right now."

A bolt of the purest lust fissures through me and I can't help the strange and warbled sound that comes out of my throat. I surrender completely by letting my head fall back onto his shoulder.

"But first, we need to talk."

What? Huh? What?

Nix releases me and pulls me to the bed as I try to shake off the lust-induced fog. He sits on the edge and pulls me to stand between his legs. His hands rest gently at my hips and I feel awkward as hell.

Looking up at me, he asks, "Do you really want to do this, Emily?" His voice is gentle, worried.

I nod my head. I have no clue why he's asking but there isn't a doubt in my mind.

"I need to make sure we are on the same page. I'm worried that you'll get hurt and even though I'm an ass to you most of the time, I really don't want to harm you."

My heart melts over his words but they aren't necessary. I think I understand where he is coming from. "I'm good, Nix. Really."

"Tell me what you expect of me."

"What? Nothing…I don't expect anything. I swear."

He shakes his head at me. "Wrong answer. Any two people, no matter the level of interaction, will always have expectations of each other. You have to want something."

That makes sense, I suppose. I think about it for a minute. I don't have any fairytale ideas about Nix, or aspirations that we will have a happy, long-lasting relationship. But there is something…

"I need you to promise you'll be monogamous…as long as you're having sex with me, that is."

He doesn't hesitate at all. "Done. Anything else?"

I shake my head as I raise my hands to his shoulders. I want to lean in and press up against him but he holds my body firmly in place.

"My turn. You need to know my expectations, too."

Well, hell. I thought I knew what they were. Wham, bam, thank you, ma'am!

"Okay. Shoot."

Nix takes a deep breath. "I'm not relationship material, Emily. I just don't have it in me to care about someone like that. You cannot expect anything like that from me."

I knew this. I knew this going in and it still hurts just a little. But I'd already made my choice and I wasn't going to change. I want Nix too much.

"But," he continues. "I promise that I will cherish you when we are intimate, and I won't intentionally hurt you."

I give him a small smile and nod my head again.

"Are you still okay with this?" he asks.

"Yes. I'm fine with everything. I know what to expect."

He releases his hands from my hips and I don't like the sudden loss of warmth.

"Good. Now…I want you to stand back a few feet."

I take two steps back, never thinking to question his command.

Nix leans back onto his elbows and watches me like a starved man. "Now…take off your clothes for me, Em. And do it slowly."

CHAPTER 20

Emily

OH MY GOD. This is way out of my league.

I want to fly out of the room because I'm achingly nervous but I want Nix more so I hold my ground. The timbre of his voice is like rough bark on a tree, deliciously grating on every exposed nerve. The look in his eyes is so sensual it makes me want to get on all fours and submit my neck to him.

On their own accord, my hands grab the hem of my jersey and pull it over my head. I'm wearing a long sleeved, white t-shirt below but I leave it on for now. Bending one knee to the floor, I quickly remove my shoes and socks. When I stand back up, I look at Nix and his position on the bed hasn't changed. He's watching me quietly…waiting. His only movement is his chest moving shallowly and his thick lashes blinking around those jade eyes.

I press forward, dispensing with my t-shirt quick enough and let my jeans follow. Standing before him, I wait to see what he does. Now that my main clothes are off, I really don't feel so self-conscious. Luckily, I'm wearing some of my nicer lingerie and the simple white, lace bra and bikini underwear set shines bright against my skin.

Nix leisurely runs his gaze down my body, then moves slowly up again. I'm holding all of my breath in and I know I should release it before I pass out. I wait for further instructions and I don't wait long.

When Nix meets my eyes again, he says, "All of it, Emily. Slower."

I think I might just incinerate right now. I didn't think Nix would be in for a slow seduction but clearly, the man has skills I didn't think were possible. And he hasn't even touched me yet.

I reach behind my back to unclasp my bra. Hunching my shoulders slightly forward, I let it slide down my arms, and drop it carelessly to the floor. Nix doesn't watch it fall and I almost groan when I see him lick his lips while he caresses my breasts with his eyes. My nipples harden almost painfully under his scrutiny.

Then his eyes travel down and he just stares at me. Without moving his gaze, he orders me, "Your panties, Emily. I need to see all of you."

My heart is pounding so hard, I'm sure Nix can hear it. Hooking my thumbs into my underwear, I push them slowly down my thighs until they just slide off. I step out of them and kick them to the side.

Now I'm self-conscious again, standing there totally naked, while Nix just peruses my body. I've never done this before, put my body under such bold examination.

"Come here," he says thickly. The way he is watching me…he's hungering and it makes me realize I have never known true passion before.

I walk to stand between his legs and he sits up on the bed. Leaning forward, he brings his hands to my hips while placing a gentle kiss on my stomach. My entire body trembles from the pleasure of that small touch and my arms glide to his shoulders. His skin is hot and I luxuriate in the burn.

Nix moves his mouth up my stomach. After placing a warm kiss in the center of my chest, he turns his face and rubs his cheek against me. My hands come up to his head and I lace my fingers through his hair. I don't have to wait long before Nix brings his lips to my breast. So hot, so wet. He kisses and sucks at my nipples, paying both equal attention with his tongue and teeth. He takes his time, he savors. He doesn't seem to be in a rush. I, however, feel like I'm going to explode from the incendiary contact of his mouth on me.

Pulling back slightly, Nix looks up at me while his thumbs smooth back and forth over my hips. "You're so fucking beautiful. The most beautiful…" But he trails off, as if the power of his own words scare him.

My heart dissolves into a puddle of emotion over his words and I lean in slightly to kiss him. He shakes his head and stands up from the bed. Taking a step back, I watch as he takes his shoes and socks off, his gaze never leaving mine.

When he's done he says, "Undress me, Emily."

I don't think twice about his order.

And it is an order.

Reaching out with shaky hands, I lift his t-shirt up and over his head. Up close, the blinded skull looks even more terrifying but I don't want to be scared of it. I don't want to be scared of anything that Nix presents to me.

I try to read the words on the scroll that floats down his ribs. I only catch brief snippets as I reach down to the fly of his jeans.

For quiet times disappear…

The way is not in the sky…

Don't let your ears refuse to hear…

The words have no clear meaning to me but they are beautiful. They are at complete odds with the skull. If I get an opportunity, I want to make a study of Nix's body, which will include all the words he finds so important to permanently ink them on his skin.

I glance up at him briefly to see the purest desire etched in his face and then lower my eyes again to watch my hands make their progress.

Popping the top button, I ease his zipper down. He takes in a sharp breath as my knuckles make soft contact with the hard bulge that is outlined below.

Taking my hands, I place them on his stomach and then smooth them around to his back. Tucking my hands into the waistband of his boxer briefs, I glide my hands down over his ass, flexing my fingers as I go. Nix growls at my touch but follows up with a whispered, "Yes".

Emboldened, I slide my hands around to his hips and push his pants down, kneeling as I go until they reach his ankles. He lifts one leg, and then the other while I take his jeans completely off.

Nix gazes down at me while I kneel in front of him, the impressive evidence of his feelings stands boldly in front of me. His body is beautiful in every way.

I lick my lips and lean forward but I'm stopped when Nix takes his fingertips and places them at my throat. He traces them gently around to the back of my head, cupping it, and then pulls me to my feet.

"Not this time," he whispers. "But later…"

I'm his puppet and I do what he tells me. I have no thoughts of trying to take charge because frankly, I'm not sure what to do. This is a sexual experience beyond anything I've ever known.

Still holding me immobile by the back of my head,

Nix just stares at me, like he's contemplating his next move.

After several painful seconds, he finally dips his head down. I think he's going to kiss me but he bypasses my lips and heads a little further south. The first contact of his tongue is on my collarbone and I sigh softly from the touch. He kisses me gently, moving back and forth, the stubble on his face divinely abrading me.

Finally, his other arm wraps around me and pulls me in closer to his body. The heat of his skin is scorching and I can feel his erection twitching between our bodies. He feels like steel wrapped in satin.

Nix finally moves his mouth upward until our lips connect, and then he is kissing me deeply. Never releasing my head, his other hand drops down and hikes my leg up over his hip. The move brings his hardness squarely between my legs and I can't help but move my hips against him.

The contact is overwhelming and I want to beg him to please just bury himself in me.

But I don't.

Instead, I gasp when he reaches down and picks me up, forcing my legs around his waist.

He turns swiftly to the bed and lays me on it, never breaking contact between our lips. He comes to rest on me, gently rubbing himself between my legs and I can already feel myself building for him.

Nix finally breaks our kiss and he sits back, kneeling between my legs.

"I'm dying to make you come again, Emily. Do you want that?"

"Yes," I whisper.

He looks down at me and places his hands on my knees. I can feel rough callouses against my skin and I shiver. He pushes gently against my legs and they fall apart at his simple request. He just watches me…hungrily…running his eyes all over my body.

The world seems to stop when he drags a finger down between my legs. My hips arch high off the bed and I can't help but softly cry out, "Nix."

A lovely smile plays across his face and I am even more turned on by the fact that he loves turning me on.

"That's my girl," he says, desire thick in his voice.

Nix wastes no time. He scoots backward then lies down between my legs, deftly pulling them over his shoulders. He places one soft kiss on my hipbone, then his tongue darts out to lick the same spot. Nix looks at me briefly and our eyes hold for just a moment before he brings his mouth down on me.

There is no way I could have even been prepared for that feeling of his mouth between my legs. The world as I know it spins out of control, faster and faster. I try to keep my eyes open, to stare down at his head between my thighs, but my eyelids keep fluttering closed.

I've never had a guy go down on me. Hell, the only

guy I've ever been with was Todd and that was a disaster. Todd would never think to want to pleasure me. I have had girlfriends that have talked about it and how wonderful it is. But I never could imagine how unbelievably spectacular the sensation is until his lips branded me there.

I have to bite the inside of my cheek to keep from screaming out. My muscles clench up and a pleasurable cramp rolls all the way up from where his mouth is latched on to me to the top of my spine.

Nix has no mercy. He licks, kisses, sucks and plunges with his lips…with his tongue…with his fingers. I'm vaguely aware of my head thrashing and when I look down at his glorious head working between my legs, I notice that my hands have fistfuls of his hair clenched tightly. He doesn't seem to care.

My climax builds fast, like a fireball massively rolling outward from the nucleus of an explosion. Pressing his face against me harder, I let out a low, long moan as I come. It goes on, wave after wave, muscles clenching and releasing, all the while Nix gently kisses at me until I plummet downward again.

Nix finally raises his head to look at me and his look is dark, almost sinister. I know he's not finished with me by a long shot. "I could do that all night to you, Emily. Just to hear your sweet cries."

Oh God, did he know the right words to use in the bedroom? He is a terrible conversationalist in real life but he probably has the power to induce an orgasm just from his wicked thoughts translated into erotic conversation.

He licks his lips and pushes back off the bed. Rummaging around in his jeans, he brings out a foil-wrapped condom.

Nix comes to stand at the edge of the bed and I have a clear view of him while he rips open the packet. He has no modesty but there's no reason why he should. His body is beyond glorious.

I've never watched this before. My sexual experiences were always fumbles in the dark. Nix is deft and efficient, and he's quickly sheathed. I want to do that for him next time but those thoughts are banished when he crawls onto the bed, back between my legs.

Kneeling between my thighs, Nix runs his hands up my stomach and over my breasts. He rolls my nipples back and forth, causing a pleasured sound to gurgle up from my throat. He glances at me. "Tell me what you want."

"You."

He smiles. "Where, Emily? Be specific with me."

I suck in a small breath. "I want you inside of me."

My words inflame him and he covers my entire body with his own. His lips find mine and he is ferociously kissing me. He lays thick and heavy between my legs, rubbing himself against my heat. Nix takes one arm and loops it under my leg, the back of my knee coming to rest in the crook of his elbow. He raises me up, spreading me wider.

He pushes inside of me with gentle precision. He goes slowly, working his way in, even though I can feel that I'm wet and ready. The sensation is almost unbearable. He's huge but my body is melting to accommodate him. I have no control over my hips as they undulate to help move him deeper in me.

Finally, with one strong push, he's all the way in and our pelvises are locked together. Nix pulls back from my mouth and lets his gaze travel down to our union.

"Look, Emily. Look at us…together." His words are rough, his breath heaving. I can feel his arms trembling as he holds himself above me.

I look down and I find the sight to be erotically overwhelming. Pleasure pulses through me and my muscles involuntarily clench around him. He feels it and grits out, "Fuck, Emily."

Then Nix starts moving and my eyes close. I can feel his lips on my neck, kissing me. One arm is still holding my leg but he takes his other and wraps it behind my head, fusing our bodies tighter together.

There is no way possible we could be any closer. I can almost feel him touching every part of my body with every part of his. There's nothing that feels neglected.

Our movements become faster, harder. We find a sympathetic rhythm that is pushing me higher and higher. He's hitting me so deep, he's awakened something inside of me that I didn't know existed.

Nix's breaths are coming faster and he's gasping in my ear, "You feel so fucking good, Emily. I'll never get enough of you."

Those words evoke an unparalleled emotion in me and already I feel another orgasm coming on. And it's coming fast but the wave of it is no less forceful.

"I'm going to come again, Nix," I warn him, almost with fear that I won't be able to contain my reaction.

"Damn right you are," he growls against my neck. His thrusts become more focused, intent on wringing every bit of pleasure that he can out of me.

Without warning, it crashes through me and I bite down on his shoulder, riding the pleasure until it starts to recede like an ocean wave at low tide.

I can just feel the last rumbles easing up my spine when Nix gives an incredibly deep push, shuddering violently.

"Emily," he groans as he unloads inside of me. My name on his lips sounds like a prayer and a curse.

I'm vaguely aware of Nix pulling back off my body a bit, the cool air soothing our sweat-soaked bodies. He rolls to the side, taking me with him.

I am boneless yet I feel invincible.

As the frantic beating of my heart starts to calm, all I can think is that this is the best experience of my new and improved life. I'm positive it can't be topped.

CHAPTER 21

Nix

I LOOK AT my watch for what seems like the tenth time in an hour and take another sip of the beer I've been nursing for precisely that long. Emily should have been here already and I'm starting to get worried.

Which, as with everything involving Emily, I just don't understand. Since when did I start worrying about a girl? I am hoping some clarity will shine through at some point.

I had texted Emily earlier that I needed a ride. I had delivered a finished custom motorcycle to a customer and I am sitting in a biker bar outside of Newark. On the barstool next to me is said customer...John "Wolf" Camarino. He's a bear of a man, standing just as tall as me but twice as wide. He has long salt and pepper hair tied at the nape of his neck and then tightly braided into a long tail down his back. His face is covered with a wiry, salt and pepper beard that reaches halfway down his chest.

I'm not sure what Wolf does for a living but he had no problem coming up with the $31,000 I charged for this bike, although he did pay it in two installments. And now that it was finished, he asked me to deliver out here to him. I didn't mind as it was a nice day for a ride and I figured Emily could pick me up as part of her workday.

But she should have been here by now. I think about calling her, just to make sure she's okay but then quickly quash the thought. I need to control my thoughts about her a bit more.

Reflecting about last night with Emily has pretty much ruled my thoughts today and it's irritating the crap out of me. I had been hoping that I would have her once and then she would be out of my system.

Stupid thought.

I had her three times and she still isn't out of my system. And this thought is actually a burden to me because I don't like being beholden to my feelings.

Last night was beyond amazing. Emily was amazing.

When I told her to take her clothes off, she looked at me with those amber eyes and I could tell she was intimidated. But just as quickly, determination washed over her face, quickly to be replaced with desire.

Yes...Emily was inexperienced. No doubt. But I so enjoyed teaching her things last night. And I have more to show her.

After our first time, as I was lying there, trying to get

my heart rate to slow down, Emily rolled on her side, propping her head on her hand. She reached out and lightly laid her hand on my chest. Her words were reverent when she said, "Thank you, Nix."

I had jerked my head in surprise at her.

Thank you? For what? An orgasm?

I was kind of offended so I asked her what she was talking about.

She just leaned over, kissed my chest, and said, "For going outside of your comfort zone. For taking a chance on me. I know it wasn't easy."

I know I just stared at her dumbfounded. It twisted something deep inside of me as I realized that she is…had always been…perceptive of my feelings. She knew all of this had been a struggle for me and she was grateful for the dice I decided to roll.

Her words alone provoked me to hardness and I rolled back over on top of her. The second time between us was almost frantic. As if the world would end if we couldn't be together. There was nipping, hard sucking and fingers digging into soft skin.

As we lay gasping beside each other after that round, she had looked at me and said, "You don't have to stay the night. I know it's not your thing."

And she was right. That wasn't my thing. Except…I didn't seem to want to leave. And I told her so. She just smiled and said I was welcome to spend the night if I wanted.

We ended up falling asleep, on our sides, just looking at each other.

This morning, I woke up with Emily sprawled across my chest, her legs twined with mine. Her arm was wrapped around my waist and her hair was tickling my nose. Her body was soft and warm against mine…oddly comforting.

And arousing.

I had her for the third time before I left. That time was slow and soft. I left her with a smile on her face—and mine—when I left to head back across the river.

And now…I'm officially worried. She had texted me when she left Manhattan and she should have been here almost thirty minutes ago. I get up from the barstool and head out the door of the bar so I can have some quiet when I call Emily to check on her.

When I'm about ten feet from the door it opens and Emily strolls in. She looks like she is wrapped in sunshine. Her hair is in a high ponytail and it's swinging jauntily with her steps. She's wearing no makeup, but then again, she doesn't need to. Her casual Abercrombie outfit sticks out like a sore thumb in this place…sinfully short khaki skirt, a blue tank top, and a dark denim jacket. Her feet are encased in a pair of shimmery, silver sandals that scream, "I'm Out Of Place In A Biker Bar."

"Hey. Sorry I'm late. There's a bad wreck on the

turnpike and traffic is spilling out onto all the side roads."

She's standing there, so casual, with her hands tucked into her front pockets as she looks at me. I'm so used to a woman making some sort of play on me that I'm kind of at a loss as to what to do with her serendipitous approach.

"I was worried something had happened to you," I grouch. "Next time try calling."

She tilts her head at me. "Seriously? Since when did we enter into the realm of calling each other about things?"

Indeed. When did we do that? Or rather, when did I do that?

She walks up to me and stands on her tiptoes. My body eagerly bends so she can place her lips near my ear. She continues in a whisper, "Last I heard, we were just fucking each other."

Her words are like a slap in my face and a punch of lust to my dick all at once. Emily is right…she owed me no phone call, and I have no right to be pissed at her for that. But hearing her say the words that we were "fucking each other" was hot as hell. I didn't know Emily had it in her to drop the "F" bomb like that.

I straighten back up and merely say, "Touché."

Emily gives me a winning smile and looks around the bar. I see her eyebrows rise up as she takes in the scenery.

It's mid-afternoon so it's not that crowded, but there are still enough rough-looking characters in here that a girl of her social element would feel uncomfortable.

Every guy is decked out in denim and leather, and every woman is wearing tight clothing with no bras. Most everyone is covered with tattoos and piercings. Emily is probably ready to bolt.

I start to walk toward the door to get her out of here when she steps past me and says, "I'd like to stay for a beer. It's the least you can do for dragging me out to Newark."

I turn around slowly and just watch stunned as she heads to the bar and plops down on a stool to sit next to Wolf. He looks down at her, raking his gaze from head to toe. She looks like she walked out of a fashion runway magazine and she sticks out like a sore thumb.

She gives him a cheerful hello and he grunts an acknowledgment at her. He's not the biggest conversation maker and I'm sure he's shocked as shit to see someone like her in this bar.

I walk back to my beer and pick it up, taking a seat next to Emily.

♦

THREE BEERS LATER and Emily is having the time of her life. She's playing pool with Wolf and he's actually treating her like the daughter he never had. I'm on my stool—watching her—with my legs stretched out in front of me.

She is pure, walking sin and for the past half hour, I've been trying to think how to get back home with her in the same car without mauling her.

When Emily had asked for a third beer, I stopped drinking as it looked like I would be driving us back. I now sipped on a bottled water while she hung out with her new friends…The Hell's Angels.

Well, that's exaggerating but Wolf is a pretty rough dude and I've seen him pound a few people into the ground before. Emily has him completely charmed though.

It isn't long before more people start coming in. Emily's sweet exterior and obviously different background make her the center of attention. Most dudes are pleasant but I see a few ogling her in a not so nice way.

One dickwad, clearly drunk as hell, comes up behind her while she is bent over the pool table to take a shot and grabs on to her hips. Red clouds haze my vision and I shoot off my stool, intent on fucking this guy up ten different ways. Halfway to my target and my rage doesn't diminish even though my mind is telling me to calm down. My body isn't responding and I feel a clenching in my gut. I'm actually fearful of what I am getting ready to do, but I am not stopping until this asshole is taught a lesson.

No one touches Emily but me.

Luckily, just steps before I reach the guy, Wolf lashes out and grabs the guy around the throat. He slams him viciously into the wall and two other men quickly move in to throw the drunk out.

I turn to Emily, ready to offer some comfort, but she is just standing there with an amused expression on her face. She doesn't seem bothered in the slightest. In fact, when Wolf comes back to the pool table, she high-fives the bastard for saving her.

Shaking my head, I walk up to Wolf to tell him we have to head out. He shakes my hand and then Emily gives him a hug. He tells her to come back and party with him anytime.

Un-fucking-believable.

I ask Emily to give me her keys and soon we are headed back toward Hoboken.

"That was so much fun," Emily gushes. "Thanks, boss for letting me hang out there for a bit."

I glance over at her. She has a grin a mile wide on her face.

"I don't get you," I say.

"What do you mean?"

"That bar is the last place in the world that Congressman Burnham's daughter would be hanging out."

She's silent for a minute while she digests what I said. "Maybe the old Emily Burnham wouldn't. But the new

Emily Burnham is finding a fond appreciation of people like Wolf."

"Well," I snort. "You were certainly on the 'new experience train' back there."

"I sure was. But I'll admit I was a little afraid walking in there."

My eyebrows shoot up surprised. "Really? I never would have guessed. You have a great poker face."

"Yup. Seeing all of those motorcycles when I pulled into the parking lot, it was a little intimidating. But I knew you were in there and wouldn't let anything happen to me."

Her words are said innocently, I know that. But my stomach tenses up and I have to do some silent calming breaths. That sounds a little too much like dependency to me. No way did she need to be looking at me for care or protection.

"That Wolf is a nice guy," she continues. Her comment breaks into my thoughts. "I think I might go back and hang with him sometime."

I'm not prepared for this new wave of emotion. Something feral rises up in me and I can't even place it. "Like hell you will. That is not a place that you should go to by yourself."

"Really? They seemed so nice."

"Don't do it, Emily," I warn. "It's not a safe place when people start getting drunk."

She doesn't say anything in response.

I continue to drive, fuming at myself that I just freaked out that Emily would look to me for protection, only to have the basic instinct to protect her rise up viscerally within me when she talked about putting herself into danger.

What. The. Fuck?

I decide a change in subject is in order.

"Stay the night with me?" I ask. Linc is at an away game so we can run naked around the apartment if we want.

And I definitely want.

She looks over at me, lightly nibbling on her bottom lip. I want her to do that to me and if I'm lucky tonight, she will.

"Sure, but you owe me dinner," she says with a smile that causes my heart to thump madly. "But then I could go for some down and dirty with you."

I hold back a silent groan over her words because they make me think about hot and sweaty sex with Emily and I shift uncomfortably in my seat. I'll never think about that cliché the same way again.

CHAPTER 22

Emily

I WAKE UP sprawled across Nix's chest again. Both times we've slept all night together, it's how our bodies seem to naturally come to rest in our sleep. I love the feel of his body against mine.

Both my cheek and palm are resting on his skull tattoo, and they both feel the slow thump-thump of his heart rate while he slumbers. Thinking of the night before, I start drawing lazy patterns with my fingers over his skull.

Nix was a little intense last night…not that I minded. In fact, I liked it…a lot!

But something happened in the car on the way home from Newark that put Nix in a mood. I obviously have no clue what was said to cause this shift but he was more distant than usual after our discussion about me returning to that bar.

It's almost as if Nix wanted to prove a point. I just can't figure out what the point was. As soon as we walked into Linc's apartment, Nix took Harley for a quick walk. I waited in the living room, surfing Facebook on my iPhone until he came back.

When he walked in and unclipped Harley, he practically lunged at me. Stripping off my clothes, he pulled me into his arms. Using his mouth and hands, he had me begging him within minutes. And here's where I think he was trying to prove something.

Rather than carry me off into the intimate haven of his bedroom, Nix did nothing more than push me up against the living room wall. Turning me so that my chest was pressed flat against it, he merely undid his pants, rolled on a condom and then he was driving into me within a matter of seconds.

It was a huge turn-on, the intensity of the passion he was unloading onto my body. We may not have been in a bedroom with soft sheets and plenty of comfortable space to roll around. He had my naked body plastered to a cold wall while he remained clothed. But there wasn't an inch of my body he wasn't touching with his body, mouth, and fingers as he slammed in and out of me. I felt the burn of his chest through the material of his shirt as he pressed against me. He whispered urgent words in my ear while he drove me higher and higher.

It was primal, edgy and volatile, and while I think Nix was trying to prove it was just "sex", he ended up showing me that fast, hard, down and dirty can have a wealth of intimacy involved. In fact, there was more emotion pouring off of Nix than I had ever seen before.

The mere fact that Nix felt he had to prove something to me, although he failed dismally, tells me that he must be doubting his own expectations and needs.

My fingers are moving in lazy circles over his smooth skin and I notice that Nix's heart rate has picked up a bit under my cheek. My hand moves down to his stomach, making soft glides across the hard ridges of his muscles. I'm pretty sure he's awake and my touching him has brought that about. I glance down and see he's impressively tenting the sheet.

Yup, I'm pretty sure he's awake.

I shift my head so I can look up at him and he's staring down at me with that sizzling look that makes my breathing erratic and floods me with warmth and wetness. I think he's getting ready to pounce again, but instead, he leans down slightly and runs his lips over my forehead.

"Good morning," he says. His voice is heavy with sleep still.

"Morning." I resume tracing my patterns on his stomach, inching a little further down with each pass.

He makes a moan of appreciation. "That feels good."

"I'm glad," I tell him.

I lift up off his chest and scoot my body down a bit, otherwise, my hand will not reach down to my intended destination. When I do, my eyes catch the wicked skull tattoo and I get sidetracked. Moving my fingers up, I gently run my fingers over it, looking at the design for the first time close up.

Nix is very quiet but doesn't stop me from my perusal. I run my fingers over the words, "See No Evil", and then slowly trace the outline of the tattoo. As my fingers run over the skull's temple where the shading is slightly dark, I feel a patch of rough skin. I bend down even closer to look at it and realize it's scar tissue.

"I've never let a woman touch me there," he says and my eyes snap to his.

"Do you want me to stop?" I ask quietly.

He hesitates only a moment before he says, "No. It's okay."

I'm nosy, I know it. I can't help but ask, "Why can I touch you there when you've never let another woman do it?"

He shrugs his shoulders. "I don't know. It just doesn't seem…solicitous to me."

For all of Nix's brave words, he's watching me warily. My fingers are still lying over the scar when I ask, "What happened?"

"I was shot during my last tour in Afghanistan."

I gasp but really, why am I surprised? I see it all the time on the news, the heavy casualties that our soldiers take.

"Can I ask what happened?"

"You can," he says simply, without malice or effect. "But I won't tell you."

"Fair enough," I assure him. "Can I at least see the rest of your tattoo?"

He nods at me and sits up in the bed, while I get up on my knees. The sheet falls to my waist and Nix pulls it back up to tuck under my armpits, covering me from the chest down. He smiles at me. "I won't be able to concentrate with you examining my body while you're naked and flaunting yourself."

I roll my eyes at him. "I don't flaunt."

He snorts at my response but moves himself to sit in the middle of the bed so I can see the whole tattoo.

I only got a brief glimpse of the scroll that contained the many lines of small writing. I start at the edge of the skull where the writing starts and read the first few lines out loud.

"Do not dwell in the past, do not dream of the future, concentrate the mind on the present moment." The word Buddha is written after the line.

I look up at Nix and he's gazing at me impassively. "What can I say? Buddha's the man."

I run my fingers over the next lines as I read them, again out loud. "The sun will shine in my back door one day…"

"Jerry Garcia," Nix supplies for me even as I read

that name at the end of the quote.

I read a few more to myself and then look up at him. "I don't know what concerns me more…that you have song lines on here from The Butthole Surfers or Josh Groban."

Nix laughs out loud. "I certainly have some eclectic mix of words on my tatt."

Concentrating on reading every single word, I follow the curve of the tattoo as it slides down his ribs and curls around his back. I crawl behind him to continue reading, skimming my fingers over each line as I absorb.

He has bible verses, philosophical quotes, song lyrics…even just people's names. Some I recognize and some I don't.

"Who is Nick Vujicic?"

"Just a guy. An Australian, born without arms and legs. He can pretty much do anything you or I can."

Names I recognize pop out at me. John Lennon, Helen Keller, Tupak Shakur. Others I have no clue who they are. Ray Lamontagne, Nando Parrado, Ben Underwood.

The tattoo wraps all the way around his back to the edge of his left ribs and then stops. The end of the scroll is open, clearly meant to add more lines in the future.

"What does all of this mean?" I ask him.

I'm betting he won't tell me, and as usual, I won't push. But I will ask.

He surprises me when he scoots back up to lean against the headboard. He pulls me into his arms and I settle back against his chest.

"I won't tell you exactly what happened when I was in Afghanistan, but when I was shot, I had a few other injuries."

I'm silent. I don't want to interrupt and cease the flow of his confession to me. This is, without a doubt, the most that Nix has ever willingly given up to me and I've only had the first few words out of his mouth.

"After I was shot, a grenade exploded near me. It threw me several feet and I suffered a Traumatic Brain Injury."

I can't help myself. "What does that mean?" I'm fearful and my heart is starting to stammer around in my chest.

"It's not as bad as it sounds. At least mine wasn't...although sometimes it can be very bad. Basically, my brain was sloshed around on the inside of my skull pretty good when I made impact with the ground. It caused some physical problems for a while."

"Like what?"

"Headaches, dizziness, memory loss, mood swings. Stuff like that. But that stuff has mostly resolved." Nix picks up one of my hands and laces his fingers through it. He rubs his thumb over mine as he continues. "I was also diagnosed with Post Traumatic Stress Disorder when I returned to the States. It's why I have Harley. He's a psychiatric service dog."

"What does that mean?"

"They can be used for lots of things. Right after my injury, I was pretty messed up. I'd have uncontrollable anger. I'd panic if people walked up behind me. Loud noises freaked me out. Harley was trained to basically orient me to the 'here and now' when I feel rage or panic. His touch calms me as a simple explanation. He was actually trained to walk behind me a bit to make me comfortable that no one would approach me from behind. But honestly, most of those problems are under control now and he's more pet than anything. I've learned to control most of that stuff with some intensive therapy after I returned."

Nix doesn't say anything more for a few seconds and I'm silent. I don't know what to say to this news, because frankly, I don't understand it. I only know that my heart is hurting immensely for this man who has apparently suffered so much.

"I can understand if that freaks you out and you want to break things off," Nix says hesitantly.

I'm shocked. I didn't think this man had a vulnerable cell in his body but he just exposed it to me, clear as day.

I spin around in Nix's arms, bringing my hands to his face. "Never," I say vehemently. "I'm just not sure what to say to you. You don't answer a lot of questions so I'm not sure what is open territory for me."

Nix kisses me softly and says, "The only other people that know what I've told you are my dad and my brother."

I go ahead and sit back, now facing Nix so I can look at him. I pick up his hand and hold it between the two of mine.

"And the writing on your tattoo?" I ask, bringing us back around to my original question.

"Let's just say I had a hard time coping when I first got back from Afghanistan. I was…rageful…couldn't control my anger. The slightest thing provoked me to near violence. Harley and a lot of therapy got me through the worst of it. Like I said, I learned to use him to calm my negative emotions."

As if on cue, Harley jumps into the bed with us and snuggles up to Nix's side. He's probably not even aware but his hand immediately goes to Harley's fur, gently stroking the dog.

"Does this conversation upset you?" I ask, noticing how Harley pins himself to Nix.

"A little. I'm telling you more than anyone other than my family knows."

"So the tattoo…"

"That's my own sort of therapy. I got the skull after my first tour in Afghanistan. It was appropriate given what I'd seen over there. Part of my therapy after the

PTSD is focusing on the positive. Which, by the way, I think is bullshit half the time."

I cock my eyebrow at him and he laughs.

"What can I say…the glass is half empty where I'm standing most of the time. Anyway…anytime I read or see something positive or inspirational, I memorialize it. So I can keep it with me always."

This is interesting.

"How do you choose what goes on your tattoo?"

He gives me a slight grin, filled with mischief. "That's easy. If I read something and immediately scoff at it, then I know it's probably an important message. I have too many negative emotions running through me. I figure the more antithetical a message is to my sensibility, the more I probably need that message."

I shake my head back and forth with a bemused tilt to my lips.

"Are you laughing at me, Burnham?"

Normally, he calls me by my last name to distance himself from me, but this time he says it with a light teasing that makes my insides quiver.

"Not laughing. Just amazed. You have more layers than all the onions in the world combined, Caldwell."

Nix lunges across the bed at me, sending Harley scurrying from the bed. He drags me onto his lap, pulling the sheet down at the same time. "Here's one layer I'd like to discover what's underneath…"

I giggle but that is soon turned into a gasp of pleasure as he palms my breast and brings his lips to my neck.

"Nix?" I murmur, on the verge of a full out moan.

"Hmmmmm?" he responds, blazing a trail of fire up to my jaw.

"You know this conversation knocks us out of the realm of having just a sex-only relationship, don't you?"

His mouth stills against my skin and I feel him tense up. Then he sighs against me before resuming his gentle kisses.

"Yeah," he murmurs against my neck. "I know."

He sounds resigned yet anticipatory, sad yet happy, angry yet calm. How can he be all of those things? And then I realize that Nix probably always has a million emotions swirling around inside of him. It's probably why he takes great pains to avoid interacting with people.

And yet, he's let me inside just a little bit more. I find that to be terribly brave. And for the first time, I realize it's not only my body that he commands. My heart is now involved as well.

CHAPTER 23

Nix

THINGS HAVE CHANGED with Emily and I'm not sure how it happened. I've spent so many months, keeping myself closed off from others, that my isolation was a balm to me. And yet, here I've let this wisp of a girl inside my walls in just a matter of a few weeks. Suddenly, all of the emotions that had once been so easy to compartmentalize, are now swirling near the surface. I have to sort through them now, identify which ones are okay to test out, and cautiously poke at them to see if they'll bite me. When I can figure out the ones that won't hurt or cause me pain, I let them run free a bit. It's frightening and exhilarating at the same time.

Granted, I've not opened up completely with her. I will never be able to tell her about Paul. It's too shameful for me, and now that I've let this girl in, I want to keep her there.

For the near future, at least.

I'm not ready to see the horror reflected in her beautiful whiskey eyes if she knew the truth behind what happened.

So it ultimately matters not that I've opened the door a little for Emily. I can never fully welcome her in. There will always be a part of me that will forever be untouchable.

And that, for now, makes me feel safe enough to push forward with her. To see where this is going.

I've just arrived at Emily's apartment. Harley and I jump out of my truck and head up to #322. She invited us over to dinner tonight and I'm actually looking forward to meeting Fil.

Emily's told me a lot about her and any person, man or woman, that's able to put the fear of God into Emily's ex-douche is alright by me. Yes…I'm already on Team Fil.

I knock on the door and it's immediately opened by who I can only assume is the illustrious Mignon Larson. I think she must have been lurking on the other side, waiting for me to knock. She's a very striking woman and she gives me a warm smile.

Fil first bends to Harley and gives him head rubs, cooing at the furry monster. Then she sticks her hand out for me to shake. "Hi. I'm Mignon."

I take her hand and it's strong and sure. "Nix."

Emily walks up behind her and says, "How come he gets to call you Mignon?"

Fil grins deviously at Emily. “He doesn’t. You just interrupted me before I got to the part where I tell him that if he calls me that, I’ll cut his balls off.”

She turns to me, nefarious smile still in place, and says, “I suggest you call me Fil.”

I smirk and nod my head. “Duly noted.”

Emily walks around Fil and wraps her arms around my neck, pressing her body into mine. My arms go around her waist and she stands on her tiptoes to press a soft kiss to my mouth. This one move on her part, is probably the most intimate act I’ve ever shared with a woman. It’s not sexual, but soft and welcoming.

She almost drops me to my knees when she whispers, “I’ve missed you.”

I don’t know what to say in response. Have I missed her? I’ve thought about her. A lot. Well…almost obsessively.

And when I first saw her walk up behind Fil, I felt something akin to elation well up in my chest. When she pressed into me, holding me close, my first thought was not how to get into her pants. No. My first thought had actually been that this felt…natural. And there is no way that it should have felt that way, because there is nothing natural about what is happening between us. At least, not in my carefully orchestrated world.

Before I can even answer, Emily releases me, bends to kiss Harley on his snout and then hurries off to the kitchen, yelling over her back, "Get him a beer, Fil. I've got to pull the lasagna out of the oven before it burns. And stop threatening people all willy-nilly to cut off their balls."

Fil and I actually get along quite well. We sit in the living room, drinking beers and discussing football while Harley snoozes at my feet. His head actually lies on top of my boot, a sure sign that he knows I'm a bit introverted around people I don't know.

Turns out, it's not so hard to talk to Fil. She's a big Jets fan like me. And she's a big Emily fan…like me.

♦

DINNER WAS DELICIOUS and I was quite impressed since it was the first time Emily had ever made lasagna. We are now all sitting in the living room, talking about everything and nothing. I'm on the end of the couch and Emily is tucked into my side, my arm lying loosely across her shoulders. She has her legs pulled up with her feet curled underneath her own hip.

Emily and Fil are arguing about a TV show that I've never heard of before…*The Vampire Diaries?*

Whatever.

I use the opportunity to examine all of the sensations Emily is causing me to feel right now. With her head tucked into my shoulder, her shampoo smells fruity and clean. Her long hair feels silky on my arm. The heat of her body against mine is comforting. Her feet are bare and delicate. I find them sexy as hell.

Most of all, I've never been in a relationship where I've just sat with someone so closely, yet so naturally. Even in high school, before I went into the military, the two serious relationships I had were always so full of high school angst that I never could just be comfortably silent in someone's presence.

It's nice and I can't believe I've been avoiding attempting this for so long.

But I'm thinking some of this has to simply do with the fact that it's Emily. I'm not sure I could really have this with anyone else.

"…well I hope to God he doesn't show up. That will just be awkward all the way around, especially after your dad threatened him," Fil says as she stands up to go get another beer.

I tune into the tail end of a conversation and I have a funny feeling I know what they are talking about.

"Hope who doesn't show up?" I ask.

Fil throws over her shoulder as she walks out of the living room. "Her ex-douche."

I'm definitely on team Fil. She calls him the same thing I do. And how did they get from *Vampire Diaries* to the ex-douche in that short of a time? My observation skills are waning.

I turn toward Emily a bit so I can see her face.

"Where is she afraid he may show up?"

"My dad asked me to come to a fundraiser Saturday night. Fil is afraid Todd may show up."

Her tone is dismissive and she's not worried, I can tell. But I'm on edge about it. "Is there a chance he'll come?"

"I suppose. They are selling tickets to the event so he could theoretically buy one himself, or his dad could buy one for him."

"You don't sound worried," I point out.

"Not really. What's he going to do in a room full of people?"

She has a very good point. There is no reason why I should be worried about this. Emily will be surrounded by tons of people and no way the guy can hurt her. He might be able to corner her, make her uncomfortable, maybe even cop a feel…

Before I can stop myself, I say, "I'll go with you."

She looks at me in shock. She appraises me then a grin spreads across her face. She lightly punches me in the arm and scoffs, "Yeah, right. You almost had me there, Caldwell."

I bring my hand up and softly grip her jaw so she looks at me. "I'm dead serious. I don't want you going there alone."

But Emily isn't having any of my pushy ways tonight. "I'll be fine. Besides, I didn't invite you."

"Then invite me."

"No. You're being ridiculous. I can take care of myself."

I decide to throw a low blow. "Are you ashamed of me?"

Now, I know Emily well enough to know that she is not ashamed of me. In fact, I'm sure she would love nothing more than to drag me to every social function she has, which I would absolutely hate. It's just not my thing. But I know the mere thought that I, or anyone, would think she would revert to the old "Emily Burnham" will be enough to swing her actions in the opposite direction.

"Of course not," she practically screeches at me. "I'd be the belle of the ball if I had you on my arm there."

"Then what's the problem?" I ask softly. I lean in and kiss her, resting my lips lightly against hers.

She sighs into my mouth, her hand sliding into my hair. "Fine. You can come with me."

I pull her tight to me and our kiss deepens. Gone now is the soft comfort I was feeling before. Now I'm feeling lust, desire, and hunger for Emily. I slide my hand up her thigh, stopping just before I get to my end goal with my thumb resting on the area where her underwear races along the edge of her pelvis. I pull her on top of me to straddle my lap.

She leans over me and kisses me deeply. I harden

instantly…almost painfully.

"Get a freakin' room you two. That's just nasty."

I had forgotten about Fil. Hell, Emily makes me forget everything sometimes. For example, in the past five minutes, I've forgotten that I don't do relationships, that I don't date, that I don't go to political fundraisers, and I particularly don't worry about what happens when a girl I'm fucking is out of my immediate vicinity.

Apparently, I've forgotten a lot. Thanks to Emily.

I watch as Emily blushes and pulls back from my lips. Her eyes are sweet and warm, with a hint of underlying desire coming off the heels of that kiss.

When she looks at me, she sees more of me than most. Hell…I've let her see more of me than most. She definitely has taught me a lot in the few weeks we've known each other and Dr. Antoniak, I know, would be proud I'm going out on a limb.

A thought strikes me. I should have Emily's name added to my scroll this weekend. Nothing big or fancy…just a mention of her name because I will definitely count her as a positive in my life.

CHAPTER 24

Emily

THIS WAS A bad, bad idea.

Bringing Nix to this fundraiser.

Except…it had been good up until this point. It had been very, very good.

The day started off oh, so nice. I had stayed at Linc's apartment with Nix Friday night. He grilled out some steaks that we enjoyed with a nice wine. We played cards for most of the night, until I made some sort of sexy noise in my throat—according to Nix—when I was trying to consider the best move for my hand. He simply threw his cards down on the table and grabbed me out of my chair. He never said a word…just fastened his lips to mine and assaulted my mouth while carrying me to his room. He shut the door on Harley when he tried to follow us in, and it was a bit distracting listening to the poor pup whine to get in.

But then Nix's hands and mouth were all over my body and I couldn't think of another thing except for the man who was lying between my legs.

Waking up in Nix's arms was becoming a habit to which I was becoming addicted. Saturday morning found me sprawled across his chest again, and this time he had both of his arms wrapped tightly around me. Harley was on the other side of me, so I was sandwiched in between two impossibly, gorgeous males. I lay there quietly, listening to Nix's calm breathing and Harley's gentle snores.

It was…domestic. And I loved it, even though it was extremely dangerous to even let my feelings move in that direction. I had to respect the boundaries and expectations that Nix and I put into place. Even though I very much wanted to throw those ridiculous boundaries out the window.

Nix and I hung around Linc's apartment all day Saturday. Toward early afternoon, I had received a very interesting phone call from my mother. We had not spoken since that night when she invited Todd to dinner with us although my dad and I had been in constant contact by both phone and email. He clearly was making a great effort to work on our relationship and I was happy to oblige.

I saw my mother's ID on the phone and warily answered. "Hello, Mother."

"Hi, Emily." She was clearly nervous and the iron tone was missing. She was…hesitant…soft.

Neither one of us said anything for a few seconds, both of us swimming in the awkward silence.

And then she said, "I wanted to…no, I need to apologize to you, Emily. I'm so sorry for pushing Todd onto you. I had no idea what had happened and I never, in a million years, would want my daughter to be with someone like that. Please believe me."

The words had poured out of her and they were drenched in pain and guilt. A sob punctuated her last sentence and my heart cracked wide for my mom. "Oh, Mother. Please, don't cry. It's okay. Honestly."

"No, Emily. It's not okay. Your dad has been talking to me and he's made me painfully aware that I've been a terrible mother of late. I think I've just been so caught up in appearances, that I have forgotten what's real…what's important. But I hope you will let me work to make it up to you. You are one of the most important things in the world to me and I never should have put anything above you."

We talked on the phone for almost an hour. A record in our book. Nix sat quietly on the couch, watching college football. But his hand stayed on my thigh, stroking me lightly in support.

My mother shocked the hell out of me when she told me that she and my dad had been talking about possibly giving up their eye on the presidency. She said it was not worth any rift in our family.

I immediately tried to talk her off the ledge. I assured her we could have both if we worked at it. She said it was just something that they were talking about but they wanted to include me, Ryan, and Danny in on the conversation.

And my heart stopped.

Ryan? Danny?

I asked her what that meant. My mother sighed. "It means that you are not the only one I've wronged. I have another phone call to make after this one."

Oh, the joy. I jumped up off the couch, startling both Nix and Harley and yelled out, "Mom…I mean…Mother…that's great. I'm so happy. You're going to love Danny so much. And Ryan misses you a lot."

I was jumping up and down, dancing around the apartment when I stole a look at Nix. His full attention was on me and he was grinning at me from ear to ear.

My mother's laugh had cut in, and I remember her vaguely saying, "Mom is fine, Emily. I kind of like it now."

It truly had been a marvelous day. I was so happy after hanging up the phone with my mom that I threw myself into Nix's arms and practically begged him to do dirty things to me. We had an amazing afternoon in his bedroom.

All too soon, it was time to get ready to go to the

fundraiser.

I had brought my Monique Lhullier cocktail dress with me and Nix borrowed one of Linc's tuxedos, which thankfully they were both the same height and build.

I have to admit…Nix would look amazing in a burlap sack. Hell, I've never seen him dressed in anything other than a t-shirt and jeans, and he'd always looked edible to me. But tonight…in a tuxedo? He looked impossibly stunning. He even styled his hair a bit so it was layered back away from his forehead and temples, showcasing the beautiful lines and angles of his face. He didn't shave, which I loved. His forever look of stubble made sure no one ever forgot that Nix Caldwell was a rough man. And that was fine by me.

He was my rough man…for now.

When I came out of the bathroom after putting the finishing touches on my makeup, Nix stood there looking very nervous, holding a bouquet of flowers.

"Are those for me?" I asked, my throat dry and my eyes threatening to fill with tears.

He nodded. "I ran down to the corner grocery while you were in the shower. It seemed like a night where flowers were in order."

I took the bouquet and held them to my nose. They didn't have much fragrance but they were lovely, and they were given to me by an incredibly closed-off man. The mere fact he thought to do that for me had my heart dangerously threatening to crack wide open and suck him inside.

"They're beautiful, Nix. Let me go put them in some water."

I didn't say anymore because I could tell he was nervous and I was threatening to cry. As I went to walk by him, his arm snaked around my waist, bringing me to a stop. He put his lips against my temple and said, "I've never brought flowers to a woman before, Emily. It's a first for me."

I turned my face into his and our lips met…softly, quietly. He pulled back. "I'm having a lot of 'firsts' with you."

My heart had been hammering with excitement over those words as we drove to The Waldorf-Astoria.

Yes…it had been a practically perfect day leading up to this fundraiser.

And here I stand now…in the corridor outside of the restrooms, getting ready to go in.

And Todd Fulgram is standing here with his hand on my arm. He had appeared out of the blue, with no warning.

His move was not made with aggression, and had it not been for a slightly sad air to his whole demeanor, I would have screamed my lungs out for being trapped here. But he said quietly, "Emily…I really need to talk to you…to explain my situation."

I shouldn't trust him. I should make polite excuses and walk the other way…or run into the bathroom. But his tone is different. It's not pleading, childish, threatening or arrogant in the usual Todd Fulgram way.

It is sorrowful and scared.

My heart, damned fiend that it is, says I have no choice but to stay and listen. "Okay."

He releases my arm and pushes a hand through his hair. "First, I'm sorry for coming here. But I knew you'd be here and I had to talk to you…in person."

"I'm listening," I say carefully.

Todd leads me over to an upholstered bench set against a wall in the hallway. We both sit down, our knees angled inward. He's nervous, twining his fingers around each other.

"Emily…my father is putting an incredible amount of pressure on me to get back together with you. He wants to be tied to your father by more than just money."

I nod at him. I so get that. My mother was doing the same exact thing to me.

"He's done everything from threatening to cut me off financially if I don't seal the deal with you, to kicking me out of the family. It's why I have been so frantic for you to resume our relationship."

I almost take Todd's hand in sympathy but refrain. I don't want him to think there is any hope of something there. "I'm sorry, Todd. I know what it's like to be used for gain."

He gives me a small smile of understanding. "Your mother wants the same thing for you. You understand the importance of appearances."

I nod but I'm not sure where he's going. I thought he was on the verge of apologizing, but now I'm not so sure.

Todd is silent. He has more to say, I know it. He looks around and the hallway is quite busy. He stands and pulls me up, leading me over to a corner bordered by plants and a large four-foot vase with flowers. It offers a little bit of privacy. My back is to the wall and he's facing me. He looks left and right to make sure we're alone.

"That's not the worst of it, Em. I'm really desperate here and I need your help…"

Something is obviously wrong, but Todd doesn't come off threatening. He looks frightened and overwhelmed. I'm starting to feel scared for him now. "What is it, Todd? You can tell me."

He takes a deep breath, looks up at the ceiling, then down at me. His breath comes out in a whoosh. "I can't tell you everything, but I really need to have the appearance that we are together. My father cannot know I've failed at this."

"What? You want me to have a pretend relationship with you?" The idea is preposterous.

"Yes, that's exactly what I'm saying. Look, people do

it all the time. I know you don't feel anything for me, and I know you're with that other guy. If we could just act like we're together, I don't care what you do on the side."

Okay, now Todd has gone overboard and is verging on complete idiocy. "Todd…that's the most ridiculous thing I've ever heard. And the answer is no. Now, if you'll excuse me, I need to get back."

I move to the left to walk past Todd but he reaches his arm out, grabbing mine. He pulls me to a halt and his grip is biting. "Emily…please listen to me. This is serious."

I laugh at him. "Nothing is so serious, Todd, that we would have a farce of a relationship. I'm sorry…find someone else to play your games."

I try to jerk out of his hold but it remains tight. And then I realize I've made a mistake by even giving Todd the time of day. I try to pull my arm out one more time, but I can't break free. I decide to go with a threat instead. "If you don't release me, Todd, I'm going to scream the house down."

That seems to work and his hold eases. "Emily," he says with overt desperation, but he lowers his voice to a harsh whisper so no one can hear. "I'm gay and I'm in big trouble if it comes out."

What. The. Hell?

I can't help it but I know the look on my face is

probably a mix of horror, sadness, sympathy, and anger all at once. However, before I can even say anything, movement over Todd's shoulder catches my eye and I gasp.

Nix is walking toward us…his eyes focused on Todd. His fists are clenched and pure savagery has taken his face hostage. The first thing that pops into my mind is the fact that Nix has suffered in the past from rage issues. He has wanted to rain violence down when he gets that way.

And I'm suddenly very frightened for Todd right now. I can tell by the furious mask on Nix's face that he's witnessed the entire exchange between Todd and I. Oh, he wasn't close enough to hear what was said, but I'm sure he saw me struggling to get out of Todd's grasp.

I immediately pull my arm away and step around Todd, walking to intercept Nix. I'm scared of him…by the look on his face. He wants to kill Todd…or at the very least do severe bodily harm to him. And there is a good chance that his wrath may be inadvertently misdirected at me.

I meet Nix five paces from where Todd and I were standing. I lay my hands on his chest and quickly say, "Nix…I'm okay. He wasn't hurting me. In fact, it's not what you think at all."

Nix doesn't even look at me but continues stalking toward Todd. I, of course, have no choice but to keep my hands on his chest and now I'm walking backward to keep myself in between the two men.

Without ever taking his eyes off Todd, he says to me, "You need to get out of my way, Emily, before you get hurt. I don't have much control right now." His words are harsh and blazing with madness.

I'm terrified and I tell him. In a small voice that quavers, I say, "Nix, please. You're really scaring me."

Nix's gait falters and then he stops in his tracks. He looks down at me and at first, there is no comprehension in his gaze. His green eyes are dark, his pupils wide. His teeth are clenched and his face is full of anger. And then…it's like my words penetrate fully, or maybe it's the look of fear on my face, because I watch amazed as the heat leaves his eyes. His forehead smoothes out and his eyes soften. I tentatively reach my hand up and lay it on his cheek.

Nix blows a deep breath out of his mouth and pulls me tight into his body. "I'm sorry," he says. "I didn't mean to scare you. I would never hurt you, Emily. I swear."

I wrap my arms around his waist and squeeze him as if my life depended on it. "I know. I was afraid you'd hurt Todd and he doesn't deserve that."

Nix stiffens slightly but he still holds me tenderly. "What does he want?"

"Apparently, he wants a sham relationship…he says

he's gay. He was just telling me about it." My voice sounds as bewildered as I feel over the concept that Todd is gay.

Nix looks over at Todd with skepticism on his face. He then looks back to me, placing his hand around my throat, his thumb stroking the front of my neck with sweet care. "Are you sure you're okay? He didn't hurt you or say anything to upset you? I saw the look on your face, Emily. You were wigged out about something."

I shake my head and lean up to kiss him softly. "Just shocked more than anything. Let me have a few minutes to talk to him some more and I'll come and find you."

"Try again. I'm not leaving you alone with him."

"We're just going to talk," I say with exasperation.

"I don't give a flying fuck. The man had his hands on you. He's been stalking you. You're lucky I'm not tearing him apart right now. Talk if you must, but I'll be in the same room with you." He punctuates his statement by crossing his arms in front of his chest, daring me to call his bluff.

I sigh. There's going to be no talking Nix out of this. "Fine. You're such a bully, though, you know?"

He gives me a mischievous smile. "I'm a lot of rotten things, Emily. Bully is just one of many."

I huff but turn around to tell Todd that we can continue our talk. Before I can utter a word, Nix has my wrist in his hand, pulling my attention back to him. "I really am sorry, Em. I didn't mean to scare you."

I place my fingers over his lips to silence his apology. "Don't be sorry. I wasn't afraid you'd do something to me. I was afraid you'd do something to Todd and that you would lose yourself."

He closes his eyes briefly and lets my words sink in. He just nods his head in acceptance of what I've said.

The rest of the evening is spent listening to Todd spill his guts to me, all the while Nix is glaring at him. It had to have been hard on poor Todd. I came away with a clearer understanding of his motivations. In fact, when the full implications of what Todd was telling me sank in, it made me relieved in a way. His being gay explained a lot of things to me. Like why I always seemed to be the one to initiate any sort of intimacy with him, or why he fumbled so much when we were intimate. Heck, it even explained why he never really wanted to pleasure me.

It also made me understand that he was living a lie most of his life, just to avoid confrontation. The pressure and stress, I'm sure, had a lot to do with how craptastic he was all of the time. I offered my support to Todd if he wanted to come out, but that's all he would get from me.

Nix had the final say-so with Todd. Let's just say he left with a very clear understanding from Nix that he was never to approach me again. While I felt sorry for his situation, I am relieved that he finally got the message that we were over for good.

CHAPTER 25

Nix

THAT STUPID FUNDRAISER is over and we are heading back to Emily's apartment in a cab. She's pressed tight to my side with her head resting on my shoulder. It's amazing to me how I've become so used to the feel of her body. How much I like the feel of it against mine.

I lay my head back against my seat and think about the evening. I had thought going in that the worst part would be meeting Emily's parents.

Another first for me.

Plus, I only had a little bit of information by which I could pre-judge her parents. I knew that Emily was not close to them. Not the way I was with my Pop. I knew that Emily was struggling to get control over her life, and that many things had been dictated for her.

And I know that Emily's mother had called her today with a sincere apology. The look on Emily's face was priceless. The way she jumped up and danced around Linc's living room touched at my heart. It gives credence to how powerful a simple apology can be and that is something I would do well to remember myself.

Emily's parents were actually pretty cool to me. I know I was stiff and edgy when Emily dragged me up to meet them. I kept a firm grip on Emily's hand, ready to pull her out of there if they said anything to hurt her.

Instead, they both gave her warm hugs and they were both very gracious and kind to me. When Congressman Burnham learned I was in the Marine Corps, we spent twenty minutes talking about the war…in general terms. He said he'd love to get my personal perspective on more of it later if I could have lunch with him one day. I agreed, although I really didn't want to do it. I guess I'm just assuming that my relationship with Emily will never progress to the point where I'll be "lunching" with her father. So I said I'd be happy to just so we could move forward in our discussion.

Emily's mother was a little different. She shook my hand and her words were warm. But I could still see a little bit of a mother's appraisal going on, wondering if I was good enough for her daughter. I wanted to just blurt out, "Look lady, we have an understanding. We're just fucking each other." I can only imagine what the look on her face would be if I had actually said that to her.

The rest of the evening, up until the "Todd" incident, wasn't so bad. The food was great and I actually danced a few times with Emily, and that was heaven. It made up for all of the boring, stuffy people she had to introduce me to and the fact I was stuck in a penguin suit.

I actually shudder slightly thinking about the nuclear rage that coursed through me when I saw Todd grab hold of Emily. My mind went numb when I saw her try to pull away and his refusal to release her. I had no clue what he was saying, but the look on Emily's face was such a bevy of tumultuous emotions that I had no control over the splinter of rabidity that shot through me. All I know was that he upset Emily and therefore, I must hurt him.

I honestly don't even remember Emily stepping in front of me. I don't remember her soft hands on my chest, or the words that tumbled from her mouth. None of it mattered. I didn't try to picture Harley's warm, brown eyes or Dr. Antoniak's teachings…breathe deep, breathe deep.

I only pictured my hands wrapped around Todd's neck and squeezing the ever-fucking life out of him.

And then…somehow words finally penetrated the fog…Nix…please…you're scaring me. It was Emily's sweet voice that touched me and all of my anger simply vanished. Todd was not what was important. Emily…and the fact that she was scared of me…that was what was important.

I had looked down at her face and there was fear

brimming in her eyes. The amber color had darkened and her brows were scrunched tight with worry. Her fingertips were digging slightly into my chest.

And awareness of what I had been about to do came sweeping back into my body. I almost gasped at the sickening realization that I had been so mad that I had almost blacked out from cognizance of my situation.

I had an overwhelming need for Harley right then…to sink my fingers into his fur, and have him nuzzle up against me. But he wasn't there and I needed to get control on my own.

After pulling Emily into my arms, I felt a slight settling overcome me. Like a light blanket of peace. I credit that strictly to Emily, because I felt it the moment our arms wrapped around each other.

Emily is such a kind soul, that she feels really bad for Todd. Me? Not so much. He's still a douchebag in my opinion.

I'll give the guy a tiny bit of credit. He sat there and spilled, what he believed, to be a terrible secret to her. That he was gay and had known pretty much since high school. He also reiterated what I had already figured out, that his family would not be accepting of him at all. He's been living a lie his entire life and he's been taking it to extreme measures so he will not be outed.

I get that he is in a terrible situation. I would hate to be in his situation…to not be accepted by your family for who you are. But his troubles in no way justify the torment he visited upon Emily. I hope he takes my warning to heed because I won't hesitate to see my threat through to fruition. With that being said, I truly hope the guy can find some peace in his life, because everyone deserves it. Except maybe me.

Regardless of my feelings on the matter, Emily has chosen to forgive him and I will accept that. She feels bad that he is stuck in the same situation she was in herself not too long ago…bending to the will of her parents. She believes, and I trust her, that the situation with Todd is resolved. She has encouraged him to be true to himself and hopefully, he will take her advice.

Because if he doesn't, and decides to continue this futile pursuit, I will hurt him.

♦

FIL IS ASLEEP when we get home and Emily leads me into her bedroom. I know she's tired and probably wants to curl up and go to sleep.

But as soon as she closes the bedroom door, she starts taking her clothes off. And not just disrobing to get her pajamas on. She's slowly and seductively removing her dress, watching me with stormy eyes.

What. The. Hell?

I mean, I thought she'd want to talk some more about what happened at the fundraiser. That's what women want, right? And although I've never felt compelled to give that before, I had completely set my mind on giving that to Emily if that is what she wanted. But apparently, she didn't.

Oh, well…I'm not going to argue. Besides, my tongue practically slides down my throat when Emily pushes her dress to her feet, so I'm not in much of a talking mood. She's standing there in nothing but a strapless black, lace bra, matching black lace panties and mile-high fuck-me shoes.

"Please don't take those shoes off," I beg her as my eyes try to roam every inch of her body.

She grins at me and saunters forward. "Funny man," she says as she works at my belt and pants.

I frame her face with my hands and kiss her. She makes quick work of my pants and is sliding the zipper down. She reaches in and takes a hold of me and I surprise the shit out of myself when a long, low moan pours out of me. My body has never been such a slave to someone's touch before.

I don't mean to but my hips thrust into her hand, demanding more. Her soft hands have the power to command anything they want from me. A thought that scares and humbles me all at once.

I pull away from her kiss and start to slide my hands down to her breasts. She actually grabs my hands and turns me toward the bed. When I feel the edge hit the back of my legs, she softly pushes me down until I'm sitting.

Emily swiftly pulls off her bra, and pushes her underwear down her legs. She gracefully steps out of them, leaving her heels on at my request.

My dick is so hard right now, I'm afraid it might break.

Climbing on top of me, Emily straddles my hips. She rubs her softness on my erection, which is fully exposed outside of my pants. My hands involuntarily grip her hips…hard enough it will probably bruise…and I clench my teeth, trying to maintain some control. I slowly ease the pressure of my fingers.

Emily rises on her knees so her face looms over me. She brings her lips down on top of mine in a kiss that slings lust all the way from my mouth to my hips. She wraps her arms around the back of my neck, melding her face to mine. Neither one of us comes up for air and I use the opportunity to run my hands up her calves, her thighs, her back…and back down again.

Suddenly, Emily pushes back from me and stands up. She lays her hands on my chest, just staring at me. Her eyes are dark, smoldering. Her tongue peeps out and runs wickedly across her lower lips. Then she drags her gaze down, down, down and stares at me.

I reach to her to pull her down for another kiss but she practically knocks my hands away as she drops to her knees in front of me. She looks up at me, coyly almost, as she takes me in her hands again. My hips move—independent bastards—and she's stroking me gently.

And then my vision dims when she bends over and takes me in her mouth.

Soft…wet…magical.

My hands hold Emily's head lightly. I let her set the pace and I don't push her to give me anything she doesn't want to give. The fact that she is here, bent over my lap with her silky hair floating across my exposed skin, is a fucking wet dream.

She's not experienced, but she is oh, so unbelievably sweet and adventurous. Her mouth feels like a satin fist as she pulls me deeper and deeper in. Her sharp nails are sunk into my thighs right now and I'm not going to be surprised if she draws blood. I don't give a fuck because this is one of the most amazing feelings ever and I don't want her to stop. Except, I'll blow so fast and hard in her mouth if she doesn't slow down a bit and I want inside of her too bad to let that happen.

I gently pull her off me and she actually fucking whimpers at the loss. That right there almost has me losing it.

I stand up, pulling Emily along with me. I push her gently back to the bed and tear the rest of my clothes off. My baser instincts are telling me to drive into her…to pound my brand into her so there is no doubt that she belongs to me.

Instead, after putting on a condom, I ease slowly into her. She wraps her legs, still wearing those sexy shoes, around my back. I keep my eyes closed and concentrate on the feel of her body. The way her warmth slowly pulls me in deep, and squeezes me rapturously.

I open my ears and listen to the sounds we are making. Both of us are breathing heavy, but Emily is making shorter, raspier breaths. Mine come out in long, choppy waves. Both of us issue staccato groans and I smile when I hear the most delicate whimper come from Emily's lips. I listened to the erotic sounds our bodies make when they come in contact with another.

My pace is slow, measured. Behind the darkness of my eyelids, I try to memorize the feel of every inch of Emily as I slide in. I listen closely to her soft moan when I pull back with agonizing deliberation.

Emily's hands on my ass urge me faster but I don't give in. I keep it lazy and methodical. I build us up tortuously. I can feel Emily is close, and I can even feel the rumbling of my own orgasm starting. My body practically demands to start pounding but I don't. This exercise in fucking civility is going to kill me but I'm going to keep it slow until the end.

"More," Emily pleads.

"No," I tell her. And I go slower yet.

Somehow, our fingers become laced together. I open my eyes briefly to see them clasped together beside our heads. Our knuckles are white and Emily's nails are dug into the back of my hand. Again, I could care less if she draws blood because it feels so fucking good.

I don't pick up my overall pace but on my next push in, I go a little harder…a little deeper. Emily cries out at the sudden change.

I do it again, and her cry echoes once more.

The third time, I slam in and watch as Emily fractures apart. My name bursts out in a husky shout and her upper back arches off the bed. I can feel her wet, warmth gripping me tightly as I make one more thrust and then I'm shooting inside of her, my face buried in her neck.

My orgasm continues on and on, my hips involuntarily knocking against her pelvis with each spurt.

Finally, I'm drained and I collapse on top of her. I know she has to be suffocating but I can't even move, so deep is the post-orgasmic paralysis I'm feeling.

I have no clue what that slow dance of passion was.

I think many women would coin that to be "lovemaking".

There wasn't love involved but it was without a doubt the most sexually charged, softly passionate experience of my existence.

I know I've never come harder in my life.

I know I will probably never replicate that moment again. Ever.

I know that Emily has just become so much more to me than she was just this side of ten minutes ago.

CHAPTER 26

Emily

BY SOME UNSPOKEN agreement, Nix has stayed at my apartment every night this week. He plays my body in the most delicious of ways and it feels true and thoroughly used. It's a feeling I could get used to.

There has been yet another subtle shift in our relationship.

And yes…there is now a relationship.

Despite the earlier lines in the sand that we drew, we have progressed to something different. I just don't know what it is. It's fuzzy and not easily definable, and it feels slightly out of reach.

Nix and I don't go out on dates. We don't do things that normal couples do. I go to school, he works, and at the end of the day, we come together in a fit of blazing passion. I now know Nix's body as well, if not better, than my own.

But it's not just sex between us. After we both empty ourselves, Nix will hold me and we'll talk about everything and nothing. I've told Nix all about my childhood and he reciprocated. He's told me more about his time in the Marine Corps, mostly about his days stationed at Camp Lejeune. It seems he was quite the party animal back then.

Gone is the snarly, closed off Nix Caldwell. In his place is a different man. He hasn't completely opened up but smiles come more easily to his face and he seems to be a little lighter of spirit. I'm not vain enough to think I've single-handedly caused this change in Nix. He's proven already to himself and the world that he effectuates his own change. From what little bit he's told me of his past, he clearly is a man that can accomplish any feat he deems necessary.

But I do like to think I am a little bit of the reason he smiles more. And I want to make it my mission to create a permanent smile on his face. I don't want him to ever be scared, or furious, or angry again. I want him to only know the good and happy parts of life.

I'm such a girl.

It's Saturday morning and I'm lying in Nix's bed for the first time all week. The Rangers are out of town again so we stayed here last night. We watched the dumbest movie I've ever seen—The Human Centipede—which was not only stupid, but frighteningly grotesque.

Even its blend of horror and low budget effects couldn't make my eyes stay open. I fell asleep with my head in Nix's lap. He woke me up with the most luscious of kisses when the ending credits were rolling.

Before I knew it, both of us were stripped out of our clothes and naked on the couch. After contorting our bodies in a variety of orgasm-inducing positions, Nix finally carried my naked body back to his bedroom where we both collapsed in sleep.

I can now hear Nix banging around in the kitchen and I know he's making breakfast for us. As much as I would love to lay here and have him serve me in bed, I'd rather spend the time watching him cook and talking to him.

I slip out of bed and walk over to his dresser where I've seen him pull out t-shirts before. I don't think he'll mind if I borrow one of his. In fact, he admitted to me once that the first night I slept over when he picked me up from the nightclub, the image of me in his t-shirt the next day had really turned him on.

Maybe I could go for a repeat performance this morning.

I open the drawer and reach in to grab the first t-shirt on top. My fingers brush against something that feels both hard and soft to my senses. Pulling the t-shirt out, I see a black velvet box. It's clearly not a female jewelry box, which was my first thought. Rather, it's thicker and it's square. There is a tiny latch on the front.

My curiosity gets the better of me. I suddenly want

to see what type of jewelry Nix Caldwell favors. Because in a million years, I cannot imagine the man ever wearing adornments other than his watch.

Flipping the latch, I pull the top back and my breath catches.

Lying on a platform of black velvet is a blue and white ribbon with a medal in the shape of a cross attached. I know this is a military decoration but I don't know its significance. I wish I had my iPhone in here but it's laying out in the living room. Otherwise, I'd just GTS.

Then I see Nix's phone on the bedside table and I grab for it before my conscience can dictate otherwise. I quickly Google "military medals" and click on the "images" tab.

Right away I find that I'm holding the Navy Cross in my hand. I read a Wikipedia link that says it's awarded for extraordinary heroism while engaged in action against an enemy of the United States.

I set Nix's phone aside and pick the medal back up. I stroke my fingers down the metal surface and I wonder what happened in Afghanistan that warranted Nix to be awarded this.

And why is it shoved in the bottom of his t-shirt drawer?

There is a piece of paper folded into the top of the case and I open it up. It starts, "The President of the

United States takes pleasure in presenting the Navy Cross to Nixon Henry Caldwell, Sergeant, United States Marine Corps, Team Leader, 2d Platoon, Bravo Company, MARSOC, FIRST Marine Division FMF in support of Operation ENDURING FREEDOM…

"What are you doing with that?" I hear Nix snarl from the doorway and I jump sky high he scares me so bad.

He's staring at me with blazing ferocity in his eyes. His fists are clenched and his jaw muscles on both sides are ticking. He's not happy and I'm so busted.

I stand up and start stammering. "I'm sorry. I was getting a t-shirt to wear from your drawer and I saw this there. I was just…being nosy I guess." I'm holding the medal in one hand and the paper in the other.

Expecting my little "nosy" confession to lighten Nix's mood, I give him a small, shameful smile. He's not impressed or moved. Instead, he stomps over to me and rips the medal and document out of my hand. Opening the same drawer I found it in, Nix throws them both in and slams it shut, causing the mirror on top to rattle heavily.

He spins around on me. "Do not go through my things again. Ever."

"I'm sorry, Nix. I won't."

Some of the tension leaves his shoulders but I clearly don't know how to keep my mouth shut for I ask, "What was the medal for?"

Wrong move.

His spine stiffens again and he wheels on me. "Jesus Christ, Emily. Don't you know how to mind your own fucking business?"

I shrink back from his words. No one has ever spoken to me with such hateful menace before. And he's not finished. He puts both hands on top of his head and looks up at the ceiling.

"FUCK!" he yells to no one in particular.

It's at this point I realize that I'm completely naked, never having put the t-shirt on that I borrowed. I quickly pull it over my head because I'm feeling vulnerable under the glare of his acrimony.

I reach out tentatively to him and I feel like I'm dealing with a wild animal. "I'm so sorry…"

He takes a step back from me, fury and rage still masking his face. He holds his hands out to me in the universal sign of "stay the hell away from me".

"I just…wanted to know a bit more about you…I thought…the medal had something to do with your injuries."

Again…wrong move. I apparently don't know how to just shut the fuck up.

If I thought Nix was enraged before, I had been sorely mistaken. His face mottles red and I swear his pupils have flames in them. He lunges toward me and grabs my upper arm. It's not painful but it's not comfortable either.

He marches me to his bedroom door and with his words chopped and shaky, he says, "This isn't going to work, Emily. I need you to leave."

I dig my heels into the carpet. Oh, hell no I'm not leaving.

"Wait, Nix. I'm sorry. I'll back off. You don't have to tell me anything about what happened there."

And then the dam bursts opened. "Fuck you, Emily. You don't just get to rip this shit open and then say you're sorry. Why couldn't you leave well enough alone? I should have known better than to trust you. I thought you respected my privacy, but you're fucking like everyone else. You want to dig, and poke, and prod, and figure out what demons make my world go round. Well, FUCK YOU EMILY! I don't need this shit and I don't need you. Now GET OUT and don't ever contact me again!"

I am stunned speechless. I don't know what to say and I am devastated by the pain and hate in his words. I've crossed an unforgivable line with Nix and I can't take it back.

But I try one more time, "Please, Nix. I'm sorry—"

He's having none of it. He pushes me out of his bedroom door and just says, "You got five minutes to get the fuck out of my house or I'll throw your naked ass out of here. Don't push me, Emily."

Then he slams the door in my face.

I stand there for just a second before a sob tears out of my throat. I clap my hand over my mouth and spin from the door so Nix doesn't hear it. I won't give him that luxury…to know that he hurt me that badly.

I all but stumble to the living room as the tears are now pouring down my face. I'm not even sure how I get dressed but I do. As I'm slipping my shoes on, I become aware that Harley is there, nudging me with this nose. He's trying to get my attention and I ignore him. Finally, he gives a whine and I stop to look at his soulful face. Grief courses through me and I drop to my knees, wrapping my arms around his neck. Burying my face in his soft fur, I let loose with wracking sobs. I have a sharp pain in the center of my chest and I'm sure it's my heart breaking.

Finally, I pull back and I'm embarrassed to see Nix standing in the hallway, his arms crossed over his chest, watching me weep into Harley's neck. His face is cold and hard but I see something flicker there as he watches us.

Is he here to apologize? To beg me to stay?

I'll accept. I'll say yes.

"Harley…come," he calls. And no matter how heartbroken I am, Harley's loyalty is to Nix…as it should be. He turns from me and pads over to his master, pushing his head into Nix's hand. I notice Nix doesn't bother to pet Harley and that tells me a lot.

Nix turns his back on me and walks back to his bedroom, softly shutting the door. I would have preferred him to slam it because that would tell me he is still being controlled by anger. Instead, I'm hearing soft acceptance of the situation and that slices deeper than his rage.

I gather the rest of my things and leave the apartment, knowing that my life will not be the same again.

CHAPTER 27

Nix

2 weeks later…

I BOOT THE laptop up and grab a beer while I wait. Harley is curled up at my feet.

We've been holed up in this dingy hotel in the town of Olney, Illinois for two days. It's the last leg of our journey from California. I've been stalling, not quite ready to head back to reality. But tomorrow…for sure…I'm going back home to New Jersey.

Opening Outlook, I take a long swallow of beer. I need to send an email and it will make one person very happy, and hopefully, it will work out for two more people as well.

I need to think about what I'm going to say, so I stall by reading some email exchanges I've had over the past few weeks.

I burn with a little shame and a whole lot of guilt when I read the first one from Linc.

Date: November 10, 2012 8:17 a.m.
To: Nix Caldwell [harleydog@gmail.com]
From: Linc Caldwell [lincnlog@yahoo.com]
Re: Happy Birthday Asshole!

Nix: What the fuck dude? You take off without telling me where you're going? It's a good thing you at least let dad know you were traveling or I would so kick your ass. You have some explaining to do. I don't know what happened between you and Emily but Ryan is extremely pissed at you. If it's any consolation, I know I told you not to hurt her, and you clearly did, but I know you didn't do it intentionally. You're not that type of man. I hope you get your shit worked out. Miss you buddy.

Oh, and Happy Marine Corps Birthday!

Semper Fi
Linc

Yes, I'm riddled with guilt and shame. I didn't intentionally mean to hurt Emily the way I did. I was so angry, so afraid of her finding out the truth about me, that I had absolutely no control over my words. I never, in a million years, would try to hurt her, but I hurt her all the same. And I hate myself for it.

The next email I read represents the start of my journey back to salvation. It took me less than twenty-four hours to decide to pack my shit and hit the road after I kicked Emily out. It took me a bit longer to realize I needed help and I reached out to Dr. Antoniak.

Date: November 11, 2012 6:21 a.m.
To: M. Antoniak [m.antoniak@wrnmmc.gov]
From: Nix Caldwell [harleydog@gmail.com]
Re: Help

Dear Dr. Antoniak:

I think I may have screwed my life up pretty royally and I really need to talk to you. Unfortunately, I'm in California so I obviously can't come and see you. Can we do a phone session?

Just as a head's up, I was in a situation where my rage completely took over and I'm afraid I said some things to Emily that are pretty unforgivable. I'm not sure what to do but I would like to try to fix this. Any help is really appreciated.

Sincerely,
Nix Caldwell

I'm lucky that Dr. Antoniak responded to me almost immediately. We set up to have an hour session via phone for the following day. I spent most of the time telling her in exacting detail what transpired in my bedroom when Emily found my Navy Cross. It still came back to the same exact issue. I was suffering from extreme guilt over what transpired with Paul, and until I confronted that, Dr. Antoniak pretty much said I was fucked.

She didn't say it in quite those terms, but that's what I got out of it.

I spent the next week talking things through with

Dr. Antoniak over a course of three phone sessions. She would send me follow up emails giving me words of encouragement.

I read one such email now.

Date: November 16, 2012 4:02 p.m.
To: Nix Caldwell [harleydog@gmail.com]
From: M. Antoniak [m.antoniak@wrnmmc.gov]
Re: You Can Do It

Dear Nix:

Just a quick note to tell you that I think we had a very good phone session today. You know the answers to all of your problems. Hell, you've probably known the answers all along. You are only missing the fortitude to push past your fears and confront your guilt head-on.

You must go see Paul. You must talk through these feelings with him. Remember, it doesn't matter what he says. It doesn't matter what his perception is. It only matters that you get these feelings off of your chest so that they stop weighing you down. I personally trust that Paul is going to give you exactly what you need to heal.

Last piece of advice. You need to let Emily in sooner, rather than later. You need to trust in her too. Now get off your ass and go get it done. I have faith in you.

Dr. Antoniak

This last email has the desired effect and I believe I'm

ready for what needs to be done. I open a new email to Dr. Antoniak and start typing.

Date: November 18, 2012 10:48 p.m.
To: M. Antoniak [m.antoniak@wrnmmc.gov]
From: Nix Caldwell [harleydog@gmail.com]
Re: Here I Go…

Dear Dr. Antoniak:

I'm heading back and will be home by tomorrow evening. I plan to see her then I'll head down to see Paul.

I'll let you know how it turns out.

Sincerely,
Nix

I hit "Send" and then shut my laptop down. I sit back on the bed and finish my beer, my thoughts straying to Emily as they normally do.

I miss her so much.

I cannot believe how much I fucked things up with her. I wasn't even sure that we had anything to fuck up. But once I pushed her out of my life, it was painfully obvious how much she fulfilled me. If I thought I was only half of a person before I met Emily, I was nothing but a wasted, dried-out husk after she was gone.

Over the past two years, I have spent all of my time trying to hide from my feelings. I was afraid of the torment they brought me. What I've come to learn is that the pain of losing Emily far exceeds anything that I could ever imagine happening to me.

And that realization alone makes me understand with shocking clarity that I have nothing to fear by talking to Paul. Nothing can hurt as bad as the way I feel when Emily is not in my life.

I've probably lost her for good and that's a consequence I'll have to bear. But I need to let her know she's taught me so much in the few weeks I've known her. She's shown me the path to my own salvation and I am finally strong enough to walk it.

CHAPTER 28

Emily

IT'S FRIDAY AFTERNOON and I'm trying to study. My eyes skim over half a page before I realize that I've not absorbed a single word.

I throw my textbook aside with frustration. It's no use…I can't concentrate.

It's been this way for the past two weeks. All I can think about is Nix and how much I screwed up. My heart is broken and I don't know how to fix it. Nix is angry, and I don't know how to fix that either. I feel useless…and lonely.

I am also tired of feeling this way. I have to snap out of this funk and move on with my life. It's clear that whatever I had with Nix is no more, and there is no going back.

Unfortunately, it doesn't feel like there is any going forward either.

There's been no word from Nix. I texted him the day after our fight asking him if he wanted me to still work for him. I knew the answer to that already, but I was desperate for some contact from him…anything.

His return text was short and biting.

Just pay me when you get your trust money.

That was it. Nothing else.

I didn't have the guts to try again. It hurt too much to have this bitter freeze from him.

Danny and Fil have been great. Between the two of them, they are sporting some soggy shoulders. They've both listened to me bitch, grouse, cry, moan, and gripe to them. They've cursed Nix with me and they've defended my feelings. They both threatened to cut off his balls for me, but when it boiled right down to it, they would have welcomed him back with open arms if he walked through my door, because they both knew that would make me happy.

Ryan is another matter. I haven't really talked to him yet but Danny has filled him in on everything. I think she said it would be wise for Nix to stay away from Ryan unless he wanted a broken nose. I don't think Ryan is going to be happy if he were to walk back through my door, but it really doesn't matter. It's not going to happen anyway.

Surprisingly, I even told my parents about our breakup and they were amazingly supportive. I mean, my mother wasn't threatening to cut off his balls but she did tell me that sometimes men just need time to see the error of their ways.

I hated she told me that because it kept my hopes alive far longer than they should have been.

That's it, I say to myself. I stand from the couch and stomp into the kitchen. I'm done feeling sorry for myself. It's time to put Nix Caldwell to rest and start getting back on this crazy train of life I had been riding.

I open the fridge and pull out a bottle of wine we had opened a few days ago. I don't even bother with a wine glass but pour some into a coffee cup.

Ah, the benefits of freedom.

Heading back into the living room, I take a generous sip. Maybe I'll get drunk tonight. Just as I'm almost ready to sit down again, someone knocks on the door.

Setting my wine down, I head over to the door and look through the peephole.

And my world starts crashing as I see Nix on the other side of the door.

My heart starts into overdrive and my skin starts to itch. I suddenly realize I'm wearing his t-shirt. It's the same one I had pulled on when he kicked me out of the apartment. I walked out wearing it, not even realizing it until a few days later when I found it in my laundry bin. I didn't wash it because it smelled like him and now I'd taken to wearing it around the house when I was feeling blue.

Maybe he's here for the shirt. Surely there would be

no other reason for him to be here.

I take a deep breath and open the door. As soon as my eyes meet his, all of my false bravado and promises to move on flee my mind. Instead, I take in the beautifully damaged man that I had fallen foolishly in love with.

And the tears immediately well up in my eyes.

Hastily blinking them back, I manage a whisper, "What are you doing here?"

"Can I come in so we can talk?"

Can he? Should I let him? Or should I stay hard and unyielding?

"Okay," I immediately capitulate as I step back from the door.

Nix, as always, looks beyond mouth-watering. Simple t-shirt and jeans. Nothing different from what he normally wears but he owns that look. His hair has been trimmed a bit but he's still sporting that five o'clock perpetual shadow that I love so much.

He walks in, shutting the door softly behind him.

I try to make my words strong, confident. I need to steel myself against further pain. "What do you want, Nix?"

"You."

My legs turn to jelly over that one simple word. Does he understand the power of what he's just said? The fact that I am ready to submit to that power leaves me shaken.

I shake my head, trying to clear my thoughts. "I think it's a little late. Don't you?"

"Probably. But I need to try."

I turn away from him and walk to the living room. I can hear him follow me in. I take a sip of my wine, hoping it will fortify me. It tastes like vinegar in my mouth.

"Emily," he says softly and I cannot help but look at him, immediately getting lost in his eyes. "I will never be able to tell you how sorry I am for the words I said to you. Those were unforgivable. The only thing I can do is offer you a way to understand them."

He has my attention but I have no clue what he is trying to say. "How's that?"

"I want you to come with me to Washington, D.C. I want to explain to you what happened in Afghanistan…why I freaked out when you saw the medal…why I said those horrid things to you."

"And you can't do that here?"

He shakes his head, determination hard on his face. "No. To make it count, it has to be done in front of one other person. My best friend, Paul."

Huh? He has a best friend named Paul?

I didn't know this but why am I surprised? I didn't know a lot of things about Nix.

"When did you want to go?"

"Now."

Now? Holy shit.

"I know I'm springing this on you," he continues, "but I desperately want to fix things with you and this is the only way. The sooner we can go, the sooner you can begin to fully understand me. That is...if you want to."

I don't need to think about this. I can't help it but I love Nix Caldwell. If he is willing to go out on a limb and open up his entire pain to me, I'm ready to go to the moon with him if he asks.

I'm smart enough to know that this doesn't mean *we* will be fixed. In fact, he's offering me nothing more than a means to understand him at this point.

None of that matters, though. Not really.

There isn't anything I wouldn't do for Nix.

"Okay, let's go."

♦

OUR TRIP TO D.C. is uneventful and fairly quiet. Nix tells me he's been traveling around the country with Harley. They drove out to California and back. He said he used the time to think. He also talked to his neuropsychiatrist, Dr. Antoniak, by phone a few times. They apparently discussed me but Nix said he would tell me the details later. The only thing I knew about Paul was that he was supposedly Nix's best friend and that they served in the Marine Corps together during his last tour there.

When we got close to Paul's house, Nix actually pulled into a hotel. He explained it would probably be late when we finished up at Paul's and that we would stay the night. He came back out with two room keys and handed me my key. I didn't say anything even though the thought of two rooms saddened me. It makes me think Nix doesn't have much faith that we can work through this.

Nix drives us a few miles down the road and we enter into a small, middle-class neighborhood. He finally finds the house he is looking for and we pull in.

Turning to me, he reaches out and trails his fingers down my cheek. "I'm scared, Emily. Because what you are getting ready to hear is something that is incredibly shameful to me. I'm doing this because I want you to understand why I flipped out on you. I'm hoping it will let you possibly forgive me."

I just nod because I don't know what to say. He has me imagining the worst and I can only pray that whatever I'm about to learn about Nix is not so horrific that my memories of him will be tarnished forever. I think I may be as scared as he is right now.

We get out of his truck and Nix leads me up the front porch. With every step he takes, his shoulders become more hunched. He looks like he is marching off to his death.

After a brief knock, the door is thrown open and I

see a handsome, stocky man staring out at Nix. He has very short hair, buzzed the same length all the way around. It's blond and his eyes are bright blue. He stands much shorter than Nix but you can tell he works out. His build under his t-shirt and sweatpants is solid.

"Nix Caldwell," the man says reverently. "I never thought I'd see the fucking day you just showed up on my doorstep."

His words are soft. His eyes are sparkling with something I cannot name, although it could just be tears. Nix doesn't make a move but the guy doesn't notice. Instead, he steps towards Nix and wraps him in a big bear hug. Nix hesitates for just a second, then his arms wrap tightly around the other man.

Pulling apart, Nix steps back toward me. "Paul…this is Emily Burnham. A very good friend of mine."

My eyebrows rise. Good friend? Is that true?

I have no clue what we are to each other. If you asked me—especially with the way things ended—I'm not sure we were much more than fuck-buddies. Emphasis on the fuck part, not the buddy.

Paul sticks his hand out toward me. "Emily…it's good to meet you. Nix didn't tell me he had such a beautiful friend."

I blush prettily because that was about as sweet of a compliment as a man can dole out.

Paul invites us in. He tells us his fiancée, Marie is still

at work and won't be home for another hour. He seems truly happy to see Nix but I don't see that reciprocated. Nix has tension vibrating off of him in waves.

I can tell that Paul will chatter on and on if Nix doesn't stop him and that's exactly what he does. "Listen, Paul. I need to talk to you about something serious."

Paul's carefree smile he had been sporting fades away. "Sure, man. What's on your mind?"

I'm sitting beside Nix on the couch, and Paul is sitting in a chair opposite us. I've turned slightly so I can see Nix's face as he talks. He's clearly stressed. My gut churns at his obvious discomfort and I feel like I might puke just from Nix's fear of what he is about to do.

Nix leans toward Paul, resting his elbows on his knees. He lets his hands hang loosely for a minute but then grasps them tightly together. I want to slip my hand in between his, to give him comfort, but I don't. I'm frozen in place by fear and dread.

"Paul…I need to tell you something that I should have told you a few years ago and it's tearing me up. Worst, it's turning me into someone that I don't like, so I need to get this off my chest."

Paul looks worried and he says as much, "Nix…dude…what the fuck? You're freakin' me out here."

He's freaking me out, too, Paul.

Nix takes a deep breath and lets it out. "Okay, here

goes. Paul…I need to apologize to you. The guilt over what I did is eating me up, man. And I'm hoping you will forgive me one day. But I need you to know how sorry I am."

I'm glancing back and forth between Nix and Paul. Nix looks like he's ready to break down, and Paul? Paul just looks…angry. This does not bode well.

Then Paul does the unthinkable and starts laughing. Genuine, belly-deep amusement pouring out. I glance at Nix who looks astonished.

"What in the hell do you find so funny about this?" Nix sounds affronted, as he apparently should be. Nix just bared his soul and Paul is laughing at him.

Paul finally winds his chuckles down. He leans forward in his own chair and points his finger at Nix. "Let me get this straight…our squad gets stuck in the middle of a firefight. I get hit with a bullet. So do you. You drag me out to safety, save my life, and you're… you're…apologizing to me? Are you smoking crack or something?"

Paul no longer sounds amused. In fact, he sounds pissed off.

Nix stands abruptly from the couch. "That's not how it went down and you know it. I got your fucking legs blown off." As if to prove his point, Nix stomps over to Paul and pulls up on both legs of his sweatpants. I see teal blue metal rods poking out and disappearing into his tennis shoes.

"Look at this, Emily. You want to know what you found in my drawer. This is what I got a fucking medal for."

My eyes are wide in astonishment. I'm looking at a man with two prosthetic legs, and I had no clue. I couldn't tell. He walked…perfectly. No limp. No awkward gate.

Amazing.

Nix throws his hands up in the air. "I can't fucking do this. I thought I could, but I can't."

He walks to the door, opens it and slams out.

I just sit there in stunned silence, wondering what to do next. Finally, Paul stands up and shakes each leg, in turn, to get his pants' legs to fall down. "Want a beer?"

"Sure," I respond. Because I have no clue else what to say.

"Come on in the kitchen. I'll tell you the whole story."

CHAPTER 29

Emily

PAUL PULLS TWO beers out of the refrigerator for us and opens them up. We're sitting at his kitchen counter.

"You're more than just friends with Nix," he observes.

"Not really. Maybe once…but not now."

He watches me while he takes another sip of beer. "Why did Nix want to come here?"

I shrug my shoulders. "I'm not sure. He sort of flipped out on me a few weeks ago because I found his Navy Cross and asked him about it. I haven't seen him since then. He just bailed. Next thing I know, he shows up on my doorstep this afternoon. He wanted me to come here with him so he could explain why he flipped out."

Paul puts his beer down. He leans up against the counter. "I met Nix six years ago when we got assigned to the same unit. We did both tours in Afghanistan together…best friends…always."

"What did you guys do in the Marine Corps?"

"We were part of MARSOC. It's a Special Forces command within the Marine Corps. We were trained to do a variety of things. We are like the equivalent of the Navy SEALs. Our mission this last tour was to patrol local villages, help to protect against the Taliban, try to negotiate with the Taliban and help further train their local police and military forces."

Paul's voice is low and melodic. I'm sitting on the edge of my seat, finally getting information that I had been hoping that one day Nix would tell me.

"One of the most dangerous aspects of our job was the threat of a 'green on blue' attack."

"What's that?"

"It's basically Afghani forces attacking NATO forces. It's usually people we are working closely with. Say, for example, we may be embedded in a local village for months. We work with the local police to help train them to protect the village. Unfortunately, many of them are secretly part of the Taliban. A 'green on blue' is when one of them attacks us."

That's horrible and beyond frightening. "How do you ever trust anyone?"

"You don't. You learn to look at everyone as if at any moment they can pull a gun on you. At any rate, that happened to us. One night on patrol, several of the

Afghani police that we had been working with turned on us and opened fire. A vicious gun battle ensued and three of us got pinned down. Me, Nix and our buddy, Gary."

Paul picks up his beer and takes a swallow before he continues. I feel like I am on pins and needles, watching a scary movie and waiting for the monster to jump out and scare the living daylights out of me.

"We had to call in helicopter support to help us out, but the Taliban outnumbered us and were moving toward our position. We had no choice but to try to make our way to higher ground so we could be easily accessible when the helos came in. Unfortunately, all three of us had been hit. I had been shot in my right thigh and I'm pretty sure that the bullet had hit the bone because I couldn't put any weight on my leg. Gary, though, had taken one right in the stomach and was bleeding really bad. And Nix…he took one—"

I finished for him, "—to the chest."

Paul nods. "That's right. Luckily, the bullet he took was pretty high in his chest, going just below his shoulder. Quick in and out so he was still pretty mobile. At any rate, we had a quick discussion and it was decided that Nix would carry Gary out first while I laid cover fire. That worked nicely. Even though Nix had a bullet hole in him, he was able to carry Gary to safer ground where a helo landed right away. While they were tending to Gary, Nix came back to get me."

My heart is pounding. I'm fearful for Nix's life, even though I know he makes it out. "What happened next?"

"Nix came back, hauled my ass up over his shoulder and ran us out of there while I shot my 9mm pistol at them…hanging practically upside down on his back. I think I was giving sort of a Braveheart scream the entire time."

"But…" I know there is a punch line coming.

"But…one of the Afghani's threw a grenade at us. It didn't hit us directly but it was close enough that the blast caused Nix to stumble. We both went crashing to the ground. Nix was back on his feet, now dragging me by my arm, when the second grenade hit. I remember it landing right about five feet from my legs when it blew."

"I'm so sorry, Paul."

"Hey," he says softly and grabs my hand. "Don't. This is a hero's tale, nothing more. The grenade took my legs but it threw Nix into the air. He hit the ground so hard his brain was pretty scrambled, and of course, he had that bullet hole in his chest. None of that stopped him though. He crawled back to me and started dragging me to safety. Of course, I weighed a lot less by that time."

I gape in horror at Paul.

"Geez. You and Nix need to lighten up a bit. Both of you are too tightly wound."

I try to smile but I'm failing miserably. I clear my

throat. "Sorry. What happened next?"

"Nix got me to safety. The helo flew us out and we went to a field surgical hospital. Then we were separated. Nix was able to get medically stabilized a lot quicker than I was but we both ultimately ended up at Walter Reed National Military Medical Center."

I'm silent for a moment. Nix flipped out when I found the medal. Nix came here to apologize to Paul. It doesn't take a rocket scientist to figure out that he's feeling like he did something wrong in the rescue. But after what Paul has just told me, I can't see how.

"What happened to Gary?" I ask.

Before Paul can answer, Nix provides me the information in a voice that barely registers above a whisper. "He died on the helicopter."

I turn around to see Nix leaning against the entryway to the kitchen. He looks sad. Beaten down. "And had I chosen to take Paul out of there first, he'd still have his legs. Gary would still be dead, because he wasn't going to make it out of there anyway…not with that stomach wound. Had I just taken Paul first, he'd have his legs."

And there was the source of Nix's guilt. He has been second-guessing his decision making all of this time. Having the power of hindsight and calm conditions, he'd reasoned out that he made a poor choice.

I wanted to smack him.

But before I can say a word, Paul walks around the

counter to stand in front of Nix. "Get your head out of your ass, man. You're not the only one that made that decision. We decided that together."

"What the hell did you know? You were suffering from blood loss—"

"—as were you, you jackass. It was the right call. If we had any chance of saving Gary, we had to get him to the medics first. They ultimately couldn't save him but it was still the right decision."

Nix is silent, digesting this. Paul doesn't let up though. He grasps Nix by the back of his head and makes him look at him. "Hear me when I say…I'd make the same decision all over again, even knowing what I know now. And if you'd be honest with yourself, you'd say the same."

Nix's gaze lowers, and he seems to be processing what Paul is saying. I want to wrap my arms around him so badly, but it's not the time or place. This is Paul's job right now.

"Nix," Paul says softly but with command. "You need to let it go, man. You did the right thing and you saved my life. You hear me? You didn't cause me to lose my legs…you caused me to live. You. Saved. My. Life. I will forever be indebted to you."

I'm watching Paul and Nix through the hazy film of tears that are pouring down my face. I'm witnessing something beautiful here…something that I'll never see again in this lifetime.

I watch Nix closely. I see pain, and fear, and then hope that maybe he has the story wrong. That maybe his life might have more purpose than he once thought. I can see he wants to trust what Paul is saying, but he's afraid to take that chance. He's wallowed in so much guilt and misery for so long, I think the idea that he could actually be a true hero is too much of a foreign concept to him.

Paul finally says, one more time. "Thank you, Nix, for saving me. You are the most amazing person I know and I'm honored to call you my best friend."

And then I see it. I see the moment where Nix finally releases the pain. His body stands a little straighter. The glaze of guilt recedes from his eyes and I actually see a small smile grace his beautiful lips.

He doesn't say anything but nothing needs to be said as Paul pulls him into a tight hug.

♦

THE REST OF the night was so nice. Paul's fiancée, Marie, came home with some pizzas. She and I actually ate in the kitchen, getting to know one another. Nix and Paul spent the time in the living room, talking in hushed tones while they ate. When we finished, I gave Paul and Marie hard hugs. I wasn't sure if I'd ever see them again but I hoped so.

At the hotel, we walk to our rooms. Nix has been noticeably quiet and introspective on the ride here. I'm not sure what he expects. Hell, I don't know what I expect, but I still want some time to just hold him and to thank him for sharing that part of himself with me. And for finally giving himself permission to be free from guilt.

We get to my room and I stick my key card in. Nix asks, "Can I come in? I want to show you something."

"Sure," I say with a smile. I have no clue if he intends to show me pictures of his trip out West or if he wants to seduce me. I'll go with the second option if I have a choice but for now, I'm just thankful he wants to continue to talk.

After the door shuts behind us, I turn to look at Nix. "How do you feel after your talk with Paul?"

"Liberated. Relieved." He's silent for a second. "Peaceful."

I smile at him. "I'm so glad. Thank you for sharing that with me. I'm really humbled to know someone like you."

A shaky breath flutters out and Nix looks almost shy. "So…like I said…I want to show you something if that's okay with you."

"Sure." I'm more than curious.

Nix doesn't hesitate and pulls his t-shirt over his head. It happens every time that I see his amazing torso…all thoughts sort of melt away and all I can think of is, *Oh my, he's a god.*

He throws the shirt down and just stares at me. I don't know what he wants me to do. Does he want me to make a move? Because if so, then I'm ready to throw myself into his arms.

My gaze rakes over his body, down then up. I glance at his eyes once, and I see amusement there.

Glad I can accommodate.

I do a once over again, staring a little more leisurely this time at his chest.

And then my breath catches. I see what he wants to show me. His tattoo has been finished.

I can't see any of what the writing says, but the scroll has now taken off from his left ribs and flows up over the top of his left pectoral muscle. It drapes over the top and comes to rest right over the area where his heart is nestled deep in his chest. I can see that the end of the scroll has been closed. It's complete.

"You finished your tattoo?" I'm in awe that he found enough inspirational messages that had meaning to him that he could fill it in so quickly. I'm itching to walk closer and see what revelations he inked on his ribs and chest to complete the artwork.

"I did. Would you like to examine it?"

Oh, boy, did I.

I walk toward him on shaking legs. My fingertips are tingling with just the thought of touching his skin. I know I don't need to touch his body to read the tattoo, but I'm going to.

Walking up to the side where the tattoo starts, I note that Nix is watching me intently. I circle around to his back. I trail my fingers along his skin, appreciating the way his muscles twitch at my touch. I finally get to the spot where the tattoo had previously ended and I touch the words, *"I have decided to stick with love. Hate is too great a burden to bear. Martin Luther King, Jr. 1929-1968"*. That was the last entry I remembered seeing.

I peer at the next word. It simply says, "Emily". And the next word… "Emily".

And the next… "Emily".

I let my fingers brush the words.

I'm stunned. My name must be on his body dozens upon dozens of times within the scroll. I follow it across his ribs, making my way in front of him again. I slide my fingers over the tattoo…*Emily, Emily, Emily*…on and on, up over his chest and then coming down to rest over his heart. The last two words say, "My Emily".

I drag my eyes up to Nix who is staring at me intensely. He's holding his breath, waiting for my reaction. And he gets it.

I immediately start sobbing.

"Oh, Emily…don't cry," he tries to sooth.

His arms come around me and he pulls me into his chest. My cheek rests on top of my name.

Nix kisses the top of my head. "Do you like it?"

I nod my head and sob harder.

Finally, he picks me up, grabs a box of tissues from the dresser and carries me to the bed. Sitting on the edge, he cradles me in his lap and lets me cry. When I'm finally worn out, I lay there quietly, taking in the beauty that is this man.

My Nix.

Just as I'm his Emily.

Nix places a butterfly of a kiss on the top of my head. "Thank you for coming here with me, Em. I'm not sure I would have had the courage to talk to Paul had you not come."

I lean back so I can see his face and I bring my hand up to stroke his cheek. "I'm glad you asked me."

Nix covers my hand with his own and closes his eyes, relishing the touch. When he opens them, they are burning. "I want to make love to you, Emily. Will you let me?"

Oh, my. Words I have wanted to hear and yet I don't want to read meaning into them.

I nod my head slowly, holding my tongue.

Nix swoops in and masters my lips with his. My mouth opens readily for him and his tongue settles in for a leisurely exploration. I sink into the feeling, never wanting to let it go.

Nix suddenly pulls back. "Did you notice I said I

wanted to 'make love'?"

He's smiling at me and this time, it's different than anything I've ever seen on his face before. It's completely at ease…filled with peace.

"I did notice."

"I just wanted to make sure you heard that. Because…it's different now with us."

"How so?" I whisper.

"Well, first, don't go thinking my style is going to change. I'm still more likely than not going to drive into you so hard you'll be screaming the walls down."

Just the thought makes my toes curl.

"The difference is now…I love you more than the air I breathe and I feel so very empty without you in my life. So no matter how down and dirty we get…no matter how hard or fast we go…it will always be making love, baby."

I sit up fast and flip my leg over Nix's. I straddle him and grab his face between my hands. I behold his lovely green eyes as they look at me with unfettered love and desire. "Oh, Nix. I love you so very much. More than I ever imagined possible."

He gives me a brief kiss then pulls back. "I have never felt so lost as I have these past two weeks. I can't believe I never even recognized the depth of feeling I had for you…until I lost it. I'm so sorry I did that to you, Emily. I promise I will hold your heart with the greatest of care if you'll trust it to me."

I sigh and lean my forehead against his. I finally get it. I get how love can run so deep that it touches the very fiber of your being.

"Nix...you are the most amazing man I have ever known. I'm lost without you, too. My heart is yours for however long you want to keep it."

"How about forever?" he asks, rubbing his nose along mine.

"You got a deal."

Nix leans his face toward mine and we enter into a kiss that defies logic. It's deeper than a canyon, higher than the stratosphere and hotter than lava. It speaks of the promise of love to come and a gratefulness for what we've found together.

We strip each other quickly, murmuring sweet words of love and sexy words filled with passion.

Just before Nix slides into me, I take another look at my name inked over his heart, and I know that we have both battled improbable odds to find our way into each other's lives. We are so different from one another, yet we are the same. He and I have worked hard to overcome all of the things that had previously held us back.

We have found love together, and it is beyond glorious.

EPILOGUE

Emily

6 Months Later…

I PULL ONE pillowcase out of the hamper and hold it up to my nose. Inhaling deeply, I release a soft sigh. Nothing smells better than clean sheets out of the dryer. Working a fluffy, feather pillow into the casing, I smile over this new domesticity I've come to love.

I'm making up Nix's bed. We finally have finished fixing the water damage to his house and he's moved back home. I say "we" finished the remodels because I'm quite proud to have helped with more than just making up his bed with fresh linens. These past several months, I've spent most of my weekends here with Nix, helping him to hammer and paint. I've come to love this house and the times I've spent here with him.

But I love all my times spent with Nix, no matter where we are.

As I finish the second pillow, the phone rings. I reach over and pick it up.

"Hello…Nix Caldwell's personal maid."

Warm laughter greets me on the other end. It's Paul. "Hey, Em. My man got you in a French Maid outfit?"

I snort. "Hardly…he prefers me to do my cleaning naked."

I hear Paul suck in a large breath and it sounds like he's choking on the other end. After a fit of laughter mixed with coughs, he asks, "Speaking of the perv…is he around?"

"Yep. Hold on…"

Putting my hand over the receiver, I yell toward the open bedroom door. Nix is downstairs in the living room trying to hook up all of his electronics. I had left him down there a bit ago, cursing under his breath. "Nix! Paul's on the phone."

I hear a loud curse this time, and something bangs to the floor. Nix picks up the receiver downstairs and I hang up.

Nix and Paul sure have come a long way since that night many months ago when Nix confessed his non-existent sins to both of us. Released from pain and guilt, Nix easily fell back into the solid friendship with Paul that had developed before their injuries.

My heart nearly swells to bursting just thinking about the way Nix easily laughs with Paul. Or the way that they tease each other mercilessly. Heck…Paul even has Nix laughing at his prosthetic jokes. It's a friendship that will last beyond this lifetime.

Pulling out the fitted sheet, I snap it out and let it float over the enormous mattress. Nix bought a new king size bed when he moved back into his home. He said he had no doubt that we would use every square inch of it and my face flushes thinking of all the times we christened it. Climbing onto the bed to tuck the sheet into the far corner, I remember just last night he had me on my back with my head hanging off the side of the mattress. I could see his bathroom door from my practically upside-down view while he showered heaven on my body. I shudder from the memory.

Before I can start to move to the next corner, I can feel the mattress dip and Nix grabs hold of my waist from behind me. He pulls my hips back until they nestle against his very hard erection. Desire pools warm and deep in my belly and I rub up against him. The move is calculated to drive him crazy but he's in a mood to take his time. I know this because he does nothing more than purr in his throat before pushing me down to the mattress and slowly covers me with his body.

Rolling to his side, he brings me with him, the heat from his chest burning through the thin material of the shirt covering my back. His arm wraps snug around my waist and he squeezes me tight. I can still feel his hardness pressed against my butt, but he does nothing more than stick his nose in my hair and breathe in deeply. This will definitely be slow and soft, I can tell.

"How are Paul and Marie?" I ask, reveling in the feel of Nix wanting to just hold me for a moment.

"They're good. He said they'll probably be able to make it up to visit this weekend."

"Awesome. I know Marie wants to look at wedding dresses so I'll take her on Saturday afternoon into the city."

"While Paul and I can stay here and drink beer, right?"

I giggle. The idea of Nix shopping for a wedding dress amuses me to no end. "Of course you can stay here with Paul and drink beer. Your manliness is always safe with me."

Nix doesn't respond because he's now busy nibbling on my neck. His arm loosens around my waist and runs up my outer thigh, gently caressing me. I love when Nix wants to go slow but he drives me mad with anticipation.

Nix suddenly pulls his body away from me and pushes me onto my back. Leaning on one arm, he hovers over me, searching my face. "Move in with me?"

I blink in surprise. I'm not sure where this came from. By the hard evidence that had just been pressed against my body, I'm amazed this thought even popped into Nix's head. We've never discussed anything like this before and a serious discussion was not what was on his mind just a few seconds ago.

Reaching up to run my fingers along his jaw, I ask,

"Why, baby? We spend almost every night together between your house and my apartment."

His eyes are dark and serious, but he shrugs his shoulders as if not understanding his own needs. "I don't know…it just seems the next logical step for us to take…moving in together."

My whole heart sighs with love for this man. He wants to make our relationship more permanent, and he's right…this is what most people do. And while I would love nothing more than to call this place my home with Nix one day, I have other obligations.

Leaning up, I give him a gentle kiss. "I can't leave Fil. I've committed to being her roommate until we graduate next year."

Nix lays his forehead against mine and lets out a long sigh. "I know. And you're right."

Pulling his face back, he looks in my eyes again. One hand comes up to cup the side of my head, as if he's afraid I'll look away from what he's about to say. Stroking his thumb over my cheek, he says, "I just want you to know that this is forever. My love for you, that is. My heart is a complete slave to you and I just want you by my side…always."

I can't help my soft nature, and Nix knows me well enough that he will not be surprised by the sudden rush of tears that flood my eyes. In fact, the sight of them makes him give me a gentle smile.

"Nix…my world is you and it always will be."

We don't say anything further but another sweet kiss from Nix turns suddenly hot. Conversation is forgotten as our hands start roaming. Nix has the ability to make me forget myself when he's touching me. He says his heart is a slave to me, and that thought cuts both ways. But he also owns my body and I'm completely okay with that.

Just as Nix's hand reaches the button on my shorts, my iPhone starts ringing from my back pocket. I reach back to grab it but Nix whispers against my lips, "Don't answer."

For a split second, I hesitate because Nix now has my pants open and his hand has just slid into my panties. But then I come to my senses and grab my phone. "You know I have to answer it."

He doesn't respond but starts kissing me below my ear as a finger slides its way into me. I gasp as I look at the caller ID.

Ryan.

There's no way I can talk to my brother when Nix has his finger sunk deep into me, so I pull at his wrist. For a second, he doesn't relent, in fact moving his finger in such a way that every muscle in my body clenches tight. Then his hand slides out and he gives me a mischievous grin as he kisses me on the end of my nose.

My blood is pounding through my veins and I hope

the breathless way I answer the phone doesn't reveal the fact that Nix's hand was just down my pants.

"Hey, Ryan."

"It's time," he says simply.

I look at Nix and he chuckles at the excitement in my eyes. "We're on our way."

I'm getting ready to become an aunt.

Nix

I WATCH EMILY hold the baby and my chest constricts. Her copper-brown eyes are so soft and warm, and her lips are pursed making little cooing noises at the bundle in her arms. Little Amelia Grace Burnham. It is still incredibly humbling to me that I am at a point in my life where I am able to be moved by such a simple gesture.

I do that a lot lately…take stock of simple things. I look around the hospital room and there is a wealth of simplicity that speaks profoundly to me. Danny is lying in bed, her gaze resting on her daughter nestled in Emily's arms. Ryan's hand is holding Danny's. He has her wedding band between his thumb and forefinger, and he's twirling it back and forth as he watches Danny watch their daughter.

Linc is talking to Congressman Burnham. I'm still having a hard time calling him Alex like he's asked me to do repeatedly. Linc has his hands stuffed in his pockets and he's rocking back and forth on the balls of his feet. Congressman Burnham…I mean Alex…is laughing at something Linc has said, one arm casually propped on the door frame that leads into a private bathroom. Linc has a reporter-friend of Emily's trailing him for a sports article, and she is nervously chewing on her bottom lip while she sits in the corner trying not to be noticed.

My eyes move to Mrs. Burnham. Now there's a lady I've come to know a lot about just by watching her simple gestures. Right now, she's clutching her pearls in one hand while the other rests lightly on Emily's shoulder. She's staring down at Amelia Grace while her thumb rubs lovingly across the fabric of Emily's blouse.

Having circled the room and taken in such simplicity, perhaps I'm the only one at this very moment that realizes the depth of feelings I've just witnessed. There's a girlfriend's hope, a mother's love, a husband's gratitude, a brother's mischief, a father's joy, a stranger's nervousness and my own undying humility to be able to appreciate it all.

Emily stands up and hands Amelia off to her mother.

Celia takes the baby and sits down in the chair Emily has just vacated. Her face is equally as soft and warm as Emily's was just a few seconds ago. She is a woman who has made big changes in her life—just as I have in mine—and I respect the shit out of her for it. She is now emotionally present in her children's lives, and has even grown close to Danny. But hell, everyone loves Danny after you talk to her for about five minutes. Celia Burnham, like me, has decided that life is too short to waste moments that are simple yet precious.

Emily gives me a weird look and walks out the door. No one has seemingly noticed, so I get up and follow her out.

Looking up and down the hall, I don't see her so I walk toward the L&D lobby. Turning the corner, I see her standing at the huge wall of windows that overlooks the city street below. Her face is pensive and her arms are crossed over her belly. I walk up behind her and wrap my arms around her, sliding my arms underneath hers so mine are the ones that are crossed over her stomach now. Leaning over, I rest my chin on her shoulder.

"Penny for your thoughts?"

Emily lays her head back so it's resting on my shoulder and I squeeze her even closer. Her arms are now resting over mine, her fingertips stroking the skin over the back of my hands.

"I was just thinking about how amazing Amelia is. I've never held a baby before..."

She trails off, caught up in this new miracle of life that she has witnessed. I smile to myself although I'm sure it's apparent on the outside as well. We both just stand there, silently, wrapped up in each other and in our thoughts.

Will there be a day, when I'm doing exactly what Ryan was just doing? That simple gesture of his…twisting his wife's wedding band with his own fingers, while he gazes at her with complete love and devotion?

Such a simple act…

And I realize…there is nothing simple about my love for Emily. It is twisted and complex. It is ingrained in every cell that swims in my blood. I'd as soon lose a limb, or four, than be without her, and with a moment of clarity so pure that it rings like a crystal chime, I know that I will put a baby in this soft belly that I'm holding right now. That Emily will be the mother of our children, and those children will give us grandchildren.

I spread the palm of one hand wide on Emily's stomach and press her just a little more tightly to me. Leaning down, I whisper in her ear. "There will be a day, Emily…in the future…that our baby will be in here. And it will be the second happiest day of my life when that happens."

I can't see her face but I can feel her smile at my words. Her hands grasp onto mine. "Second happiest? What will be the first?"

Nuzzling her neck, I tell her, "The day you agree to marry me."

She startles in my arms and turns to look at me. "But…you haven't asked me yet."

Grabbing her arms, I loop them around my neck. I kiss her quickly on her lips and smile down at her. "I know."

Her eyebrows raise and she quirks her lips. "I know? That's all you have to say after dumping on me the fact that we'll get married someday and have kids together?"

"There's nothing else to say right now. I love you, baby, more than life itself. And the greatest thing about it…our happiest days are still to come."

She laughs at me then, and it is bright, and warm, and soft as the morning sun. It is one of those simple gestures that I would have taken for granted just a year ago.

But not now.

Now…it is everything to me.

Nix's Scroll

Do not dwell in the past, do not dream of the future, concentrate the mind on the present moment.

~ Buddha

The sun will shine in my back door one day...

~ Jerry Garcia

Even though I walk through the darkest valley, I will fear no evil, You prepare a table before me in the presence of my enemies: you anoint my head with oil; my cup runs over.

~ Psalm 23

Judge each day not by the harvest you reap but by the seeds you plant.

~ Robert Louis Stevenson

Retreat Hell! We're just attacking in another direction.

~ General O.P. Smith, USMC, Korean War, 1950

You can turn off the sun, but I'm still gonna shine.

~ Jason Mraz

Chesty Puller

Even if we don't understand, it's all understood.

~ Jack Johnson

I get by with a little help from my friends.

~ John Lennon
Nick Vujicic

Imagine there's no countries, It isn't hard to do, Nothing to kill or die for, And no religion too, Imagine all the people, Living life in peace.

~ John Lennon

Don't let your eyes refuse to see, Don't let your ears refuse to hear.

~ Ray Lamontagne

For quiet times disappear listen to the ocean.

~ Tupac Shakur

It's better to regret something you have done than to regret something you haven't done.

~ The Butthole Surfers

Come on, you sons of bitches. Do you want to live forever?

~ Gunnery Sergeant Dan Daly, USMC, Belleau Wood, June 1918
Nando Parrado

The best and most beautiful things in the world cannot be seen or even touched – they must be felt with the heart.

~ Helen Keller

And it's no one's fault, There's no black and white, Only you and me, On this endless night.

~ Josh Groban
Ben Underwood

No, I don't believe in the wasting of time, But I don't believe that I'm wasting mine.

~ Fiona Apple

The mind is everything. What you think, you become.

~ Buddha

I have decided to stick with love. Hate is too great a burden to bear.

~ Martin Luther King, Jr. 1929-1968

Emily, Emily,

Emily, Emily,

My Emily

Afterthoughts

If you haven't figured it out by now, I am a proud supporter of the U.S. Marine Corps and all of our troops. If you want more information about Post Traumatic Stress Disorder, Traumatic Brain Injuries, and Psychiatric Service Dogs, check out these links:

www.MentalHealthDogs.org
StiggysDogs.org
www.PTSD.va.gov

Please note that I took great liberty with the use of Harley as a psychiatric service dog. In this book, Harley ultimately is a pet but service dogs are working animals. They certainly don't jump all willy-nilly on folks and often, it can even be prohibited to approach or touch one without the owner's permission. Their training can take months and they are very disciplined animals. Forgive my latitude in giving Harley a bit more leeway in this book!!!

Looking for more Off Series? Go here to see all seven standalone titles in the Off Series.

sawyerbennett.com/bookstore/the-off-series

Go here to see other works by Sawyer Bennett:

https://sawyerbennett.com/bookshop

Don't miss another new release by Sawyer Bennett!!! Sign up for her newsletter and keep up to date on new releases, giveaways, book reviews and so much more.

https://sawyerbennett.com/signup

Connect with Sawyer online:

Website: sawyerbennett.com

Twitter: twitter.com/bennettbooks

Facebook: facebook.com/bennettbooks

Instagram: instagram.com/sawyerbennett123

Book+Main Bites:
bookandmainbites.com/sawyerbennett

Goodreads: goodreads.com/Sawyer_Bennett

Amazon: amazon.com/author/sawyerbennett

BookBub: bookbub.com/authors/sawyer-bennett

About the Author

Since the release of her debut contemporary romance novel, Off Sides, in January 2013, Sawyer Bennett has released multiple books, many of which have appeared on the New York Times, USA Today and Wall Street Journal bestseller lists.

A reformed trial lawyer from North Carolina, Sawyer uses real life experience to create relatable, sexy stories that appeal to a wide array of readers. From new adult to erotic contemporary romance, Sawyer writes something for just about everyone.

Sawyer likes her Bloody Marys strong, her martinis dirty, and her heroes a combination of the two. When not bringing fictional romance to life, Sawyer is a chauffeur, stylist, chef, maid, and personal assistant to a very active daughter, as well as full-time servant to her adorably naughty dogs. She believes in the good of others, and that a bad day can be cured with a great work-out, cake, or even better, both.

Sawyer also writes general and women's fiction under the pen name S. Bennett and sweet romance under the name Juliette Poe.

Printed in Great Britain
by Amazon

43505665R00189